AMELIA C. GORMLEY

PLAYER
VS
PLAYER

Pushing for change can be deadly when change starts pushing back...

ACG Publications
www.ameliacgormley.com

Player vs Player

Cover Art by Alexandria Corza, https://www.seeingstatic.com/
Editor: Danielle Poiesz

ISBN: 978-1-62622-616-6

First edition
December, 2014

Second edition
November, 2018

Pushing for change can be deadly when change starts pushing back...

NILES RIVER HAS his dream job, writing for a socially-conscious video game studio, and working with his best friend and his twin brother. Sure, he has to deal with incessant harassment from trolls and even protesters who take issue with his ethnicity, his sexuality, and his politically progressive storytelling, but the chance to make a difference in the world through his art makes it worth it.

Until threatening notes begin arriving, hand-delivered, on Niles's doorstep, and two cosplayers dressed as characters from Third Wave Studio's latest game are murdered. Their deaths echo plot developments from unreleased content no one except people who work at the studio could know, and Niles is one of the last people to have spoken with the young women.

Now his formerly-closeted ex is investigating the crimes, armed security guards are patrolling the studio, and the death toll is mounting—and getting closer to home. If they don't solve the murders soon, it could be Game Over for Niles.

READER DISCRETION ADVISED

Each reader is unique in their tolerance for graphic material. As such, please be aware that this novel may contain material or references which may be triggering for some readers. If you worry that this might be an issue, the author whole-heartedly encourages you take the time to read some of the reviews others have left at Goodreads and various ebook retailers to see if it contains subject matter you may find disturbing. Thank you.

Dedicated to the women and men who were injured and killed during Elliot Rodger's rampage in Isla Vista, CA, May 2014, and to all the victims of violent male entitlement everywhere.

And, as always, much love to my husband, son, and the friends and family who have supported me in my writing.

CHAPTER 1

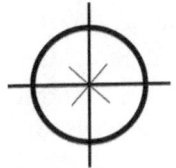

"Check that out."

Niles's gaze followed to where Rosena Candelaria, CEO and lead producer at Third Wave gaming studios—and, not coincidentally, his boss and best friend—had gestured, pointing out a cosplayer in the autograph line. A stacked woman in a form-fitting, yet combat-practical, brown leather catsuit stood amid the crowd beside another cosplayer. He whistled appreciatively. "Great costume. That must have taken some effort."

Rosie nodded. "Yeah, but notice anything about her specifically?"

Niles narrowed his eyes and looked closer. To her credit, the girl in the leather hadn't made any attempt at darkening her skin to portray Issis, who was a tall, ebony-skinned powerhouse of a mercenary in-game. The care she had taken with her outfit showed in the minute details and quality of its craftsmanship. The neckline over Issis's not-inconsiderable rack was squared off, rather than the plunging vee the marketing dickwads at EEU had slipped past them for the promo images, and hanging from her shoulder was a bandolier of ammunition, lockpicks, and various tools of the character's mercenary trade. "Oh, hello, looks like we have a beta participant. Lucky lady."

"She had to have busted her ass to get that costume completed. The limited beta just went live two weeks ago, and no one knew Issis's look was different from the promo shots until we released it." Rosie turned back to attend to the next fan in line at the autograph table, though Niles continued to watch for a moment longer, his attention drawn to Issis's companion.

The other cosplayer was shorter, and so convincingly androgynous that Niles wasn't entirely sure if the person under the dark blue-gray stage makeup was male or female. His money was on female, given the height and the fact that there weren't a lot of guys who would show up in public dressed as Gairi, *Phoenix Force 3*'s unapologetically queer character. Gairi's costume wasn't as eye-catching as Issis's, but then, there wasn't much the cosplayer could do with the homespun peasant-wear Gairi first appears in-game wearing.

The pair were still quite a ways down the line and Niles glanced at his watch, hoping they'd make it to the table before the autograph session ended.

Normally, a lead writer and CEO wouldn't have been signing autographs at all. That sort of fan interaction generally went to the voice actors doing convention appearances, but this year, Portland GamerCon had a feature aimed toward gamers wanting to break into the industry, and specifically focused on gaming companies in the Pacific Northwest. It was exciting for Third Wave, and he and Rosie were getting a little bit of celebrity treatment for the way they'd taken an unlikely start-up and managed to produce a franchise of platinum titles. Of course, the downside was that everyone who stopped by for an autograph had an idea to pitch to Rosie, which meant each auto-graph was taking longer than it should and their handlers had to keep urging people to move on.

Between signing mint-condition collector's edition boxes of

the first two Phoenix Force games and a handful of other Third Wave offerings, Niles monitored the two cosplayers' progress in line and took in the rest of the convention-goers. Amid a mass of T-shirts bearing logos for countless TV, movie, comic, and game fandoms were many other cosplayers, and Niles wished he had time to wander the floor and get a better look at them. Through the open doors of the autograph room, the main convention floor bustled, clusters of tables hosting pen-and-paper role-playing games. Booths for other electronic gaming companies lined the walls, complete with computers and consoles offering passersby a chance to sample upcoming titles.

The number of guys wearing fedoras at the gaming tables and in line at the booths and exhibits was disheartening. With the hat having been adopted by the regressives who were misleadingly styling themselves as men's rights activists, he found he couldn't see a fedora anymore without making a snap judgment about the wearer. How many of these guys here today were making a political statement with their headgear, and how many just thought they looked cool?

The autograph line continued to inch forward. The third time a ubiquitous dude-bro gamer asked "Issis" to pose for a picture with him, he noticed the young woman's smile was beginning to look a bit strained. Predictably, the guys ignored "Gairi," no doubt concerned that if they took a picture with someone portraying a gay character, the gay would rub off on them. It was the female fans—and a lot of them—who wanted their picture taken with Gairi, or with Gairi and Issis together. Equally predictably, the shots with the female fans generally featured the deadly bombshell Issis in power poses, while the guys who asked for pictures sometimes were simply looking for an excuse to cop a squeeze.

"Funny how people watching at one of these cons pretty much encapsulates every single issue with gaming we try to tackle at Third Wave," Rosie observed under her breath. To all appearances her attention was on the first edition *Phoenix Force* comic she was signing, but Niles could tell by the tension around her mouth and eyes that she hadn't missed all the interplay involving Issis.

Niles nodded. While it was the most blatant bit of harassment they'd seen, he had no doubt there was plenty happening out of their line of sight, as well. The Portland Convention Center was packed. The scent of food brought in from the outside mingled with body odor from people who had been sitting at the gaming tables or wandering—and definitely sweating—all day, making the air stifling. He'd never dare admit it publicly, but he was one geek who really didn't care for conventions.

"I'm trying to figure out how to take some of the pressure off her without creating a scene. Looks like she could use a break," Niles murmured back, refraining from checking his watch to see how much longer they had to be here. He smiled at the next fan as she stepped up to the table.

Before Rosie could respond or Niles could greet the fan, a broad-shouldered body inserted itself between their chairs. Not in a pushy way. Quite the opposite, actually. There was a questioning hesitation to the interruption. "Ms. Candelaria, Mr. River, Mr. . . . uh, the other Mr. River asked me to see if there was anything the two of you needed."

Rosie stopped signing autographs long enough to look at the stammering young man, then over to Niles. "I didn't know you'd brought an intern along to help out today."

"I didn't." Niles chuckled, giving his new intern an amused look. "Patrick, it's okay to call me Niles. And I promise, my brother doesn't need to be called Mr. River any more than I do. I didn't know you were working today. Did Jordie bring you along?"

And if so, just what was Jordan doing co-opting Niles's writing-staff intern?

4

"Uh, no, Mr.—um, Niles. I'm here with my stepbrother and some of his guild-mates from his old MMO. They're around . . . somewhere." The intern frowned. Patrick Rutledge was a nervous kid, Niles had noticed, even here in a social setting. He glanced around the crowded meeting room with the same discomfort he normally exhibited every time Niles tried to get to know the skittish intern. The kid's anxiety seemed to get worse when referring to his family, especially his stepbrother or stepfather. "I just bumped into Mr. River on the floor, and he asked me to check on you."

"Leave it to your brother to wrangle a hapless convention-goer into free labor." Rosie shook her head. "Tell Jordan he can bring us a couple more bottles of water, and he can do it himself. Don't you dare let him make you do it for him. If you paid admission and you're not on the clock, go have fun."

"Oh, I don't mind helping out," Patrick protested, blushing. "I'm not sure where Mr. River is just—"

"He's there." Niles jerked his chin toward the line of people still waiting for autographs, which was steadily creeping along. A fedora-wearing dude had hit Issis up for a picture, and judging by the way she stiffened and jerked away after the flash had gone off as the guy's friend took the picture, Niles was willing to bet the kid had tried to grope her. He saw her face flush and her mouth twist as she struggled with the impulse to retort angrily. But just then, Jordan appeared beside her, his voice loud enough to carry across the ever-shortening line.

"Hey, I just have to say I *love* your costumes!" he gushed to her and Gairi. Niles blinked at the amount of camp in his tone because that wasn't Jordan's style at all. He managed to sidle up to Issis without actually disrespecting her space and turned to give a salacious look to the handsy guy she'd posed with. "*Who's your friend?*"

Never had a dude-bro backpedaled quite so quickly. He practically fell on his ass in his rush to put several steps between himself and Jordan, as though Jordan were going to launch himself at the guy and shove his tongue down his throat at any second. Gairi looked wryly amused as the guy righted the fedora on his head and stammered defenses of his masculinity, but Issis seemed peeved with the display. She stepped away from Jordan as soon as she could politely do so, and Jordan dropped the camp act.

"Thanks," Niles heard her say, looking from Jordan to her accoster and back. "But I was about to deal with it." She paused for a moment and gave Mr. Hands a stern look. "Dude. Not cool. Grabbing someone like that without consent is considered assault, you know. If you grope anyone else, I'll report you to security, and maybe the police."

"Oh, good girl," Rosie whispered.

Mr. Hands scoffed, his alarm turning quickly to indignation. "Whatever, bitch. Don't bother dressing up if you don't want the attention." He thumped his companion, the one who'd been wielding the iPhone, on the chest. "Come on, let's go. There's fucking fags and bitches all over this place."

They walked away before Issis could answer, and a dozen or so frustrated responses played across her face, stuck on the tip of her tongue. Niles could still hear the guys complaining—and not discreetly—about "crazy sluts" halfway across the convention center. Gairi laid a consoling hand on Issis's arm.

He didn't really even need to glance at Rosie to know what her reaction was. Her knuckles whitened around her metallic Sharpie, and he wondered if it could actually be used as a stabbing implement if wielded with enough force. She seemed ready to give it a try. She jerked her head in a "come here" gesture to Jordan, and he got the cosplayers' attention without invading their space.

"You two want to jump to the head of the line?" he asked with a reassuring smile. "Ms. Candelaria wants a better look at your costumes."

The two cosplayers grinned at each other, Issis's irritation with Jordan melting away in an instant, and they nodded eagerly, following Jordan to the autograph table. Niles heard a sigh behind him and looked over his shoulder to see Patrick staring at Jordan with stars in his eyes, as though Jordie had just single-handedly rescued the ladies from a whole army of boss mobs. He continued staring the entire time Jordan guided Issis and Gairi past the queue.

Biting his lip against the urge to smile or say something that might embarrass Patrick, Niles murmured, "I thought Rosie told you to go have fun? We're okay here. I'll see you later."

Patrick nodded, swallowing as he tore his eyes away from Jordan, and left. Niles sighed and turned around to accept the next game box to autograph, exchanging a few words with its owner until Jordie and the cosplayers reached the table. Jordan gave them a friendly nod good-bye and slipped away, leaving them with Niles and Rosie.

"What's your name, Issis?" Rosie asked when they arrived, giving the young woman a smile as she produced a booklet of concept art that had come with the collector's edition of *PF2*. Niles smiled at the young woman—on closer inspection, it was obvious his assumption regarding the sex of the player had been correct—cosplaying Gairi, who had a copy of a trade rag Rosie and Niles had done an interview for after the original *Phoenix Force* had gone platinum.

"Charity Anspach," Issis replied, glancing sideways at her friend, and Gairi eagerly stuck out her hand somewhere between Niles and Rosie, as if she couldn't decide who she wanted to shake hands with first. She looked ready to bounce off the walls.

"Lakshmi Agrawal," she said as Niles set his pen aside and came to his feet to accept the proffered handshake.

"Nice to meet you, Lakshmi," he said, smiling in an effort to encourage her to relax. "We've been admiring your costumes from up here. You did a great job."

Rosie likewise stood and shook their hands before sitting again, with Niles following suit. "How are you enjoying the beta, Charity?" she asked as she began inscribing something on one of the glossy pages of the booklet. Niles lifted an inquiring eyebrow, and Lakshmi spelled her name for him as Charity effused over her play-through so far. Niles and Rosie traded off the items to autograph while the girls bantered.

"I'm still so freaking jealous you won that drawing for the beta key," Lakshmi interjected, nudging her friend. Then she gave Niles a long-suffering look. "Don't worry, she's following the NDA. She won't even give me spoilers."

Lakshmi grumbled, and Niles laughed. At a fleeting glance from Rosie, he produced a card from his shirt pocket and offered it to Lakshmi. "Here. Your very own beta key, for having such an awesome costume."

Her dark eyes grew huge, and she and Charity beamed at each other. Niles and Rosie handed their memorabilia back and stood to shake their hands again, Rosie adding an extra pat and a squeeze when she clasped Charity's hand.

"You did good, standing up to those guys out there," she said sincerely. "Keep it up. Don't let them win, okay?"

Charity nodded eagerly, and the young women hurried away to make room for the remaining fans to slip in before the autograph session closed.

CHAPTER 2

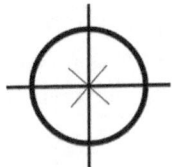

"Oh, great," Rosie muttered as the line continued to shuffle past, rubbing her temple where it felt like someone was trying to drill into her head with an ice pick. Her senses were kicking into overdrive. The smell of the place was turning her stomach, and the flickering of the overhead lights had her eyeballs ready to crawl out her skull. "I never got a chance to tell Jordan to bring us some water. Where's he off to now?"

"Prince Valiant, you mean?" Niles chuckled, flashing her a characteristically wry smile. It always astonished her how two identical men could have such different smiles. Same olive-brown Mediterranean complexions, same dark hair and star-tlingly contrasting pale gray-green eyes, but Niles's smile was gentle and sweet, Jordan's sharp and wicked. There was no way to confuse the two.

"Hunting down some con officials to report the harassment to, if I had to guess," Niles said. "If he catches another glimpse of those kids that bothered Charity, he'll make sure they're kicked out. He probably also wants to keep negative incidents like that from affecting the studio's public image."

"Ouch." Rosie lifted her eyebrows at the harsh assessment, and Niles gave a self-effacing shrug.

"You know Jordie. He defines enlightened self-interest. He'll always do the right thing, but he likes it better when the right thing happens to also have a pragmatic upside."

She considered it a moment, conceding the point with a small nod. "Well, where's your intern, then?"

"You mean the one you told to go have fun?" Niles snorted, and Rosie rolled her eyes at her own about-face. This headache was screwing with her memory—and her ability to think rationally. "Probably panting at my brother's heels," he continued.

She gave him a pointed look, and Niles waved a hand at her. "C'mon. You know Jordie better than that. He's not going to mess with an intern. Patrick's virtue is safe, and his crush doomed to pass by unrequited." He lowered his voice. "Especially since I'm reasonably certain he isn't even out yet."

Another pause for autographs, then Rosie murmured, "How do you know?"

"That he's not out or that he's pining for my brother?" Niles shrugged and stretched, nodding as their handlers approached the table and a con official announced the autograph session was over. "Just a feeling. He winces every time I ask him about his family."

Rosie dropped the subject as their handler escorted them away from the table and to the conference room where she and Niles would be doing a Q&A next. Outside the door, they were stopped by a trio of college-aged guys. In addition to the casually sexist and homophobic slogans emblazoned on their T-shirts—seriously, did anyone even make that "fake gamer girl" joke anymore, much less the "back to the kitchen" schtick?—they had an air of nervous bravado, as if they were girding their loins for a confrontation. Apprehension masked with arrogance. One of them had a cell phone out, apparently taking a video.

"Excuse us. Rosie, could we talk to you for a moment?"

She cleared her throat, trying to ignore the spike of pain in her temple. There were times she wished she didn't have quite the level of notoriety among gamers that she had. Most gaming studio CEOs wouldn't be recognizable on sight, but then, most gaming studio CEOs were cis men who had never had to deal with their faces being plastered all over sexist and violent internet memes. "Do I know you gentlemen?" she asked briskly.

The one who appeared to be the ringleader hesitated for a moment but charged on. "No, but we've got this pet—"

Her face stiffened. Jesus, she needed some water. "If I don't know you, then it's Ms. Candelaria. Now what can I do for you?"

The three didn't seem to know how to respond to that, trapped somewhere between indignant defensiveness and embarrassment at being called out on a breach of simple courtesy their mothers should have drilled into them. It took one of the silent pair nudging him to get the ringleader to continue.

"Um, actually, we were hoping to present the petition to Mr. Lott, since he's the producer on *Age of Valiance*," he said, referring to Third Wave's low-fantasy single-player RPG, the first game of a new franchise still in development.

The bottom dropped out of her stomach at the first surge of adrenaline, which wasn't helping the nausea any. Years of practicing, years of studying the societal and cultural scaffolding that taught women not to make waves, and it was still a daily effort to force herself not to retreat. Be conciliatory. Head off a confrontation. "Drew Lott is the lead animator and concept artist for *AoV*, not the creative producer," she corrected them, her voice and smile brittle. "And he couldn't be here today. Now, I'm about to be late for our Q&A, so if you young men could get to the point . . .?"

The spokesman glanced at his companions, as though looking for moral support, and then the set of his jaw became more belligerent. "It's just that we'd be more likely to get an unbiased hearing from him."

Another spike of pain. It wasn't doing much for her temper. "Drew Lott works for me. I am his boss, not his coworker or subordinate, which means whatever your issue is, any decisions made regarding it will have to come from or be approved by me." She crossed her arms over her chest, turning her wrist to check her watch before tucking her left hand into the fold. "Now, your choices are to present your petition to me within the next ninety seconds, or email it to Drew, who will then bring it to me. Which will it be, boys?"

Another exchange of glances between them all. In her peripheral vision, she saw Niles cover a smile. How likely was it that these guys' worldview would adapt to the idea that, yes, a woman did actually run the show at Third Wave Studios? It wasn't a secret by any means, but these sorts of situations came up with exhausting regularity: fans assuming that she either had someone she answered to or that some male would know better than she would about issues pertaining to her studio and game franchises.

Finally, the spokesman held up a sheath of papers. "All right. Rosie, this is a petition—" her jaw tightened, her eyes narrowing "—signed by five thousand seven hundred and fifty-three loyal Third Wave fans—both online and here, today, at the convention—requesting the removal of Niles River as a writer from *Age of Valiance* and as a writer at Third Wave entirely." He glanced down at the papers, clearly reading the petition's text. "There are rumors that there are going to be gay characters in *AoV*, just like there are in *Phoenix Force*. It's clear from the direction Third Wave's titles have been going that Niles has an agenda he's trying to push with the writing he does on these games. We feel Third Wave is neglecting its largest paying demographic, which is the straight male gamer. We're determined to boycott *AoV* if

Niles continues to write for that game and forces more gay characters on us."

Rosie stared at them silently, one after another, and they began to squirm when she refrained from speaking. They kept peering at Niles as if they expected him to jump into the conversation, but he took a step back. His mien was sober, but Rosie could see the small sparkle he was trying to mask, the slight crinkle in the corners of his eyes, the twitching at the edges of his lips. He knew what was coming, and he was more than pleased to let Rosie handle it.

"What's your name, young man?" Rosie finally asked the ringleader.

"Jeff Whitfield," he answered, his Adam's apple bobbing as he swallowed.

Rosie saw their convention handler step close and murmur to Niles that they needed to get going to the Q&A, but at least the poor guy had the sense not to interrupt.

"Well, *Jeff*." She heard the coldness that imbued her tone and wished she had the patience to extend civility a little further. But she didn't. "I'm curious. Which part of what you just did do you think was okay?" Except for the one with the video camera, the boys began stammering, and Rosie could see the defensive bluster gestating on their lips. She didn't give it a chance to birth. "Was it the part where you completely disregarded my request not to address me familiarly? The part where you intimated that because I'm a woman, you wouldn't get an unbiased hearing from me? Or the part where you attempted to undermine my authority at the studio *I* created by assuming that decisions there regarding our game franchises are made exclusively by men—both Niles *and* Drew?"

The boys shot more glances at Niles, but he merely shrugged, the gesture clearly saying, *You're on your own, dudes.*

"Or was it the part where you presumed that you, as cisgender, heterosexual, white male gamers, could tell me how to run my business?" Rosie drew a breath, and the boys swallowed, hard, in unison when her lips curled in a particularly nasty smile. "At any rate, in this case, Jeff, your arrogance is only outpaced by your ignorance. Niles River is not, and never has been, a writer for *Age of Valiance*. He's far too busy as the lead writer for the Phoenix Force franchise, where he—with my full and enthusiastic support —oversees the development of storylines that represent the *entire* gender and ethnic spectrum of the actual gaming audience. He's presently at work on a collection of downloadable content expansions that will be coming out after *PF3*'s release. And because I do not and never will make my staffing decisions by committee or public referendum, you may be assured that he will continue in that role until I, and only I, decide to use his talents elsewhere. Now, you've wasted enough of our time. Get out of my way."

When she'd brushed passed the boys to enter the conference hall, and their handler had closed the door safely behind them, Niles finally spoke. "You okay?"

"Hm? Yeah." She pressed her fingers against her temple and rubbed so hard her short nails dug into the skin.

"You have your migraine meds with you?"

"Why do you think I wanted the water?" She opened her eyes to look at their handler. "If you don't mind?"

"I'll get you a bottle," he murmured as he led Rosie and Niles backstage. He disappeared into the conference room that was gradually filling and returned with the water. Niles sat beside Rosie silently as she downed the pills and prayed the headache would dissipate before she had to face the Q&A.

"Fuck," she muttered finally. "I think I almost preferred the tumor in my skull to the headaches after having it removed."

Niles offered her a crooked smile. "I think I prefer you alive and capable of speech."

Someone came backstage to speak with their handler, who warned them they would be introduced in ten minutes and left again. Rosie sat up, her energy lifting at the prospect. Public address was where she shone. She could have made a mint on the lecture circuit if she hadn't decided to develop video games.

She tapped her fingers on her chair while they waited. "You know, I keep thinking back to the *Star Trek* conventions and such I went to when I was a kid, back when conventions were run for fans by fans and weren't such a huge corporate affair. And I don't remember shit like *that* happening." She chucked her thumb over her shoulder in the direction they'd entered from. "Guys groping women, calling everyone fags and bitches, trying to push women around. Was I just too young and ignorant to notice, or has it actually gotten worse?"

"I'm not sure. I think maybe the attitude was always there, but that internet culture and the anonymity it affords have amplified everything. Lack of accountability has given those sorts of people the idea that it's okay to behave that way, so they maybe don't have the filters they used to?" Niles shook his head and sighed.

"Maybe. Or maybe I'm just getting to be a tired, old, bra-burning bitch ready to yell at kids for walking on her lawn." She snorted. "What the hell possessed me to prance out of college with my women's studies and computer programming degrees and decide to reform video game culture?"

Niles grinned. "The fact that no one else was doing it and it needed to be done."

"True, that." She closed her eyes and fell silent a moment, then asked, "Vault of Reminiscence raid tonight, since we'll be out of here early enough to sync up with the guildies on the East Coast. You in?"

He nodded eagerly, but before he could say anything, their handler appeared again, and Niles stood. Rosie could see the effort it took for him to suppress his urge to offer her a hand up, because he knew she wouldn't want it.

"Come on." She rose on her own, squeezing his elbow in

passing. "Let's go enlighten some of today's misguided youth, then kick some undead ass."

———

THEY DIDN'T CATCH a glimpse of Niles's twin until later that afternoon as they were about to leave for the day. As she scanned the crowd, she saw their intern in the company of a young man who was probably about Patrick's age and a slightly older man with a camera. The stepbrother and guild-mate, she assumed. They were with Charity Anspach and Lakshmi Agrawal, the stepbrother laying an arm around Charity's stiff shoulders and mugging for the shot. Lakshmi and Patrick stood beside them, but Patrick carefully kept his distance from her. He looked distinctly uncomfortable in the company of the androgynous young woman cosplaying the unapologetically gay video game character, reminding Rosie of Niles's assertion that Patrick was in the closet. Was his reticence due to the fact that Gairi was actually a girl, or was Patrick keeping his distance because the character was gay? He could apparently devour Jordan with his eyes, but only when people who knew him weren't around.

She was debating with herself about interrupting to say goodnight to their intern when Jordan caught up to them.

"Hey, we going to dinner?" he asked, looking every bit as fresh and polished as he had when they arrived at the convention that morning. Rosie envied him that. She felt greasy and exhausted from too much exposure to too many people in too close of quarters.

Niles glanced at his watch. "Actually, Jordie, Rosie and I have a raid forming up in about a half hour."

"Seriously?" Jordan rolled his eyes.

"If Rosie wants to bring her laptop over to my place," Niles said with a flick of his eyes in her direction, "we can all order pizza."

"Right. And I'll sit there watching TV while the two of you are on raid chat with your guild. No, thanks."

"You could always play with us," she taunted.

Jordan snorted. "Thanks, but I have better things to do on a Saturday night. I'll go out and get laid, like people with lives outside a computer sometimes do."

"Grotesque stereotyping!" Niles elbowed his brother in the ribs.

"Which happens to be true. When's the last time you picked someone up?"

"When's the last time I wasn't working eighty hours a week?" Niles shot back.

Jordan turned an arched eyebrow to Rosie, and she held up her hands. "Don't look at me. I've been trying to get him to go dancing for months." The arched eyebrow shifted in Niles's direction, and he shrugged helplessly. Rosie smirked. "Okay, here's the deal: if I score the killing blow on the last boss in the Vault tonight, then tomorrow night you go out to a club with me and Jordan for a few hours."

"Wait a minute!" Jordan protested. "You know Niles and I don't go clubbing together."

Rosie narrowed her eyes at him. "You want to get him out having fun for a few hours? Deal with it."

"It's not exactly a fair bet—for *you*," Niles taunted, laughing. "I'm your healer. I can make sure you don't live to make that killing blow."

Rosie narrowed her eyes. "Hey, I'm the tank that keeps your acolyte ass alive in your tissue-paper excuse for armor. Remember that if the temptation to play dirty gets to be too much to handle."

Niles sighed. "Fine. It's a bet."

Jordan fist-bumped Rosie and led the way out the door. When she turned to make sure Niles was with them, he was watching the cosplayers. Charity was putting some distance between herself and Patrick's stepbrother with a smile that looked a little forced. Another unwanted advance? She almost asked Niles if he'd seen what had preceded it, but he just shook his head and turned, following them out of the convention center.

CHAPTER 3

Jordan smiled at his brother as Niles juggled three bottles of beer from the bar to the sofa where he and Rosie sat. They were shouting a conversation at one another above the driving beat of the music, which pulsed through them so heavily Jordan could feel it rattling in his lungs.

"Bless you!" Rosie yelled as Niles set the bottles down. She abandoned her empty to grab one and took an enthusiastic swig of the cloudy microbrew. "Isn't this better than sitting around moping?"

"I don't mope!" Niles denied, grimacing. Jordan could practically hear his twin's internal mutterings about how ridiculous it was that simply carrying on a conversation was going to strip his voice hoarse by the time they left the club. After the convention on Saturday and now the club tonight, his introverted brother was no doubt reaching the limit of his ability to cope with the unwashed masses. Jordan, on the other hand, loved the noise and the activity.

"Speaking of last night's raid, what did you think of our new off-tank?"

Jordan rolled his eyes and tried to tune them out, but Niles squirmed uncomfortably beside him. "Bolment?" He cleared his throat. "After you logged off, he made some remarks on voice chat that required me to give him his first, last, and only warning about slurs and hate speech in guild spaces. I don't think he read the guidelines very well before he applied to the guild."

"What did he say?" Rosie's eyes narrowed. Never a good thing for whoever was the cause of that particular expression. Jordan spared a moment of sympathy for whoever or whatever the "off-tank" was.

Niles sighed. "When I mentioned that our raiding schedule isn't particularly demanding because of the hours you and I work. He apparently thought we'd raid more frequently than that, and complained that his last guild didn't have a tight enough raiding schedule because it was run by a bunch of 'pussy-whipped faggots' with 'family obligations.'"

"Seriously?" Rosie's thunderous expression lightened a little bit, and her mouth lifted in a sardonic smile.

"I tried to take a light-handed approach at first. I assured him that as a rule, unless our partner happens to be a trans man, we faggots are rarely pussy-whipped." Niles shrugged. "He didn't find it as amusing as I did. Which was why I had to bring the hammer down and give him his warning."

Niles sounded unhappy about that, which probably had as much to do with the fact that Niles hated confrontation as it did with however this Bolment guy had responded. Jordan laid an arm around his shoulders.

"How did he take it?" Rosie asked. She must have picked up on Niles's discomfort because her smile gentled.

Niles cleared his throat again. "We're now back to searching for a new off-tank."

"Oh, brother." Rosie sighed. "Ah well, it was clear he overstated his qualifications to begin with. He was one of the first to die on the Recollector, because he didn't have a clue about the mechanics."

"Unlike those of us who knew damn well what taking that AOE nuke was going to do to us if we didn't get out of line of sight, but stuck around to heal your ass anyway," Niles muttered, taking a swig of his beer.

"Sore loser!" Rosie taunted.

"It was a fucking wipe!" He leaned forward, growing more animated. "You were down to five percent health when the Recollector went down."

"Well, that's why I'm the boss." Rosie grinned and took another lusty drink.

Niles narrowed his eyes at her. "You could work on being a more gracious winner."

"Relax, bro." Jordan drew his tense body in close. "You're just cranky because Anthony called again."

"Now, see, I knew you should come out tonight. A breakup is *definitely* cause to go to a bar with friends and get hammered." Rosie smiled over the mouth of her bottle. "And hey, I finally got the two of you to go to a club together."

"This time only." Jordan shook his head with a small smile, tipping back his own beer.

"Okay, I don't get that!" She looked back and forth between Niles and Jordan, nearly pouting. "What the hell do the two of you have against going out together? You do everything else together. You even work for the same company!"

Niles caught Jordan's eye and then turned his head, jerking it in a subtle nod toward a guy who had been cruising them since Niles had walked up to the bar. "*That's* why."

Rosie gave him a puzzled frown. "What, because someone is checking you out?"

"No, because someone is checking *us* out." Niles sighed. "We can't go out together without every guy in the place assuming we're a package deal here to fulfill his twin fantasy. And we don't do that."

"*Anymore*." Jordan buried a smirk behind his beer. After a

bad breakup in college, Niles had had a brief slutty period, and they had quite a few fun memories from that time.

Rosie's eyebrows shot up, and she took a long swig of her beer. "Sorry, I need a moment alone with that mental image."

Niles snorted and leaned his head on Jordan's shoulder. He wondered—not for the first time—what exactly was troubling Niles. Something was going on he wasn't talking about. Jordan could just tell. And it wasn't that Niles was heartbroken over the breakup with Anthony, that much he knew. Niles had already admitted the chemistry between the two of them hadn't been working for quite a while. Jordan suspected he simply didn't want to have to start the search for a relationship all over again. Jordan was perfectly happy taking home a different guy every night, but with their thirty-second birthday looming, Niles was over the singles thing and counted himself among the ranks of the husband hunters.

"Careful, Rosie, you're bordering on becoming a stereotype." Jordan grinned at her, and Rosena shrugged.

"Come on, a *pair* of you, both gay. How often do you see that?"

"It's more common than you think." Niles took a slow drink of his beer, comfortably pressed against Jordan's side as she looked askance at him. Jordan let himself enjoy the fact that Niles was unwinding a bit. "I'm serious. If you're a gay identical twin, there's something like a fifty-two percent chance that your twin is gay too. It's one of the strongest arguments there is for a genetic component to sexual orientation."

"I bet it's actually higher," Jordan mused. "I bet whatever method they used to calculate that fifty-two percent figure doesn't take into consideration the twins whose siblings might be in the closet."

"That's a good point." Rosie hummed thoughtfully as Niles's pants pocket vibrated against Jordan's thigh. "Though, I imagine when the person who's pretty much literally your other half comes out, it'd make it a bit easier for the second twin to come out, no?"

"It definitely did for me." Niles set his beer down and dug in his pocket for his phone. He glanced at the text and rolled his eyes, stretching to stuff it back into his pocket, but Jordan snagged it from his hand first.

"Another one?" He frowned. No matter how many times Niles assured him that harassing messages were part and parcel of what he and Rosie were trying to accomplish at Third Wave, nothing was going to make him feel better about the fact that strangers were saying vile, threatening things to his brother.

Niles shrugged, smiling wryly. "Well, what did we expect after that 'petition' to take me off the writing staff before the Q&A yesterday? It's not like it's news to us that I'm considered a blight on gaming culture, what with me spreading my faggy influence all over the games."

Rosie grimaced at the mention of the petition. "I guess you have to admire their chutzpah, however misguided."

Niles grinned and saluted her with his beer. "I especially liked the assertion that we were 'forcing' the same-sex romance on the player by writing Gairi so that he flirts unless and until you tell him you're not interested."

Jordan scrolled through the texts on Niles's phone, anger beginning to sizzle in his gut. "Fuck, is there anything these guys won't say?"

Niles shrugged and grabbed it back. "You become inured to it after so many times of being told you should drink bleach and jump off an overpass into heavy traffic while fellating yourself."

Rosie snorted into her beer. "That's more inventive than having your body type and ethnicity disparaged while being told to get back to the kitchen before you make gamers into pussies and succeed in having all female characters dressed in nuns' habits."

Jordan looked up to catch her rueful smile. With her broad

shoulders, thick waist, large breasts, and wide hips—she was a good forty or so pounds over the near-anorexic "ideal"—Rosie was a prime target for cruel remarks concerning her appearance. Even though she seemed to be completely happy with her body, and was as outspoken against body shaming as she was on every other issue, the constant barrage had to be hurtful. "I don't think *inventive* is a word that belongs in the same sentence with these dickwads." Niles's phone vibrated again almost the moment he'd stuffed it back in his pocket. He ignored it, grabbing his beer instead.

"How often do they do that?" Jordan demanded, gesturing to the outline of the phone beneath the denim.

"Do what?"

Another vibration. Jordan resisted the urge to jerk the phone back out himself and see what they were saying to his brother now. "Actually threaten you?"

"That wasn't a threat."

"'Get fucked with a chainsaw, you worthless cunt,' isn't a threat?"

"Probably not in the legal sense. Not unless the person in question is saying, 'I'm going to fuck you with a chainsaw'—"

"I've got a few thousand of those in my files, if you want to compare," Rosie muttered.

"—That would be a threat. This is just . . . some basement-dwelling trogg using his mom's computer to talk like a big man about a game he bought with his dad's credit card."

Rosie gave him a censuring look. "Niles. Seriously? You, of all people, stereotyping gamers?"

"Sorry." Niles gave her an apologetic smile. Jordan understood all too well. As Third Wave's marketing director—and a staunch nongamer—he'd been the target more than once of a lecture about the truth behind gamer demographics, but it really was all too easy to assume this sort of behavior was the province of kids, given how immature it was.

He wasn't going to let the two of them divert him, however. "How many of these do you receive in a day?" Jordan demanded. "And don't try to parse semantics of what does and doesn't constitute a threat."

Rosie shrugged and answered for Niles. Jordan knew no matter how vile the abuse and harassment heaped on his brother, it was nothing to what Rosie was regularly inundated with. "Depends on the day. If we've recently released news or done an interview that pisses someone off, it could be hundreds. If it's a slow news day, maybe only a few. This week will be interesting, because you *know* that video of my response to that petition is going up on YouTube. There will be another wave of rape and death threats for me, threats of violence and homophobic slurs for Niles. Same old, same old. They're persistent but not particularly original."

"Have you thought about hiring security staff for Third Wave?" Jordan leaned toward Rosie, bracing his elbows on his spread knees. Unlike the two of them, Jordan wasn't going to accept that such treatment was the cost of doing business.

Maybe it was because he had more of an outsider's point of view on the whole issue. He hadn't come on as Third Wave's marketing director until after the furor over *Phoenix Force 2* had died down, and Niles hadn't ever been particularly candid about the harassment until Jordan had been in a position to witness it firsthand. "And I don't mean those rent-a-cops who patrol the building at night to keep someone from stealing the equipment or the guy at the front desk trying to prevent industrial espionage. I mean a security team whose job it is to track down the source of threats like this and analyze them to make sure they're not coming from legitimate crazies."

"'Crazies.' Nice ableist language, there." Rosie gave him a brief censuring look, and Jordan dipped his head apologetically. "Want me to hire bodyguards while I'm at it?" she asked with a roll of her eyes.

"Relax, Jordie." Niles pulled on Jordan's shoulder, urging him to recline against the back of the sofa again. "Finish your beer, go dance, pick up someone to take home tonight. You're making too big a deal of this."

He scowled at Niles. "My brother is being threatened. Pardon me if I take that seriously. I want to know who these people are and take legal action until they back the fuck off."

"Last I checked, freedom of speech was still a thing, even when it comes to hate speech," Rosie offered with a wry smile.

"Last I checked, harassment wasn't protected by the First Amendment."

"True, but there are hundreds, maybe thousands of these guys, and we can't track them all down and file complaints against them." Rosie sighed and patted his knee. "Look, I'm the first to adopt a zero-tolerance policy on unacceptable behavior, but we have to be careful here. Too much of a reaction will just egg them on. They're attention whores. The worst thing you can do is let these guys think they've had an impact. I've gone on record supporting Niles and made it clear that Third Wave values him. There's nothing else to do. Shrug them off. Go dance. I'll get us a fresh round of beers."

"Hi, everyone!"

Niles startled under Jordan's arm at the voice behind them, and Rosie laughed in delighted surprise. Jordan turned to see the writing staff intern—what was his name? Paul? Peter?—standing there.

"Hello, Patrick! How are you tonight?" Rosie asked with a smile.

"I'm doing good!" The intern licked his lips, his eyes darting around the club nervously. His smile looked eager and yet a little forced. "Thanks for inviting me, Mr. Riv—er, Niles."

"My pleasure. Seemed like you could use an evening out when I bumped into you back at the con today. Did you ditch your stepbrother and his friends?" Niles asked carefully, and from the way Patrick's face shuttered and the avid light went out of his eyes, Jordan could tell Niles knew something Jordan didn't about the dynamics the intern had with his family. In fact, judging from Niles's solicitous demeanor, Jordan would bet Niles bumping into Patrick and extending an invitation to come out for the evening was no accident. He certainly hadn't had a work-related reason to return to the convention that afternoon.

"They, um, they don't know I'm here." Patrick rubbed the back of his neck, looking at the floor. Ah. Okay. The kid wasn't out yet. Sympathy warmed Jordan's regard of the guy. "I didn't want to hang with them again after yesterday. They don't— I mean, I-I haven't—"

Niles reached over the back of the sofa to lay a sympathetic hand on Patrick's arm, bringing his stammering to a halt. "It's okay, Patrick. We get it."

Rosie smiled softly. "You're fine here. Don't worry. I assume you're twenty-one, since you got through the door?" Patrick nodded quickly, watching her with attention that suggested he thought he was still on the job and talking to his boss. Rosie dug in her pocket and came up with a folded bill. "Here. Go buy yourself a beer, then come back, and we'll dance for a bit. Okay?"

Patrick nodded again, his eyes wide as he took the bill. "Yes, ma'am." He scurried off before Rosie could suggest he call her anything else.

Niles, Jordan, and Rosie all settled back with identical indulgent smiles and sighed nearly in unison. The wistful *Ahh, kids these days* was unspoken, but the sentiment hung in the air. Silence settled among them as Rosie scanned the club.

Niles's pocket vibrated again, and he groaned quietly, but not quietly enough that Jordan couldn't hear it, as he dug for his phone.

Go suck that Candylandia dyke's dick and quit fagging up our games, Jordan read over his brother's shoulder.

Niles sighed. From what Jordan understood, the trolls were always looking for clever ways to get in a dig about Rosie's weight and/or sexuality. Which was interesting because no one —including he and Niles—knew exactly what her sexuality was. Rosie liked it that way, because then she could take people to task for making assumptions.

"Hey." Jordan looked up when Rosie spoke, and she tipped her head, nodding off to the side. "Over there at the cluster of tables by the door. Be subtle."

Niles peeked first and then groaned again. Affecting a casual glance around the club, Jordan looked too, noting a pair of guys not much older than Patrick, neither of whom was dressed remotely as though they'd come to the club with the intention of attracting company. In fact, their clothing screamed *Straight dude* so loudly that everyone in the club was giving them the side eye. One of the guys kept gazing around with an expression of distaste, while the other was typing something into his phone.

A moment later, Niles's pocket buzzed.

Jordan's brow furrowed and he glanced at Rosie, confused. She snorted. "It's our petitioners. Well, two of them, at least. They *actually* came into a gay club?"

Yeah, they came into a gay club to pursue and harass his brother. Jordan gritted his teeth. "What the fuck?"

"Want to bet they think they're supersleuths or some shit, trying to get dirt on me? Maybe hoping to catch me getting sucked off in an alley?" Niles sighed and shook his head, looking —to Jordan's mind—more amused than he should be.

They discreetly monitored the guys for another moment, until the timing between the one using his phone and the arrival of harassing texts was irrefutable. Setting his jaw, Jordan rose and began to unbutton his shirt. "That's it. I'm going to handle this."

Rosie grabbed her own phone and followed, leaving Niles to scramble after them.

With his shirt hanging wide open, his skin damp with sweat from the heat generated by the sheer crush of people, Jordan sauntered up to the pair and draped an arm around each of their shoulders, pulling them in intimately close, not letting them jerk away. He pasted his best barracuda smile in place, the one Niles said meant he was about to eat someone alive. "Hey, guys, having a good time?" A second later, the flash of Rosie's phone camera lit them up as they stood there with identical expressions of panic on their faces.

He plucked the phone out of the texting guy's hand and began scanning through it while Niles shook his head at them.

"You know how many federal and state communications laws you're in violation of with these?" Jordan asked conversationally, shoving the phone back at the guy. He didn't wait for an answer. "I don't, either, but I imagine it's enough to face some pretty hefty fines. Maybe even time in prison."

Rosie looked up from admiring the picture on her phone, her grin positively evil. "This is going to look great splashed all over the Third Wave fan forums. *Homophobe petitioners party with Third Wave staff in gay bar.* Thanks to that petition, we even have their usernames, so I can tag them in the caption."

The two young men scrabbled to get away, rushing out of the club like it was on fire, and Jordan looked over to see Patrick coming up behind Niles, who was watching them with a bemused expression.

"What's going on?" Patrick asked.

Rosie patted his shoulder. "Just handling some trolls. Come on, I want to dance. Niles, Jordie, you guys in?"

"Nah." Jordan tossed his shirt to Niles and looked around the crowd. "I think I'm going to take my brother's advice and find someone to take home tonight. Catch you later."

He felt someone's eyes on him as he melted into the crowd, probably the intern watching him with that puppy-dog look Jordan sometimes caught the kid giving him. He'd be okay with

Niles and Rosie, though. Better than with him. He wouldn't touch Patrick even if he wasn't an intern with Third Wave. Jordan didn't do closeted guys, or guys so inexperienced that the new-car smell hadn't even faded yet. And right now, Jordan had some anger he needed to burn off.

———

"YOU ALL RIGHT?" Niles glanced over at the tipsy intern in his passenger seat. Patrick still swayed a little unsteadily, but his babble had faded away and his demeanor grew more sober the closer they got to his house.

"Hmm? Yeah, sure." He was staring out the side window as if afraid to look anywhere else. Niles had been almost certain he'd seen someone lure Patrick into the back room around midnight, but Patrick wasn't acting much like a guy who'd gotten laid or sucked off or whatever he'd done back there. He was acting like a guy going to his execution.

Once again, Niles found himself wondering just what Patrick's relationship with his family was like. He'd nearly panicked when he'd realized that he'd missed the last MAX train, at least until Niles had offered to give him a ride so that he didn't need to call home or take a cab. It was out of his way— Niles could almost have walked home from the club to his historic Victorian in Northwest—but Patrick had been so distressed that he couldn't leave the guy hanging, especially since Jordan had already taken off and Rosie was heading in the entirely opposite direction.

"You know, Patrick . . ." Niles sighed and rubbed a hand through his hair as he pulled to the curb in front of the Crafts-man-style bungalow his intern pointed to. He wasn't really sure what he wanted to say, but Patrick seemed like he needed something, even if Niles had no idea what. If he was right that Patrick wasn't out to his family yet, but moving in that direction, the least Niles could do was offer him a sympathetic ear. "Look, my cell number is on the list of employee contact numbers. If you ever have any trouble or need anything, even just to talk, you can give me a call, all right?"

The intern nodded, never meeting Niles's eyes. "Sure, um, Niles. Thanks. I'll see you tomorrow. Well, later today, I guess."

"Yeah. See you then."

With his head hung, Patrick closed the car door behind him. Niles tracked his progress up the front walk to the house and waited while he fumbled with his keys. The back of his neck prickled; the sensation of being watched sent a shiver rippling down his spine, but all the blinds and curtains he could see seemed to be closed and the street was deserted at nearly 2 a.m. Then the porch light came on and someone opened the door for Patrick. The feeling faded, and when the door shut again, Niles drove away.

————

HE GAVE up trying to sleep at five o'clock, after a few hours of staring at the ceiling and dozing fitfully, his restlessness fueled by a nameless and shapeless anxiety. The elegantly cozy house he'd bought after the first *Phoenix Force* game went platinum felt too cold and empty, each creak of the house startling Niles just as he'd started to nod off again.

Finally, he flung the covers back, pulled on a sweatshirt and flannel pajama bottoms over his boxers, and shuffled downstairs to his desk in the living room. At some point since he'd gotten home, it had begun raining in earnest, a stiff wind pelting water against the leaded glass windows. Even with all the city lights, there were too many shadows in the house, and Niles circled the room, switching on table lamps and lighting the gas fireplace.

A crash from the front yard brought him springing to his feet, his heart racing. With a longing look at the empty coffeemaker, Niles bypassed the kitchen and undid the chain and dead bolts on the front door. His porch furniture was all still in place, despite the best efforts of the gusting wind, but the gate between the tall hedges that bordered his front yard swung wildly, knocking against the stones lining the path from the sidewalk to the porch.

Sighing at his own jumpiness, he slipped his bare feet into the nearest pair of shoes and clutched his robe around himself. The stinging rain drove against his cheeks like needles as he dashed up the walk to close and latch the gate. His glasses were quickly becoming too water-spotted to see much, but it was useless to look around anyway. Whichever passerby had decided to unlatch the gate, they were no doubt long gone.

As he reached the porch again, his cell phone rang from where it sat on the hallway table beside the mail. Cursing over yet another delay between him and a hot cup of coffee, he toed off his shoes and removed his useless glasses. And promptly slipped on an envelope he'd either missed or dropped when he'd gathered up the mail from beneath the slot in the door on Saturday. He caught himself on the table and snatched the phone to his ear in a single, graceless lurch.

"Yeah?" he gasped.

"Niles? You okay?"

"Yeah, I'm fine, Jordie." Shivering, he crouched to pick up the letter, frowning at it. "What the hell are you calling me for this time of morning?"

"Well, you're awake, aren't you?"

"Doesn't answer my question." He squinted and turned the envelope over in his hands. There was no return address, but that wasn't unusual for things like leaflets and credit card offers. His address was neatly printed in Times New Roman on the front, but there was no "To the resident at . . ." to indicate it was junk mail. Weird. It was probably still junk, but curiosity compelled him not to drop it in the shredder.

He could practically hear Jordan's nonchalant shrug. "I'm just heading home. Thought I'd offer to take you to breakfast before I went in to work."

"Damn, whoever you went home with must have been good if you're just now leaving."

"Eh, he was okay. I just need to give up on twinks. Think I'm getting too old for them. Not enough experience to give a really killer blowjob. Kind of fun to show them how it's done, though."

Niles huffed a brief laugh, shaking his head. "Whatever floats your boat, man."

"So, you in for breakfast or not?"

"Yeah, okay, breakfast sounds good." He dropped the envelope on the table with the rest of the mail and gave the coffeemaker one last yearning glance before heading upstairs.

"Thought so. I'm almost there. See you in a few."

"Mm-hmm. Just let yourself in. I'm hopping in the shower."

"Right. Okay." There was silence on the line as Jordan failed to disconnect as Niles expected him to. He waited, letting his damp robe fall at the threshold of the master bath. "You sure you're all right?" Jordan finally asked, concern evident in his voice.

"Sure. Why wouldn't I be?"

"Something seemed wrong when you answered the phone."

"Nah, I just nearly killed myself trying to get to it in time. I'd had to go outside to close the gate. So except for being way too short on sleep—for which I hold you and Rosie completely responsible, in case you're wondering—I'm fine."

"Okay." Jordan didn't sound convinced, but Niles wasn't going to stand around shivering, trying to reassure him.

"I'm starting the shower now. See you in a few." He hung up before his brother had a chance to fret any further.

CHAPTER 4

"Jesus, what did he do, hit her with a brick?" Detective Timothy Wyatt stared down at the remains of what—judging by the rest of her—had once been a young blonde woman. He tried to get a sense of her features, but it was near impossible due to the massive bruising that mottled her face. Tim glanced up through the barren branches at the misting sky, breaking away from the sight long enough to distance himself from it a little. All around him, the park was ripe with the scent of decaying greenery as autumn's fallen foliage decomposed. He let it fill his lungs before looking down again.

Nathaniel McDermott, the medical examiner, shook his head. "I'm going to tentatively call it a two-by-four. There's a broad bruise across her back, and in the abrasions are splinters of what I'm fairly certain is processed lumber, since I'm not finding any bits of bark along with them."

There was no evidence of any sort of weapon in the vicinity. "And the killer kept it?"

Tim's partner, Detective Angela Payne, ducked under the crime-scene tape and came to a stop by his side. "Could have just been whatever was lying around. Or it could have been planned out. It's an easy weapon to dispose of." She looked down at the body. "All you need is a fireplace."

"What would a two-by-four be doing in the middle of a million trees?" He rubbed his chin for a moment, frowning. "That bruise across her shoulders . . . Are we thinking he—or she—got the drop on her? She comes around the corner, he hits her from behind, knocks her down, and goes to town?"

McDermott nodded. "It's possible. There's blood spatter on the ground and tree trunks. The attack took place right in this spot. We're going to have a hard time getting footprints with all the leaves on the ground, though. If this drizzle had fallen twenty-four hours ago, we'd have an easier time of it."

"I'll be sure to register a complaint, see if we can do something about that." Tim gave McDermott a wry smile.

"What would someone wearing *those* boots be doing in Forest Park?" Payne frowned, her eyes moving up and down the corpse. "Take it from me, Wyatt, you don't wear spike heels where it's not paved. They punch into the sod, and then you break your fuckin' ankle."

"What would someone dressed like her be doing in Forest Park to begin with?" Tim eyeballed the tight, shiny brown leather pants wrapped around the young woman's legs. Tatters and shreds of dried leaves stuck to her clothing where blood and rain had wetted it, as they did to her bruised face. "Was she out at a club? Sex worker? What call girl meets a john on a hiking trail?"

Payne shrugged. "Maybe she was just on a date and the guy brought her here? Though, if you ask me, those aren't date clothes, either. They're not easy-access enough for her to be a stripper, and they'd be damned inconvenient if she was turning a trick." She looked up from the body. "Besides, what are those pockets by her shoulder? Could it be a costume? Maybe she was a model?"

McDermott snorted, tucking away his measuring tape. "Not likely. She's only five foot four."

"Not like a fashion model. A personal one," Payne clarified. "Some private photographer wanted to do a fetish-wear shoot, maybe? That would explain the outfit and location."

A uniform came jogging over, forestalling Tim's reply.

"We found her bag," he panted. "It's over in the trees back that way. Documenting the scene now."

Tim glanced at his partner and followed the rookie over the uneven ground to another cordoned-off area where a backpack lay at the base of a shallow gully.

"We just finished photographing the area," a tech informed him. "We think it was thrown down from that jogging path up there."

"How many sets of footprints are we going to find on a popular jogging path?" Payne grumbled.

The tech grimaced. "Too many. I'll let you know what we find."

"No wonder it took so long to find the bag." Tim pulled on a pair of gloves, squatting down beside the pack. "We thought we were looking for a purse or a handbag, something to match the clothes."

Payne drew closer as he unzipped it. "No change of clothing, so if she was doing a photo shoot— Wait. A parking pass for the Portland Convention Center?" She hummed thoughtfully. "That could be our answer. Maybe she was a booth babe. A lot of strippers moonlight doing that sort of thing."

"Wouldn't it be sunlight?" Tim shrank away from the flat look Payne gave him. "Anyway, I thought they only had those at conventions in Las Vegas. But we'll check the venue, find out what events were going on there over the weekend." He rifled carefully through the printouts and notebooks stuffed into the pack. "She was a student. This is all schoolwork. Media trends. Feminist theory. Looks like notes for a paper. Any ID?"

"Here it is." Payne located a wallet in one of the outer pouches and pulled out a student ID. "Charity Anspach, enrolled at PSU. Assuming this is her bag. We'll have to make sure the ID matches the body."

"Which could take a while, considering the condition of her face, especially if she hasn't been fingerprinted before."

She sighed. "Fuck. And then we get to tell her parents they're not going to see her graduate. Come on. Let's see if there's an ex and work our way through it."

———

JORDAN'S PHONE had already been vibrating with texts, warning him, before he arrived to see that there were people with signs picketing on the sidewalk outside the Third Wave Studios offices. Signs which read, "Protect our Children!" and "End the Violence." There were even a couple about stopping the homosexual agenda. That was new, at least as far as the real-life picketers went. It wasn't the first time antigaming crusaders had taken aim at Third Wave for their content, and those groups had been on a rampage since the Sandy Hook shooting, courtesy of the NRA attempting to divert blame to the gaming industry. The *Phoenix Force* franchise was no more graphically violent than any other first-person shooter game, nor was the sexual content any more explicit than any other RPG. It was considerably milder than many titles in the genre, in fact, and none of the violence was sexualized, which couldn't be said for many other games.

But logic had little to do with the protesters' platform.

Great. Just great. Because the harassment Niles was already getting wasn't enough.

Jordan frowned again as he recalled the texts Niles had received last night. It was harder than he would have thought, seeing what some of the trolls were saying to and about Niles. Now the occasional glum and besieged phases Niles and Rosie went through made a lot more sense. He hadn't been able to stop thinking about it since, even after he'd left the guy he'd picked up.

He'd lied to Niles about where he'd been all night. After leaving the twink, he'd gone into the office and started looking through the stacks of fan mail, as well as the email from the contact box on the studio website. There was much more where the harassing texts had come from. There were entire fan forums dedicated to malcontents who were unhappy with the gay storylines in Third Wave games. The shit the twerps said on the various forums, showing their internet dicks and talking big to try to impress one another, seeing who could say the vilest thing, was even worse. Jordan had started making accounts on every board and forum and mailing list he could find to keep track of them all, under the rationale that as Third Wave's marketing director, he should know what the fans were saying, even the negative stuff. They kept egging each other on, prompting ever more extravagant threats and insults, and the big brother in him—admittedly only by six minutes, but still—wanted to start bashing heads together.

Sighing, he drove past the protesters, then hung his laptop case on his shoulder, and headed inside to where Niles and Rosie were talking in the door of the break room, cradling cups of coffee and looking far more tense than the picketers accounted for.

"So what's their beef today?" Jordan asked, striding toward his office as they fell in step with him.

"They found a new angle," Rosie nearly growled. "That video went up on YouTube just like I predicted it would, and now Niles is the poster boy for fags everywhere trying to push the gay agenda on unsuspecting kids."

Jordan set his bag down a little harder than necessary in his chair. "Wait. They got that from you informing them that Niles wasn't on the writing staff for *Age of Valiance*?"

"He's our lead writer, even if he's not working on a specific title. Or that's the argument they're using."

Niles grabbed a remote off the filing cabinet and turned on the TV on the wall in the corner of Jordan's office. "They've called the news outlets. There are going to be interviews."

"Shit." Jordan closed his eyes, imagining declining sales after the news broadcast claimed that Third Wave was shoving gay storylines on people's kids. This was going to take some spin control. "We need to get ahead of this. Start a marketing campaign immediately touting the message of acceptance and diversity inherent in Third Wave's games. Get it out to liberal parenting sites, not just LGBT and ally sites. We need to hammer home the message that equality is the ultimate family value. I'm going to draft a post for our social forums to be released immediately and start scheduling interviews."

"Get on it, then," Rosie said shortly. "In the meantime, we've got another problem."

"It's not a problem." Niles spoke between gritted teeth.

"The fuck it isn't!" She snatched an envelope from his hands and threw it on Jordan's desk. He picked it up. It had Niles's name and address on it and inside was a plain, white sheet of paper with two large, stark words:

WATCH YOURSELF

Jordan blinked at it. "You still going to tell me they're not threatening you?"

"Don't make a big deal out of it." Niles ran a hand through his hair. "We might not get many of these sorts of fan letters by snail mail, but they do come."

"To your *home address*?" Rosie folded her arms across her chest, her posture aggressive. Yesterday, she'd been on Niles's side of this issue, but today she was clearly in Jordan's camp. "It's bad enough that they've got your personal cell phone number."

Niles rubbed his forehead as if he were getting a headache. "It doesn't matter. It's still just a bunch of punks talking big."

She narrowed her eyes. "If they've tracked down your physical address, we have to assume it's more than talk."

"Oh, come on! Finding someone's physical address is a search away these days. I don't remember you reacting this way when the Google Earth images of your house went online."

Rosie went very still. "You're right. I didn't react. I just sold the house I loved and moved into a cookie-cutter high-rise condo building downtown with a doorman and a security system." The ragged edge to her voice cut through the heated debate, and Niles fell silent. "I let them make me afraid. I let them drive me out of my house, Niles, and if you didn't see me react to that, you weren't paying attention."

"Rosie—" Niles reached out to her, but she was still closed off, pulled into herself. Making an admission like that had to have cost her.

A detail caught Jordan's eye, and he felt himself go cold. "*Jesus!* Niles, there's no stamp on the fucking envelope."

"So?"

"You didn't notice?" Jordan slid it across the desk back at him, and Niles stared at it, blinking. "Whoever sent this hand delivered it."

"Oh Christ." Rosie covered her mouth with her hand. "Niles, they were at your house."

"Fuck." Niles dropped into a chair, closing his eyes and letting his head tip back.

"Okay, we should call the cops about this." Jordan picked up the envelope Niles had left sitting on his desk, and studied it again.

Niles scoffed. "And say what? A bunch of gaming geeks are stalking me because they have a stick up their ass about queer characters in their games? The cops aren't exactly well-known for taking gay issues all that seriously."

Jordan rolled his eyes. "C'mon. This is Portland, not the Deep South, and you know it. Besides, getting them to investigate isn't the point, at least not yet. Starting a paper trail of complaints is, so if it escalates, they can see that it's an ongoing problem."

"Or if it ever does get serious—which it *won't*—they won't believe me because they think I've been overreacting to every troll who tries to bait me."

Rosie gave him a flat look, leaning against the wall. "Okay, Niles, I get it. You know I do. It's nearly impossible in gaming culture to separate out the genuine threats from the usual smack talk. You don't want to overreact because you don't want to make it look like you can't cut it. You don't want to seem like some precious snowflake. *I get it.* But *this* is not trolling. *This* is menacing. They've crossed the line. At the very least, whoever left that note for you was trespassing. And probably in violation of some postal laws."

"Fine. Okay." Niles's jaw shifted as he glanced back and forth between them. "If I make the complaint, will the two of you quit nagging me and let me get back to writing? In case you've forgotten, I've got a production deadline for the Gairi DLC."

"I'll go with you to the police bureau at lunch." Jordan gave him a tight smile, and Niles tensed as though he was going to argue again. Then he pushed himself up out of the chair and strode from Jordan's office. They stared after him.

"I get why he didn't want to overreact, which is why I backed him at the club last night." Rosie slipped into the chair Niles had vacated. "But why am I getting the vibe that his resistance to the idea that this might be a problem goes deeper than that?"

"He's a pacifist." Jordan tapped the end of a pen against his desk blotter. He was far more edgy and energized now than he'd been when he'd arrived at the office. He hadn't slept in over twenty-four hours, either, and this wasn't going to do a thing to help him rest tonight. "Always has been. I don't think he's really ever internalized how serious homophobic violence can be. He can't conceive of someone having that much hate in themselves."

She smiled at him, her eyes soft. "I don't think you realize just how sappy you get when you talk about him."

Jordan ducked his head, coloring. "He's my brother. Good thing, too. Someone's got to look out for him because he'll never look out for himself."

"You think *they* realize that about him?" She jerked her head toward the exterior wall of the building and ostensibly the picketers outside. "This guy they're so up in arms about, who is such a threat to their kids, is just a gentle little lamb who wants to write stories about people like himself finding love and being heroes."

"Do you think it matters to them?" Jordan grimaced and turned up the volume on the TV. The local morning show had just cut to the reporter outside Third Wave's headquarters, where an officious-looking guy had handed off his picket sign to act as spokesman.

"What we're seeing here is a clear-cut agenda, an insidious attempt to work fringe liberal ideology into the hearts and minds of our kids through what is commonly perceived as harmless entertainment. We, the concerned citizens who form the Coalition for Responsible Media, are making a point of bringing to light this sort of brainwashing that's being embedded in music, television, movies, and even video games, and bring back family-friendly entertainment . . ."

CHAPTER 5

"All right, Patrick. Run these to the printers, and then go ahead and take your lunch."

"Sure, Mr. River . . . Niles." Patrick accepted the thumb drive with the files on it and tucked it into his breast pocket, none of his usual puppylike eagerness present. "Anything else?"

"Nope. How are you? Everything still going okay?" It was as close as Niles could come to prying without invitation.

"I guess." He shrugged. If he'd seemed subdued Sunday night after the club, today he seemed downright depressed. "I'm looking for a roommate. I really don't feel like I can stay with my stepdad and stepbrother much longer."

"Any trouble after you got home last night?"

Patrick shrugged, staring at the wall past Niles's shoulder. "Um, just, um, well, you know, my stepdad is sort of intense." *Read: homophobic*, Niles interjected mentally. "And my stepbrother, Charlie, he hangs out with his cousin and some of their guild-mates a lot." He shuffled his feet. "A few of the guys came into town for the con this weekend and headed out yesterday."

"Sounds cool. You ever play with them?"

"Um. No. Not anymore." Something in Patrick's eyes flashed,

as though he were near tears, but he wouldn't look at Niles, and his body language was screaming for Niles to shut up. Suppressing a sigh, Niles tried shifting the conversation in another direction.

"That's great that you're trying to find your own place. A little harder to cut on an intern's wages, but sometimes you just need to be on your own. Any prospects?"

Patrick nodded. "One guy. He's a little older, but he's cool, though. Found him in a local game store. He's got the most amazing gaming rig, and he said he wouldn't mind if I use it while he's working."

"Awesome." Niles smiled encouragingly. Anything that would help Patrick get comfortable in his skin could only be a good thing. He was tired of seeing a shadow on the kid's face every time his family was mentioned. Patrick didn't quite manage to smile back, but he practically genuflected on his way out the door, leaving Niles shaking his head.

"Hey." Jordan's head popped around the door to Niles's office just as he was trying to turn his attention back to his work, and Niles looked up at his brother. Over the course of the morning, he'd managed to get a grip on his irritation at Jordan's and Rosie's overreaction to the note in his mail, but seeing Jordan reminded him about their agreement to go down to the bureau of police, and he felt the tension creeping in again.

"Lunchtime already?" He glanced back at the script on his laptop. So much for his hopes of finding his stride again. *PF3*'s first expansion—which would be offered as downloadable content—was due to be released just two months after the game went live, so they were under the gun to finish it. It was an important DLC pack because it dealt heavily with Gairi's background and upbringing, some of the mystery that shrouded his past becoming clear. It also had the potential to escalate matters if the player character was involved in a relationship with Gairi when they reached the end of *PF3*. That sort of continuation in an expansion pack was always hugely important to players who had invested themselves in the emotional storyline.

"Actually, I'm not going to be able to make it." Niles's head came up as Jordan squirmed. "Sorry. I began scheduling some of those media appearances I was talking about and one of the webcasts I contacted had a last-minute opening for this afternoon because another guest canceled, so now I'm doing that. You're still going, though."

"Oh, am I?" Niles snapped his laptop closed so he could focus on his brother.

"Come on, dude. Don't make me babysit you through this. Just file the damn report, nothing to it."

"Nothing except that it's ridiculous and unnecessary."

"Maybe, but humor me, okay? Or I'll sic Mom on you."

"Now, that's just mean."

"You know I'll do it."

Niles laughed, hanging his head. "Fine, fine. I'll go." He stared at the mirror image of his own face across the desk. "I'm not sure you aren't worse than Mom."

"Hey, at least I don't force-feed you while I nag." Jordan grinned and pushed himself away from where he'd been propping up the doorjamb. "I'll see you after I'm done with the webcast and you can tell me about the hot cops."

"Right." Niles snorted. "Assuming I spot any through the mass of potbellied desk jockeys." He stood and smoothed the Oxford shirt he had tucked into a comfortable pair of jeans. Third Wave, like many gaming studios, didn't have a stringent dress code for the office. Jordan wore suits more often than not because he never knew when he was going to have to take a marketing meeting, but being a writer, Niles could get away with going casual. He shrugged into his light leather jacket, stuffed his teeny MacBook Air into his messenger bag, and hung it over his shoulder. Maybe he could get some writing done while he was waiting for someone to take his report.

The picket line hadn't dispersed even though the morning-show broadcasts were over. Niles couldn't hear what they were saying as he opened his car door and shut himself inside. At least they kept their protest safely on the sidewalk and off the property of Third Wave Studios itself, though he thought they'd gotten a little louder when they saw him emerge from the building. He couldn't let himself dwell on the monumental injustice of their making him and his stories the scapegoat for whatever they felt was wrong with society. Most days it was easy to shrug off, but today he felt particularly raw about it.

Maybe it was just Jordan and Rosie getting to him.

His phone rang while he was driving past the protesters—not the buzz of an incoming text message this time, thankfully—and he answered it as he turned out of the parking lot.

"Niles?" Anthony's aggressive tenor filled his ear before he had a chance to regret not checking the caller ID. "Where are you?"

"I'm in the car, Anthony. I have to pay attention to driving. What do you need?"

"I tried calling you at home on Saturday, and you weren't there. Were you out?"

At the intersection, Niles began to drum his fingertips on the steering wheel, the turn signal clicking rhythmically under the sound of the phone at his ear. "I had a convention to go to in the afternoon, and then Rosie and I were raiding that night."

"I was expecting you to be at work right now. You usually don't take lunch this early."

"I have things to do today. What do you need?" He didn't like repeating himself, but apparently Anthony was too fixated on knowing exactly where he was and what he was doing at all times to get to the point.

"What sort of things?"

Niles sighed. "Anthony, I don't mean to be rude, but this is why we broke up. Because you have to be all up in my business every minute of the day. I wanted a boyfriend, not a warden. But now we're broken up, so I have no obligation to account for where I'm going or why or with whom."

"Sorry. Sorry." Anthony's voice was instantly contrite. "I'll stop being so nosy. I just thought I'd ask if you wanted to get together for lunch."

What part of broken up don't you get? "Sorry, but I have to take care of some stuff."

"You sure? I'd really love to see you. You *did* say we could give being friends a try."

Fuck. "Yeah, I did, but today isn't a good day." Niles hit the accelerator when the light turned, gnawing on his lip as he debated how to respond. "Maybe in a week or two, but things are a little crazy just now. We'll have to see."

"I'm not sure being friends is going to work if you're never around when I ask to see you."

"Yeah, well, it's definitely not going to work if I can't have space to take care of things when I need to, either. Look, I've got to go. I'll talk to you sometime, okay?"

He hung up, cutting Anthony off midprotest, and spent the rest of the drive irritated with himself for ever letting Anthony hold on to that bit of hope that they might be friends. He'd wanted to soften the blow because Anthony was sweet, even if he was clingy, but it wasn't going very well. Anthony obviously wasn't getting the hints that it wasn't working. If this continued, Niles was going to have to be a dick about it because the kind-but-blunt approach only seemed to offer Anthony encouragement.

Once he got to the police station, Niles walked toward the building in the misting November not-quite-rain. He stood outside for a minute, staring at the doors and willing himself to go in and report this stupid incident. He briefly debated simply leaving, taking a long, leisurely lunch at Veritable Quandary or Kell's Irish Pub, and telling Jordan and Rosie he'd reported the harassment. But Jordan always knew when he was lying, so what was the point?

"*Niles?*"

Oh fuck. He knew that voice. Knew it in the "sometimes still dreamed of it even ten years later" sense. Swallowing, Niles turned slowly from the doors to face his ex. If you could call a guy who had, in the end, denied the relationship had even existed an "ex." Timothy Wyatt had been the first guy Niles had ever known who was so determined to remain in the closet that he'd be downright cruel to anyone even thinking of urging him to come out.

Tim was approaching from the on-street parking reserved for cops, dressed in a suit with an equally well-dressed woman beside him. His slightly gingery hair was curling a little in the humidity, which made him appear ruffled and rakish, and his blue-gray eyes were alight, as if he were thrilled to see Niles.

Damn. It really wasn't fair that he looked that good after all this time.

"Tim. Wow. Hi." Niles ventured an uncertain smile, wondering just how familiar he should be with a one-time college classmate. "What the hell are you doing in Portland? Is this your wife?" He extended his hand reflexively, his smile firming up as he found his equilibrium.

"What?" Tim looked startled and quickly shook his head as the woman beside him guffawed. "Um, no, of course not. This is my partner, Detective Angela Payne. I'm with the Portland Police Bureau now. I've been here for . . ." He glanced at the woman for confirmation. "Seven years?"

"S-seven years? Really?" Just like that, Niles's composure staggered again. "Um, pleased to meet you, Detective Payne. I'm Niles River." She shook his proffered hand, looking wryly amused. Niles glanced back at Tim, who was blinking and seemed a little stunned himself, as if he couldn't quite believe he'd run into Niles.

That makes two of us, honey.

The detective gave him an inquisitive half smile, eyes sparking in her dark-brown face. She was almost as tall as Tim was, which was impressive. He would get a crick in his neck if he had to stand here and talk with them both for too long. "Niles River? So, when you were in school and they called your name out, they said, 'River, Niles.' Your parents did that to you on purpose?"

Niles laughed. He'd had to develop a sense of humor about his name long ago, or he'd be pissed off anew with every introduction. Bantering with the other detective also gave him a reason to avoid Tim's gaze, which had shifted from disbelieving to taking in Niles as if he'd been starved for the sight of him.

Not very circumspect for a guy so firmly in the closet you could hang clothes on him.

"Yes, they really did. They're both MDs and did a lot of travel for Doctors Without Borders and decided they should commemorate the journey which resulted in our conception. My twin brother is named Jordan."

"Oh *God*." She groaned, laughing with him.

"So, what are *you* doing here?" Tim asked when they sobered, recovering his own aplomb. "I mean, right here, at the precinct?"

"What? Oh, um, debating whether or not to waste someone's time." Niles shook his head ruefully. "I've been getting these harassing messages, you see. It's no big deal, just trolls being trolls, but one of them actually came to my house and now Jordie is worried. He wants me to report it, and you know how he gets when he goes into protective mode."

"Do I ever." Tim rubbed his jaw as if the memory of Jordan's fist still pained him. The strawberry-blond scruff on his face was new. And very nice. "Well, hey, I was just about to head out to lunch after dropping Payne back here. Why don't you come with me, fill me in on the situation, and I can help you decide whether it warrants a formal report or not?"

Niles gnawed his lip uncertainly, wondering if it was a good idea for the two of them to spend any amount of time together. Especially with Tim still devouring him with his eyes. Finally, he shrugged. "Yeah. Sure. Okay."

He could have kicked himself as soon as he said it. Staying would be a monumental clusterfuck.

"Bring me back a sandwich," Detective Payne instructed before jogging up the stairs and into the building, leaving Niles and Tim facing each other on the sidewalk.

He should walk away. Niles shuffled his feet, trying to figure out a good excuse to do so, when Tim jerked his head toward a car parked at the curb. "Come on. I'll treat."

The silence as Tim unlocked the door for him was heavy. Niles wasn't sure exactly what it was okay to say so close to where Tim worked. Being in a car with Tim was an experience he remembered well. Like the car needed to be bigger, because there was too much man there for such a contained space. Pushing away the eerie feelings of déjà vu, he turned a curious —and slightly bitter—gaze toward Tim, observing the way his thick, blunt fingers clenched the steering wheel before he started the ignition. Niles stared at them a moment before he noticed what was different.

No wedding band.

"So what happened?" His voice came out so hard and aggressive that Niles himself damn near flinched at the sound. He suspected he was taking his mood—already poor after the letter and Jordan's overreaction to it and the protesters and Anthony—out on Tim. He made a damn convenient target. "Last I heard you were heading back to Klamath Falls to take a job with the county sheriff's office and marry your high school sweetheart."

"Yeah, it didn't work there." Tim shook his head, pulling into traffic. "Largely because I had too many things I kept thinking about that I couldn't let go of. Like you."

"Me?" Oh look, there was that old bitterness again. He tried to laugh it off, but the joke came out with a bit of bite. "I thought I was just your *college experimentation.*"

"Ouch. Guess I had that coming," Tim muttered, gripping the steering wheel so tight his knuckles turned white. "Well. Funny thing about denial. It doesn't quite work as well as you think it's going to."

Niles tried to rein back the urge to rub it in and settled for repeating himself. "So what happened?"

"Um, tried to have an affair with the wrong guy on the down-low, got outed, Kayleigh divorced me, things with the good ol' boys in the sheriff's department got tense." He rattled it all off in a single, rushed breath, as if he wanted to get it out as quickly as possible and move on. "Then I was injured and I ended up on medical leave and desk duty for several months, and while that was happening, my dad passed away and my brother bought me out of my half of the ranch. I decided it was time for a change, so I left before they found a reason to fire me that wouldn't result in a discrimination lawsuit. I've been up here ever since."

"I see." Niles looked down at his hands, clasped on his knees, and didn't look up again until they reached the restaurant. Tim chose Virginia Cafe, which made sense. It had much more standard fare than Veritable Quandary or Kell's or some of the other Portland classics. Much more Tim's type of food.

The wait for a table was short but excruciating. Tim was tense beside him, and it was a familiar tension. It was the same tension he'd felt vibrating off Tim back in college when he'd been fighting to try to keep himself from touching Niles.

Niles made sure to order a Rueben sandwich, confident that he wouldn't wind up flinging himself at Tim if he smelled like sauerkraut.

"So tell me about this harassment," Tim urged, finally

breaking the game of verbal chicken as the waiter set their food down and left.

Niles took a deep breath and blew it out, then blazed through the explanation the way Tim had done with his own history earlier in the car.

"Okay. Well, here's the situation: I write scripts and story for video games, specifically a studio run by a woman with a mission statement of making games that are more accessible and appealing to women, people of color, and queer gamers. We've got queer and POC characters who actually come out on top, the highest ratio of POC to non-POC characters—and also writers and designers—in the industry, and female characters who are more than just tits and ass." Niles idly swirled a fry in a pool of ketchup. "Predictably, this means a lot of cis-het male gamers—who are used to being considered the only audience that matters in gaming culture—are interpreting this as a frontal assault on the bastion of their privilege. Which, to be fair, I suppose it is."

Tim's eyebrows went up, and his lips twitched. "So you've got a bunch of pimply, adolescent geeks pissed off at you."

"Heinous and incorrect stereotyping of the gaming audience aside, yeah, pretty much." Niles pulled out his phone and brought up an archive of the text messages he'd been saving. "This is the sort of thing they say. I've got thousands more emails, private messages on our social forums, and tweets just like that. I don't even dare look at Reddit."

Tim's frown was reminiscent of Jordan's as he scanned through the texts. "Jesus Christ." He set his burger aside as though his stomach had turned. "Do these dudes have no filter at all?"

"Of course they don't." Niles shrugged, taking another bite of juicy corned beef on grilled rye. "They're used to anonymity, so they say just about anything with no fear of being held account-able. If you think those are bad, you should see what Rosena—

my boss—has to deal with. She's got bigger balls than me, because I couldn't handle that without having a nervous breakdown."

"Seriously?" Tim's eyebrows rose skeptically, and Niles could practically hear the thought as if he'd spoken it aloud: *how bad could it be?*

"Seriously. Death threats. Rape threats. Racial slurs." Niles gritted his teeth, though he wished the outrage he'd used to have over it all was still as hot as it had once been. Weird how that sort of abuse had become . . . commonplace. "There are memes out there with pictures where people have drawn dicks pointed at her mouth and spooge on her face, or written captions of things she never actually said, imploring some sort of sexual violence. Reading her email has almost made me puke a couple times. It's bad."

Tim—always a good ole country boy and raised with that sort of good-ole-country-boy gallantry—began to grow red around the ears. "Sounds like these twerps need a good ass kicking and a few manners."

"It's not an isolated case." Niles set his sandwich down, gnawing on another fry. "Jennifer Hepler, who used to work for BioWare. Anita Sarkeesian, who has a blog called Feminist Frequency that deals with women in gaming. A lot of women in the industry have to deal with it." He sighed. "I get quite a bit of it too, because they see me as one of the driving forces behind the queering up of their games—which I am—but it's always worse when it's aimed at women."

It took Tim a moment of gritting his teeth before he handed Niles's phone back. "So, this has been going on for months?"

"Years. It's been three years since we began PR for the first *Phoenix Force* game and revealed that there would be characters who would represent the full gender, sexual, and ethnic spectrum, and gameplay that would make a concerted effort to avoid problematic tropes. The hostility waxes and wanes, depending on how recently we've been in the gaming news."

"So what's changed? Why does Jordan think you need to file a report now?"

"Because of this." Niles lifted his messenger bag into his lap and withdrew the buff-colored file folder in which he'd stored the problematic note. "He thinks it's a threat, particularly since it appears to have been hand delivered to my house."

Tim flipped the folder open and stared at the envelope for a moment before reaching for the coat he'd hung on the back of his chair. He pulled a pair of nitrile—he remembered all too well discovering that Tim had an allergy to latex—gloves out of the pocket and put them on before touching the letter, which he handled carefully by the edges.

"Not very verbose compared to some of the other messages you've gotten. Which means it smacks less of bluster and big talk and more of direct action. I can definitely see why Jordan would consider it a threat."

"Do *you* think it's a threat?"

"I think it's a deviation from the pattern, and that usually means something's changed. Maybe someone has hit the breaking point and decided to escalate. I don't think caution is a bad idea under those circumstances."

"Spoken like a true detective." Niles sighed, pushing his half-eaten sandwich aside and scowling at the letter.

"Did anything happen recently that might have prompted it?"

"I take it you don't watch the morning news shows."

"I was at a crime scene this morning. What's going on?"

"We're being picketed by the Coalition for Responsible Media, who are concerned that we're trying to turn America's precious children gay by having queer characters in the games." He rolled his head on his neck, trying to stretch out the kinks. "There was a petition to have me removed as a writer because some dude-bros thought I was pushing an agenda."

"But this came before the protest, over the weekend?" Tim asked.

He nodded. "I think so. I'm not sure if it was delivered on Saturday or Sunday; I was busy most of the weekend."

Tim made a note. "Okay. Any idea specifically who might have left this?"

Niles started to shake his head, then hesitated. "Um, it's probably nothing, but—"

"Even if it's nothing, it's still something we should make note of. Helps with the process of elimination if an investigation becomes necessary."

"All right." He licked his lips. "The guys who delivered the petition to have me fired . . . They followed me, Jordie, and Rosie to a club last night."

"Actually followed you?" Tim's eyebrows rose and his pen came down. Something in the intensity of his look suggested that he'd just started taking this *very* seriously.

"Well, I don't think they did the whole secret-agent 'follow that cab' thing." Niles tried for a smile, but it felt limp. "They probably got my location from one of those social media GPS check-in things and decided to make an appearance."

"Do you know their names?" Tim asked.

"No, but we have the petition, which has that information on it."

Tim nodded. "Okay. Make sure I get a copy of that, please."

"Okay. What else do I do? Do I really need to make this a report?"

"Who all has handled this note? Just you?"

"Jordie and Rosie have too."

Tim frowned. "I could try getting fingerprints off it, see if anything comes up in the database, but it won't do us a lot of good unless I print all of you to rule you out. If you get any more of these, don't touch it with bare hands. Pull on some gloves, bag it, and bring it to me."

Niles nodded, sobering as he realized it wasn't merely a case of Rosie and Jordan being overprotective. "Okay, I can do that."

Tim stared at it a moment longer. "There's probably not enough here to launch an investigation. We would certainly consider this menacing, but the only indication that it might have overtones of a hate crime is the potential connection to your work."

"Potential?" Niles frowned. "What other reason could there be?"

"I couldn't say. Any chance someone unrelated to your work has a grudge?"

"No, absolutely not." Niles shook his head firmly. "You know me, Tim. I get along with everyone."

"Yeah, I remember that." The corner of Tim's mouth tipped up in a wistful smile before he got back down to business. "I could run it by my captain, but the substance of the threat is vague, and unless there's an undamaged fingerprint or DNA that is already in the system, we're not likely to get anything off this that would take an investigation anywhere."

Niles sighed, his shoulders dropping. "So I was right. This is nothing and Jordie's overreacting." Great. He'd just lost a couple of hours of writing time on a pointless errand.

"I didn't say that. I'm going to keep this, pull a case number, and book it into evidence, on a 'just in case' basis. That way, we have it if there are further incidences that warrant starting a full investigation." Tim shrugged, humming thoughtfully as he tucked the letter safely in the file folder and stripped off his gloves.

"Seriously?" Niles gnawed on his lip anxiously. Damn it, he did *not* want this thing blown up into a big deal.

"We should at least monitor the situation. If you get any more letters, or if the tone of the harassment seems to shift, so that it feels more immediate and less general, let me know." Tim pulled a card out of his breast pocket and slid it across the table. "Also, if you can compile a ZIP file of all the harassing emails and texts, along with that petition, send them to me, and I'll add that to the evidence as well, for future reference."

"Right." Niles sighed. "You really *do* think this could be serious."

"I think it could go either way. It's worth monitoring, at the very least." Tim flagged down the waiter for take-home boxes and their check.

They didn't talk about much as Tim drove Niles back to the precinct, but as Niles was reaching to open the door, Tim caught his other arm. "Go out with me."

He scoffed, scowling at the police station where Tim worked. "Good job sneaking that in before we got out of the car, but no. There's no way I'm going down that road again."

"That wasn't what I was doing." Tim shook his head adamantly. "It wouldn't be the same. I'm out. I made sure they knew it before I was hired on with the Portland Police Bureau. I didn't want history repeating itself."

"Oh, well, at least some good came from that broken heart." Jesus, when did he become such a queen? Maybe it was easier to flounce than let that spark of interest that tried to kindle in his chest flare up into something hotter.

"I can't really apologize enough for what I did back then." Tim drummed a nervous rhythm on the steering wheel. "It was completely unfair to you, and Jordan was absolutely right to slug me for it. But I'd like a chance to get it right."

Shit. Niles held his breath in a futile attempt to deprive the spark of oxygen and extinguish it. "Thanks, I appreciate the gesture, but I really don't want to go out with someone who just feels guilty for crap that's in the past."

The gaze Tim slanted at him from those blue-gray eyes might as well have been wired straight to his balls for the way it tugged at them. "Niles, come on. Do you *really* think the only thing going on here is guilt?" There was something hot and a little raw in Tim's eyes, and it made fluttery feelings happen in Niles's stomach. "You're still the most beautiful thing I've ever seen. That hasn't changed, not even in ten years."

"Jesus." He didn't have to hold his breath now; he couldn't have drawn a lungful of air if he wanted to. It really, really wasn't fair that after ten years and a devastating breakup, Tim could still make his blood rush and his body sing with nothing more than a look and a few words. He groped for sanity, struggling to remember how much it had hurt when Tim had decided his perfectly planned, *straight* life back in the farming and ranching community where he'd grown up had been what he really wanted. He tried to recall how crushed he'd been when the relationship that had come to mean the world to Niles in no time flat had been dismissed as nothing more than a curiosity on Tim's end.

Finally, he found the wherewithal to stand his ground. "Yeah, no, I appreciate the invitation, but I don't think it's a good idea. I just broke up with someone last week, and it's probably not a good time to get . . . confused."

"What's there to be confused about? I'm asking you to have dinner with me, maybe see a movie or a show or go dancing. That's all." Tim gave him a lazy smile that had once turned Niles's knees to Jell-O.

"Like hell that's all."

Tim tipped one shoulder up in a cocky shrug. "It's a good start, at least. Give me back that card I gave you."

Frowning, Niles pulled it out of his coat pocket, still trying to put into words why going out with Tim was a bad idea. Or at least put it in words that didn't boil down to, "I don't want my heart broken again." Because that was just pathetic.

Tim laid the card on the steering wheel, scribbled something on the back of it, and handed it to Niles again. "There.

That's my home phone. And my personal cell. And my address. You ever want to talk or stop by and have a drink, whatever, you're welcome to do so. I'm not seeing anyone; I'm not even hooking up all that frequently. There's nothing in my way. So, think about it."

With a too-perfect smile that flashed too-perfect teeth, Tim opened his own door and stepped out of the car, leaving Niles staring at the digits and address on the back of the card.

CHAPTER 6

J ordan rapped on the door of his brother's office after the sky had grown dark and most of the staff had already gone home. "Hey, staying late? Wanna order takeout?"

Niles nodded, staring at the monitor. "Yeah, sounds good. I really need to get the dialogue for this scene done."

Jordan knew that expression. That was Niles's *I refuse to let myself be pulled away from this, so I'm not going to make eye contact until you realize you're interrupting and leave* look. Unfortunately for Niles, Jordan prided himself on having immunity to it and had no qualms about breaking his brother's focus on whatever he was obsessing over.

He withdrew his phone from his pocket and turned the browser on, calling up the website of their favorite pizza joint and thumbing in an order for the combination pizzas they had saved. As he ordered, he glanced between Niles and the touch screen. "After you're done with that, what does the rest of your week look like?"

"Pretty packed until I leave on Friday, but I can make room." All of that without ever breaking his concentration on the screen, but Niles's hands were motionless on the keyboard. "What do you need?"

"I got a call from Daniel Fortesen at *The LEET News*. He heard about the protests today, wants to arrange an interview. He's willing to come down from Seattle for it, or if you don't have enough time to actually meet up, he's happy to do it via video chat."

Niles frowned and finally glanced up from the computer. Jordan ducked his head to cover his smile. It was impossible for Niles to write when someone was in the room, much less talking to him. He got flustered and lost his train of thought. Strangely, though, Niles didn't seem as irritated with the interruption as he normally would be, which made Jordan wonder just how much writing he'd been getting done to begin with.

"I've been too busy to keep up on the trades. I feel like I should know that name."

"He's the first editor of a major gaming news mag to come out, and a large portion of why he did so was because of *Phoenix Force* and the entire first generation of games that now include queer characters."

"Ah," Niles said absently, his attention drifting back to the dialogue on the screen as if he wished Jordan would go away and let him get his concentration back. If he hadn't actually been writing, what was it he was trying to get back to, though?

"So do you think you can make time?" Jordan debated with himself, then eyed Niles and made himself at home in Niles's office.

"Yeah, go ahead and tell him to come down. Any day except Friday." Niles sighed and closed the laptop. "We'll show him around the studios, give him an exclusive peek at Gairi's story in the DLC. That should make his day." Niles laid his computer glasses on his desk and rubbed his eyes, leaning back in his chair.

"How did things go with the police?" He frowned. Niles

looked exhausted. Of course, they had all been up late last night, and he and Niles had gone to breakfast early that morning, but every one of his senses was pinging an alert that something was eating his brother.

"*Pssh.* Don't ask."

"Okay and now I have to ask. How did things go with the police?"

"Fine. Fine." Niles flapped one hand, the other still covering his eyes. "They're not going to open an investigation now, but the . . . detective I spoke to is going to keep the letter on file so if there are any more incidences, I can bring them to his attention. If there's a next time, we're not to get our fingerprints on it."

Interesting hesitation there before "detective."

"Right. Okay. Sounds good . . . So what's with the reaction?"

"Nothing. It's nothing. I'm just tired. And distracted. And I need to get this fucking scene done, and apparently the universe doesn't want to let me do that."

Jordan grinned. "I'll be out of your hair after the pizza arrives."

Niles made a dismayed sound. "No, it's not you. It's just too much going on all at once."

"Is Anthony still calling you a lot?"

"Yeah, but nothing I can't handle."

"Are you letting those assholes get to you?" Jordan gestured at Niles's closed computer with an open hand. "I mean, you've been talking a good game about not giving it any attention, but—"

"No. *No.*" Niles groaned and let his hand fall away from his face. "Timothy Wyatt."

"What?" It took him a moment to place the name, the hunky country boy from college who had been Niles's lab partner and first love on pretty much every level. Mostly what Jordan remembered was how long it had taken his bruised hand to heal when he'd belted the guy for blatantly using Niles's infatuation with him to check out the action on the other side of the tracks. "What about him?"

"He's here. In Portland. He's the detective I spoke to." Niles scoffed and covered his face again. "I let him take me to lunch. Stupid, stupid, stupid. I should have turned him down."

"He asked you to lunch? Mr. I'm-Not-a-Fag-I-Just-Fuck-Guys-for-Science?" Jordan snorted, scratching at his jaw. "Let me guess, he wanted to keep you out of the police station so you wouldn't say anything that might out him?"

"Oh no. He's divorced now. And apparently out and proud. He has a whole new life, or so he says." Niles peeked between his fingers. "He wants me to go on a date with him."

"Wow. That takes some balls after what he pulled. Jesus." He scrutinized his brother as Niles dropped his hands. "What did you tell him?"

"What do you think I should have told him?"

"*Pfft.* Uh-uh. Not going there. When it involves sex or relationships, you're on your own unless someone needs their ass kicked."

"I turned him down."

Jordan nodded slowly. "Not necessarily a bad idea. Having second thoughts?"

"No. Yes. Damn it, I don't know." Niles's chair squeaked as he squirmed in his seat, rubbing his fingertip up and down the armrest of his chair. "He turns my head around. He always has."

"He turns your head *off*, and he always has. At least the one that holds up your hair."

"That too. Jesus. I'm so pitiful." Niles made a dismayed sound, closing his eyes. "If you had asked me ten years ago, I would have said this was everything I ever wanted handed to me on a silver platter. Tim. *Out.* Apologizing to me. Wanting to be with me. Hell, *pursuing* me. Hard to let that go even if it's not a good idea. My inner twenty-two-year-old is practically squeeing."

Jordan smiled, remembering a time when Niles *had* squeed like a preteen girl with a celebrity crush over Tim Wyatt. "And your inner thirty-two-year-old?"

"Thinks there's too much history there. Too much hurt. It's too good to be true. I can't trust it."

"Well, who can blame you after what he did?"

"I know, right?" Niles sighed. "Past is past for a reason. We don't get do-overs."

"Oh, I wouldn't go that far." Jordan smiled wryly, brushing a speck of lint off his slacks. "I'm not saying you should consider it, nor am I saying you shouldn't, but people do sometimes manage to redeem themselves on second chances. Whatever you do, just w—" He almost said *watch yourself* before he remembered the note delivered to Niles's house and flinched. "—be careful."

"What, you don't want me to get hurt again?" Niles mirrored his smile.

"I don't want to break my fist on that fucker's face again."

"Your protectiveness is touching, truly." He tipped his head back, staring up at the ceiling panels. "I don't know. Maybe I'll just sit on it for a while. Wait until the trolls and the protesters crawl back where they came from and I'm not under so much pressure."

A wistful look crossed Niles's face and with the perfect clarity of understanding they often shared, Jordan could nearly hear the thought as if it were his own: *fucking Tim would sure relieve some pressure.*

Ducking his head to hide another smile, Jordan started resigning himself to the prospect of his brother taking another trip on the Tim-Wyatt-Go-Round.

The night security guard called to tell them their pizza had arrived, and Jordan excused himself to retrieve it. When he returned to Niles's office with the grease-stained box in-hand, steam seeping out around the edges, Rosie was there, her grin far too toothy.

"Oh shit, what is it?"

"I am about to make your year," she practically sang, hitching herself up to sit on the edge of Niles's desk. Niles still reclined in his chair, watching with an amused smile.

"Well, don't keep me in suspense." Jordan set the pizza on a filing cabinet and started laying out napkins.

"We're going to be picketed again later this week."

His eyebrows crept up, and he turned to face her. That cat-in-cream, gloating look was pretty fucking disconcerting. "This is a good thing?"

"It is when it's the Guiding Light Fellowship doing the picketing."

"*What*?" His own face split into a wide grin. "Those douche bags out of Nebraska with the 'Fags Will Burn' signs who even conservatives hate?"

Rosie bit her lip and nodded, her eyes dancing.

"Holy shit." He laughed, a giddy, incredulous hoot, and visions of counterprotests and letters of support campaigns blossomed in his head. "*Thank you*, Coalition for Responsible Media or whoever the fuck you are. This is excellent. They just put exactly the right spotlight on us to undo the results of their own negative PR. I'll see you guys later." He snagged a few steaming slices of pizza onto a napkin and headed for the door. "I've got work to do."

"SHE WAS A NURSE'S AIDE." Tim stopped digging through papers on the cluttered desk to glance over at Payne, who was rifling through a closet in the late Charity Anspach's apartment. "Still nothing to explain what she was doing out in Forest Park dressed like she was, though."

"She had a lot of pictures of herself in that outfit." Bryan Rommel glanced up from his laptop where he was scanning through pictures they'd found on a USB stick in the desk. There was a laptop charger cable as well, but they hadn't found the computer yet, or a cell phone, two items which were suspiciously absent. There was no way a young woman Charity's age didn't live on one or both. "Look at these."

Tim abandoned the pile of unopened mail to lean over Bryan's shoulder. Payne joined them a second later. There was a directory with hundreds of shots of their murder victim in the outfit she'd been wearing when she died, the skintight leather and knee-high boots.

"She's posing in martial arts stances." Payne frowned, leaning closer. "Some of these are really aggressive. Did she do some theater acting? Or was she sending out audition tapes of some kind?"

"You'd think there'd be playbills and posters around if she had been into theater. Besides, what sort of theatrical production has someone dress and pose like that? She looks like something out of an action movie."

"Or a comic book," Bryan interjected. Tim and Payne turned in tandem to peer down at him. "Well, she does. These are classic superhero-masquerading-as-a-sex-kitten poses." He flipped down to some thumbnails they hadn't gotten to yet and opened one of the pictures. "See? She's got a gun here."

"There aren't any comic books around the apartment, though." Payne pushed her tongue into her cheek, humming. "I'm starting to think the booth babe notion wasn't such a bad thought. What sorts of events were at that convention center she had the parking pass for?"

Tim pulled out his phone and scrolled through the notes he'd jotted down when he'd followed up on that lead. "Nothing about comic books. Something about role-playing games. The convention center manager I spoke with said it was an annual event—bunch of *Dungeons & Dragons*-type geeks sitting around for three days with dice and miniature figurines. She doesn't look much like the gaming geek type to me."

"She was a *cosplayer*." Bryan's voice had an edge of impatience, as though they were being unbelievably dense for not knowing that yet. They glanced at him, and he shrugged. "She made costumes and dressed up like her favorite characters. It's really popular in a lot of fandoms. Comic books, anime, movies, TV shows, video games. I bet she has a sewing machine somewhere."

"She does." Payne pointed to the closet she had just been inspecting. "It's on a shelf in there."

Bryan nodded enthusiastically. "Cosplayers take a lot of pride in making their own costumes. It's a form of fan art." He lifted his brows at their dubious looks. "Really."

Tim jerked his head toward the living room. "There's a game console by the TV and a large DVD collection. Let's see if we can find out what she was into."

Payne nodded, trailing him into the living room. "The neighbors say she was a shy girl, though I'm not sure how shy you can be if you can go to conventions dressed like that. They say she didn't have many friends, that they only ever saw one or two people visiting. But without her cell phone, we can't even track down the friends she did have until we get her records. Her parents back in Utah say they don't know who her friends are out here, only that she never mentioned having a boyfriend. Or girlfriend, though they admit she might not have told them if she was a lesbian. Big Mormon family."

"Well, don't these gaming consoles have, like, internet and social networks and stuff on them now?" Tim squatted by a shelf next to the entertainment center, perusing the DVDs while Payne pulled out the game console from under the TV.

"Nothing doing. This is dusty. Whatever she was into recently, it wasn't on here."

"There's a pretty extensive DVD collection here, including a lot of anime." Tim brushed his gloved finger along the top surface of the DVD clamshell cases. "But they're dusty, too.

She had a new interest. Something that wasn't shows or games."

"Maybe the outfit wasn't cosplaying after all." Payne flipped through the small selection of games. "There weren't any other costumes in her closet."

Tim shrugged. "Unless she didn't keep them here. Or maybe this was her first time."

"Jesus. How is it that absolutely no one knows anything about a pretty, young woman like that?" Payne shook her head in disgust. "Her parents said she moved out here to live near some internet friends while she went to college, but no one seems to know who she was. Teachers and other students remember seeing her, but they barely remembered her name. Her coworkers say she was quiet, did her job, and left. Said she always seemed to be lost in her own head, didn't talk much, really introverted. They couldn't begin to tell me the first thing about her family or friends. And obviously her neighbors don't know her."

Tim nodded. "We find that computer, we find her social circle. I bet it's all on there."

"And probably why it's missing."

"Okay." He pushed himself to his feet, stripping off his gloves. "There's nothing here. Let's see if we can get the security footage from the convention center, if it's available. And records of the admissions pass sales. Maybe she was there with some-one. If we can find that person, we can begin to retrace her foot-steps the day she was murdered."

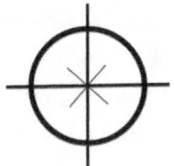

CHAPTER 7

In many ways, Daniel Fortesen was more Niles's counterpart than Jordan was. While he and Jordan might be twins, there were distinct differences in personality and that carried over into the way they dressed and groomed. In *that* regard, looking at Daniel was like looking in a mirror. Same sort of brainy-yet-attractive glasses; same longish, wavy, unkempt hair (in dishwater blond, though, rather than dark brown); same casual jeans and button-down combo.

It only took a few minutes to realize that Daniel was a kindred spirit.

"So what do you think about these sorts of accusations, that you're trying to press an agenda forward and that you're targeting youth in order to advance it?" Daniel asked, taking a sip of his latte in the Sisters Coffee Company shop in the Pearl District, not far from Niles's house in Northwest Portland. Daniel had decided to take the Amtrak down from Seattle, and Union Station was in Old Town, only a few blocks from the Pearl, which made it an ideal location for them to meet for their interview on Daniel's second day in town, before he caught his train back. Daniel spent his first day with Rosie and Jordan at Third Wave's studios, playing alpha tests of their upcoming titles, so Niles had spent the day finishing Gairi's dialog for the DLC.

Daniel's phone sat on the table in front of them, acting as a digital recorder so that he could give Niles his full attention.

Niles shrugged, fingering the side of his cup of chai. "I think those sorts of claims say a lot more about the accuser than the accused. It seems to me that the people who are most worried about someone trying to indoctrinate the youth are those who are intent upon indoctrinating the youth themselves. They're determined to force their ideas upon the next generation's impressionable minds, so they're convinced everyone else must be, as well."

"But let's be honest: you *do* have an agenda."

"In a manner of speaking, I suppose so. My agenda is to tell stories about people like me: brown people, queer people. People like a lot of the audience out there who might be confused or struggling with who they are and not seeing any positive reflections of themselves in the media. To show other people like me that we can get proportional and accurate representation. That we can be the heroes, the central characters, the romantic leads. And yes, Third Wave has a mission statement. We don't just deal with queer issues in gaming, we deal with feminist—under Rosie's guidance—and racial issues, as well. Last month, I attended a panel on women in gaming with her." He offered Daniel a quirky grin. Normally these sorts of interviews were difficult for him, but Daniel knew just the right questions to ask to keep Niles responding enthusiastically. "These people could just as easily accuse me of pushing a feminist agenda upon their children as a homosexual one."

Daniel tipped his head to the side with an inquisitive look. "Why the interest in feminist issues in gaming?"

"Because we're natural allies. Misogyny is the root of homophobia. People blurring the lines between masculine and feminine wouldn't be threatening if it didn't undermine the perception that ultramasculinity is a gold standard that needs to be preserved from any taint of femininity."

Daniel seemed mildly amused. "And how's that philosophy working out for you?"

"Just fine except for the moments when I realize that gay men aren't immune to being terrible misogynists and that straight women can be so full of their own heterosexual privilege that they fail to see anything wrong with making themselves the centerpiece of discussion of LGBTQIA+ struggles in the name of being allies." Niles sighed, picking up his chai and cradling the warm cup between his fingers.

"True that," Daniel conceded.

"So it's understandable that conflicts arise. But we have to overcome that, because it's in everyone's best interest to make gaming culture into something that represents every gamer equally. And with gaming being the fastest-growing form of mass entertainment, hopefully those messages will have ripple effects and spread into society at large, rather than remaining contained in the microcosm of gaming."

"I like that." There was something in the way Daniel gazed across the small table at Niles that changed the tenor of the conversation from professional to something far more personal. In just the space of a few seconds, he'd stopped looking at Niles as a subject and begun looking at him as a man. "I think I'm out of questions."

Niles cleared his throat, letting the frisson of awareness prickle the hairs on the back of his neck and up and down his arms. After the week he'd had, the attention was nice, and the interest was flattering. "I hope I gave you the answers you needed for your article. I'm looking forward to reading it."

"So obviously the *PF3* DLC wasn't ready for me to play yet, but off the record, can you tell me what's in store for Gairi in this expansion?"

Niles glanced at the phone, but Daniel had apparently forgotten its presence. "I can do that, but just how spoiled do you want to be?"

"Tell me everything. I'll play it, of course, but I want to hear the story the way *you* tell it, as the storyteller."

Niles smiled. If Daniel was trying to sweet-talk him, urging Niles to discuss his writing was definitely the right tack to take. Frankly, after Anthony's persistent calls and texts, and the way seeing Tim Wyatt had thrown him into such emotional chaos on Monday, the simplicity of a potential one-off with someone like Daniel—who would return to his own city and his own life afterward—sounded pretty damned appealing. It would be a nice way to relieve some stress and remind himself that there were single men out there other than the one ex who seemed to be increasingly fixated on pressuring Niles to come back and the other who had shattered him once upon a time and was now hoping for a second chance.

He was way too interested in Tim's offer of going out for his own comfort. He'd spent three days waffling on whether or not to call. Maybe Jordan had the right idea, limiting himself to tricks. So far the search for a steady, committed relationship didn't seem to be doing him any favors.

Daniel was still smiling at Niles, waiting for him to answer, so Niles set that vibe of quasi flirtation aside and pulled himself back to the subject at hand.

"All right. Well, as you saw in the *PF3* beta, prior to joining the Phoenix Force, Gairi was from an outer colony planet where the settlers have grown quite conservative and intolerant. When it became apparent that Gairi, who already has a mark against him for being half-indigenous, wasn't going to be big and strapping and manly, his father smuggled him away on a supply ship and took him back to Earth to live with his grandparents."

"Right." Daniel nodded as Niles paused for a drink of his rapidly cooling chai. "I have to say, I love that while Gairi is small and femme, he's actually one of their most badass, deadly fighters. It subverts the trope that effeminate gay men are weak and cowardly and only good for comic relief." He grinned and winked. "He's just liable to swish at you before he snaps your spine."

Niles laughed, giving a delighted nod. "Exactly. Thank you for getting that, that's *precisely* what I was going for with him. So, anyway, where the DLC picks up . . ."

It felt good to tell the story to a new audience, especially now that the tale was fully formed. He'd worked it all through with Rosie and his writing staff, of course, and he'd even discussed it with Anthony, but with the inevitable vanity of a writer, Niles wanted to share his creation with the world. And Daniel was eager to listen, nodding as Niles described the plot of the DLC. He even leaned in, fully engaged in the tale of Gairi's struggles with returning to his home planet, being taken captive and beaten by a group of radical settlers who want to put the native people back into slavery.

". . . So, the leader of the reactionaries, who believe that half-breed mongrels should be drowned at birth, decides to throw an injured Gairi off a cliff and into a river when the PC and the rest of the companions arrive." Niles wrapped up his narrative to realize his drink was long since cold. "This leads to some rather hard-hitting questions between Gairi and the PC during Gairi's convalescence, especially if they're romantically involved, which could make or break their relationship. If the player character has made certain choices leading up to that point, Gairi can and will walk away." He ducked his head and grinned. "Or it's possible he just might propose marriage."

Daniel blinked and began to smile. "Seriously?"

"You didn't hear it from me. If that spoiler gets out, I'll deny it."

"We're off the record." Niles lifted an eyebrow at the phone still on the table. Daniel snatched it up and turned off the voice recorder app. "Oh, sorry. I'll delete that as soon as I transcribe my notes. You really enjoy this sort of storytelling, don't you?"

"I really do. It's . . ." Niles pursed his lips thoughtfully. "It's not just writing a novel or even a movie script, you know? It's interactive. Each scene can go in multiple directions, each story-line can have multiple endings. It's fascinating because it gives me a chance to really examine all the permutations arising from the choices the PC has made and how the companion characters will react to them."

Daniel nodded and continued to study him, a small smile flirting at his lips.

The hell with it. Niles drew a deep breath, running a finger around the rim of his cup. "So when does your train leave?"

Daniel shrugged. "I probably won't make the eleven o'clock train, but it's an open ticket, so I can take the one fifteen or the three thirty. Hell, I can even catch the morning train tomorrow. You know, if I decided to stay another night." Niles looked up, and Daniel gave him a questioning look. "I assume you have to go into the office, but what time do you get off work?"

"I do, but I won't have to work late now that the script is written. Didn't you already check out of your hotel?"

"No reason I can't get another room."

Niles leaned forward, his elbows on the table, feeling far more aggressive than he usually did about these sorts of things. Typically, he liked to be the one propositioned, but this was too good a chance to pass up. Daniel was giving off all the right vibes. A night of friendly, no-strings sex to get his mind off all the other crap.

"Or better yet, my house is in Northwest, about twenty blocks west of Union Station. Play tourist for the day. Or come back to the studios with me and test the games some more.

Then I'll cook you dinner and take you to the station in the morning."

Daniel sucked on his cheek for a moment, then nodded slowly, with a boyishly pleased smile that Niles found he really liked.

CHAPTER 8

"How long has she been in the water?"

Medical Examiner McDermott looked up from the bloated body with its grayish-brown pallor of death to meet Tim's questioning gaze. "Less than a day."

"What is that clothing? It looks like something a medieval serf would wear."

"That's not the only thing medieval going on here." Now that the body and surroundings had been photographed and searched, McDermott rolled her onto her side and lifted the back of what looked like a rough, loosely woven tunic. Dark bruises striped what had once been the light-brown skin of her back.

"Jesus, are those what I think they are?"

"If you're thinking lash marks, probably. Someone whipped her pretty badly."

"Those aren't fetish clothes. There's no way this is S&M gone wrong."

"No, I doubt it was." McDermott released the shoulder of the corpse and let her settle back onto the ground, pushing himself up and gesturing the techs over to transport the body. "Technique varies, of course, but BDSM practitioners tend to be a lot more precise, and the lashes are given over a limited stretch of time to ramp up the pain endorphins, give the bottom a high. The force and angle of these strokes are all over the place, too irregular, too much wrapping around the ribs, which is the mark of someone not very good at controlling the whip, and/or someone using a cheap implement."

Tim pointed to a few bruises that looked more faded. "Those don't look like they were done immediately premortem."

McDermott shook his head. "They weren't. Some of the marks are older than the others. I'd say these lashes were administered one at a time over the course of several days. And there's a waffleweave imprinted in some of them that suggests she was beaten through the shirt, rather than on bare skin."

Tim squinted at the body as the techs lifted it into the bag, particularly the silver-blue shimmer near the hairline at the temples and under her jaw. "What is that around the edges of her face?"

"I won't know for sure until I get back to the lab, but I think grease paint, or something similar. Theater makeup."

The detail snagged his attention. They had wondered if Charity Anspach was into theater, as well. "Was she—"

Tim was interrupted midthought as Payne approached.

"Thanks," she muttered before hanging up her phone and shoving it in her jacket. The drizzling mist was beginning to form beads of water in the tight curls of her close-cut Afro. Her phone buzzed with an incoming text, and she pulled it back out, opened it, and showed Tim a picture. "I had them pull up any missing persons reports matching our vic's description. There was only one recent one, so I had them send a picture."

Tim looked between the picture and the body. If one discounted the bloating and pallor that came from the body being in the water, the resemblance between the two was close enough for a solid preliminary ID.

"It's her."

Payne nodded. "Lakshmi Agrawal, age twenty. Her parents reported her missing on Monday. She went out with a friend to, and I quote, 'some event,' on Saturday and never came back. Guess who that friend was."

"We just found Charity Anspach's social circle?"

Her eyebrows shot up. "Good guess."

"She's wearing stage makeup. Face paint. Anachronistic clothing. She was a . . . whatever those costume people Bryan was talking about are. And she disappeared the same day Charity was killed." He scowled. "I'd almost managed to convince myself Charity's murder was random. What do you want to bet they were at that convention together?"

"Just because they disappeared in the same general time frame doesn't mean it wasn't random. It just means the killer or killers may have grabbed them both at the same time."

"Then why didn't they kill them at the same time? Dump them at the same time, in the same place? Why keep this girl and torture her for days?" Tim shook his head, watching the coroner's assistant and a few uniforms carry the body bag up the bank of the Willamette.

"Maybe Lakshmi was the target they really wanted and Charity was just extra baggage," Payne hypothesized. "They had to get her out of the way to carry out their plans with Lakshmi."

"Okay, that works. But why her?" Tim looked once more around the riverbank, where techs were still searching for any other scraps of evidence that might have washed up with the body, then turned to begin trudging up its rocky, muddy incline. Lakshmi was almost genderless, especially compared to her friend Charity. Few curves, boyish haircut, unisex clothing . . . "Could it be a hate crime? Was Lakshmi trans?"

"Not according to her parents. The missing persons' detectives asked about any gender and sexuality issues when they were trying to get more information."

"Well, that doesn't tell us much. Parents aren't always in the know there." Payne nodded in agreement, and Tim continued, "What about the convention?"

"Looked over the schedule and guest attendance information. Your friend was there."

"My friend?"

"The one we ran into Monday at the precinct. The River Niles."

Tim's gut lurched with a kick he only felt when he thought of Niles. "I thought it was some sort of *Dungeons & Dragons* thing. Niles writes computer games."

"*Pfft.* The convention center staff you spoke with didn't really have a clue what it was about." Payne rolled her eyes. "They just book the space. Some of the security I had the uniforms interview called it a *Star Trek* thing. Someone else said *Lord of the Rings*, someone else mentioned *Doctor Who*. Which I guess isn't entirely inaccurate, since there are apparently tabletop and video games within most of those franchises, but it was about video games, as well as the kind you play in person."

"The techs gotten back to you about the video footage?"

"Dozens of cameras, three days' worth of footage, thousands of attendees. Charity—and we'll assume Lakshmi—were there both Friday and Saturday, according to the registration records. The facial recognition software has picked Charity out of the crowd a few times, but so far there hasn't been anything in the shots to indicate who might have gone after her." Payne hit the button on the key fob remote to unlock the car ahead of them. "Her costume got a lot of male attention, though."

Tim opened the passenger door, speaking over the top of the car. "Bryan says it's pretty commonplace for female cosplayers to receive unwelcome advances at conventions."

"Typical." Payne shook her head and ducked into the driver's seat while Tim closed his door and buckled up. "Girl just wants to dress up as her idol and some dude assumes she's putting it on display for him."

Tim nodded, frowning out the front windshield as Payne pulled off the shoulder and into traffic along Macadam Avenue. "You know, I feel like I'm in some cop movie trying to understand crimes committed in an underworld I know *nothing* about."

"That's a little dramatic, don't you think?" Payne smirked at him. "They played video games. It's not like we're trying to infiltrate the mafia or crack the codes of the Masonic temple."

"Maybe, but seriously. These girls lived in a sort of counter-culture most of us aren't even aware of, much less comprehend. Look at the way the convention staff all had no clue about what the convention was actually for. Charity's neighbors were clueless about her hobbies. Lakshmi's parents had no idea what she was doing when she went out the day she disappeared."

"*Young Women Keep Lives Secret From Family*: news at eleven," Payne deadpanned, and Niles flashed her a grin.

"We're not talking about who they were dating." He shrugged, staring blankly out the window as he let his mind spin. "Back in college, I would just tune out Niles when he started going on about the stuff he was into."

Payne frowned. "Really? Because I think some of it sounds cool."

"You gonna be making your own costume soon, Payne?"

"Why not? I'd rock the shit out of a Wonder Woman outfit. If there was ever a character who *needs* to be a sistah, it's her."

Tim chuckled. "I'd pay good money to see that." He tapped this thumbs on his knees, listening to the background chatter over the police radio. "I guess I just don't get it. People spend days on end at these conventions, hundreds of hours playing these games, billions of dollars on comics and DVDs of things the rest of us have never even heard of, and according to Bryan, small fortunes and countless hours making those costumes."

"What's your point?"

"They fly under the radar. Unless you're into it, you don't know they're there. Or if you do, you dismiss them as being out on the fringe." He remembered the way he'd listened with condescending amusement when Niles had talked about his computer games back in college. "Stereotypes of Trekkies and Princess Leia impersonators run through our heads, and we think their activities are a joke. But for them, it can be practically a lifestyle."

Payne hummed in what might have been agreement. "So you're thinking to understand who killed Charity and Lakshmi, we need to understand their world?"

"Maybe. There are no exes in the picture that we've found. No enemies we can pinpoint. Nothing we've seen so far indicates the crimes were sexual, or I would say it was just some pervert and it had nothing to do with their hobbies. But this says pattern to me, and right now that convention and those costumes are all we have to go on."

"So, we need to talk to someone who knows that world. What about Bryan?"

"He only knows about it because he's had roommates who are into it. He doesn't go himself. I was thinking of Niles."

Payne made a face. "If he was at that convention, we need to rule him out."

"I'll do that before I discuss any details with him. I'm just not sure he wants to talk to me."

He couldn't blame Niles for not calling. Asking to let bygones be bygones had been a long shot after the horrible way he had treated Niles when he'd graduated and left him behind.

"Can't hurt to ask." Payne flicked a glance at him out of the corner of her eye. "We got two girls who won't be going home to their mamas. I think he can suck it up and answer a few questions."

Tim sighed and tipped his head back against the headrest, closing his eyes. "Right. Okay."

He pulled his phone out of his coat pocket and thumbed through his address book until he found the number he'd taken down when talking about Niles's harassment case. The phone rang four times and seemed on the verge of going to voice mail when Niles answered, sounding a little out of breath.

"Hello?"

"Niles, hi, it's Tim."

"Oh . . . Hi." Tim's heart sank at the hesitation in the greeting. He wasn't sure if it was only surprise, or genuine reluctance, but it didn't feel very welcoming. "Give me a minute," he heard Niles murmur to someone, and then the sounds of people shouting and chanting suddenly erupted in the distant background. "Shit. So much for stepping outside for privacy. Sorry about the shouting. Fucking protesters. Anyway, what can I do for you?"

Tim forced himself not to inhale nervously in front of Payne and just plunged in. "I was wondering if we could meet up tonight. I have a case I'm working, and I need to pick your brain about something."

"A case? And you want to ask *me* about it?" He heard Niles sigh on the other end of the line. "Tim, look. I appreciate the offer of dinner and the apology, but really, I don't think it's a good idea."

"What? No. No, I swear it's not a line. I'm not looking for an excuse to get you to go out with me. I told you to call me if and when you decided you wanted to, and I meant it." He laughed humorlessly as Payne turned her eye to lift an eyebrow at him until the light changed to green. "I admit I was hoping you'd see your way clear to taking me up on that, but it is what it is. I get it. I wouldn't be calling right now except I really do need some information, and Payne's gonna kick my ass if we have to dither

trail down the side of Niles's neck, making him shiver. Fuck, he was horny. There was just too much shit going on, and all of it too overwhelming. He'd been anticipating the oblivion of a really good, uncomplicated, no-strings-attached orgasm or three. "I'm going to hold out hope for beating the odds."

A grin stretched his face, and Niles reached down to adjust himself un-self-consciously. "I am too."

CHAPTER 9

Tim was waiting at an isolated table in the back corner of the tavern with a pitcher of soda and a basket of chips and salsa when he saw Niles walking past the window. They were only blocks from Niles's house, according to the contact information he'd given Tim when they'd had lunch, and considering the parking situation in Northwest Portland, Tim imagined Niles would have walked, despite the drizzle.

He allowed himself a moment to observe Niles as he took off his leather jacket and swept his unruly curls back from his face. He really was still the most gorgeous thing Tim had ever seen, and Tim's pool of experience had broadened considerably in the decade since he'd been a closeted and confused criminal justice major at U of O. The darker complexion and thick, sooty lashes that were the legacy of Niles and Jordan's Turkish mother set off the pale gray-green eyes he'd inherited from their British father. A hint of dense hair played peekaboo at the open collar of his soft, denim-blue button-down, and his jeans looked well-worn and comfortable, grasping his ass and package like a lover's possessive hand.

Niles gave him a wary look and approached the table, saying

nothing when he filled a glass for Niles from the pitcher. "Thanks for coming," Tim murmured, expecting Niles to take a drink and browse the menu, but he pushed that aside.

"I'll be having dinner later, thanks. I've, um, I've got a house-guest I need to get back to." The way Niles's gaze stuttered away from his told Tim all he needed to know about the sort of company Niles was entertaining. "What is this all about?"

Right, Wyatt. Focus.

"Yeah." Tim puffed out his cheeks, sighing slowly. He glanced around to make sure the hostess hadn't seated anyone near enough to overhear their conversation, despite the volume of the music. "First, I need to ask you what you were doing Saturday night."

Niles stiffened. "Excuse me? Why do you need to know that? What business is it of yours?" He ran his hand through his hair. "Jesus, what *is* it with me and nosy exes?"

"What? No. *No*, this isn't—" Tim stopped himself, scratching at the stubble on his jaw. "Sorry, I might have phrased that wrong. It's not personal. Just answer the question, please."

"Fine." Niles sighed, slumping in his chair. "Saturday I was at a convention until late afternoon, and then I was online gaming most of the night."

"Can anyone confirm that?"

"Jordie and my boss, Rosie, were at the convention with me. And in the evening, I was on voice chat with my guild the whole time, including Rosie."

"Good enough, thank you." Tim made himself relax.

"Now what the hell is this about?" Niles demanded.

"How much have you been following the local news this last week, about the young women whose bodies were found in Forest Park and then today, down on the riverfront near Sellwood?"

Niles shook his head, frowning. "I haven't even had a chance to check the news this week. I heard something about a girl in

Forest Park on the radio, though honestly I've been too busy to pay much attention to anything lately."

"Well, Payne and I are working that case, and I'm trying to get some insight into these girls' hobbies because that seems to be the best connection we've found so far. They were into, um, dressing up like characters—"

"Cosplay."

"Right. They went to conventions. Specifically, the one that you were at this past weekend."

"Wait, *what*?" Niles gave him a stunned look. "They were gamers? Holy shit."

Tim nodded gravely. "Yeah. Which is why I had to clear your alibi before I could talk to you about it."

"What are you saying? There were thousands of people there! You can't honestly think—"

"God, no, not at all. But my captain would have my ass if I talked to someone and didn't cover my bases." Tim shrugged helplessly, watching Niles visibly work on lowering his hackles. It was a process he remembered well from the times they'd argued—usually about Tim's denial of being gay—in college. "As far as we can tell, most of their social life was online and not in person, so we're having a hard time tracking down their acquaintances and what the victims might have being doing. The first victim was on her own out here. The second had family in town, but she didn't discuss her activities with them much. Payne and I just got done interviewing them, and they just sort of hand-waved it when we asked, and said it was silly kid stuff."

Niles nodded, though he seemed shaken, and took a sip of his drink. "That's pretty common. We geeks are plenty happy to talk about our obsessions in the hopes of converting someone and sharing the joy, but we get dismissed a lot." He gave Tim a look, reminding him that he'd been one of those dismissive types. "It's why we tend to be so insular. Stick with our own kind." He reached for a chip, though he seemed more inclined to stare at it thoughtfully than nibble. "You know what fandoms they were into?"

"The first victim had an extensive anime and console game collection, but the second victim's family said she had been playing video games on her computer lately."

"Any titles I know?"

"No clue." Tim growled in frustration. "Both girls' computers are missing. They apparently took their laptops with them when they went out the day they disappeared and the computers haven't been found, nor have their cell phones. Which gives us reason to suspect they had contacts on there who don't want to be found."

"You think they knew the people, or person, who killed them?"

"Either that or there was something on their computers and phones that could connect them to the killer."

Niles ran a thumb up and down his pint glass. "I have to admit, I'm a little hesitant to believe that a gamer could be responsible. Gaming gets an undeserved rap for promoting violence. I would hate for this to trigger a witch hunt. Geek culture is . . . It's about sharing the love of something. People with similar interests coming together to indulge those interests. No different than a knitting club or sports fans who get together and go to games. Gamers are harmless."

"Ask any European country how harmless sports fans are when they riot after the World Cup," Tim said with a smirk, taking a long drink. "Not to mention all those messages you receive."

"Yeah, but that's just smack talk. You can't look at it that way." Niles began to gesticulate, a mannerism Tim remembered him lapsing into whenever he'd start to get worked up.

"Well, how should I look at it? What do you get from it, hanging out with people who send death threats?"

"If you just look at that, then you're missing everything else that fandom does for people." Niles sighed. "You're missing the millions of dollars raised for charity in fan-led activities. You're missing the kids saved from suicide because they have one bright spot in their life, a circle of people with a hobby in common. You're missing the isolated and disenfranchised outsiders whose lives are made better by knowing there are other people like them out there. It's not just harassment."

Tim nodded. "Fair enough. But gamers are just like everyone else, right? You get your good; you get your bad."

"Yeah, I guess, but generally speaking, even when it gets vitriolic, it is, as I said, harmless."

"Noted. But *harmless* didn't kill two girls."

Niles's shoulders tensed visibly. "You don't know it was a gamer who did that."

"Of course I don't. If I make any such assumption, it will be because that's where the evidence is pointing us. And that's what I'm trying to find right now: evidence, one way or the other." Niles blinked, then nodded and settled back in his chair. Tim gave him a comforting smile. "Okay. So, let's talk about these gamers and the sort of people these girls might have hung out with."

"It's like any other fandom, really, except that TV and book fandoms are frequently dominated by female fans, and comic, sci-fi, and gaming fandoms tend to be dominated by male fans, or so the male fans think."

"Explain that to me," Tim prompted, pulling out a notepad.

"In reality, the numbers suggest the demographics are nearly equal. Women make up forty-eight percent of the gaming market." Niles grimaced. "The guys claim that's because they play more 'casual' games that don't require a lot of skill, but there's no data to back that up. I know plenty of hardcore female gamers, including my boss. As I've mentioned before, the male fans are a little resistant to the fandom trending toward serving female fans equally."

"You mean like the harassing texts and emails you receive? I thought that was mostly homophobia."

"No. The homophobia is bad. The misogyny is much, much worse. The default male gamer assumption is that if a woman has entered into gaming or comic book fandom, it's to garner male attention. They've been known to try to make the environment very unwelcoming for female fans."

"In what way?"

"Check out Fat, Ugly, or Slutty—all one word, no spaces or punctuation—dot com if you want to see some samples. One common response to a female fan bringing up *anything* is 'Tits or get the fuck out,' by which they mean, 'If you're not here to entertain and titillate us, you're not welcome.'"

Tim frowned. "Couldn't that be chalked up mostly to the age demographic?"

"The average gamer is around midthirties." Niles sighed. "And male gamers, specifically, don't want to see gaming change. Homophobic and gendered slurs are common, and they like that female characters in games and comic books tend to be designed to appeal to the male gaze—unrealistically dressed, objectified, anatomically impossible, hypersexualized poses."

"And it's grown men defending this?"

"Well, as you've seen with my harassment, guys can get very vitriolic when their preeminence is challenged. It's basically the whole anti-sexism-racism-homophobia debate in a microcosm: 'I, the privileged demographic, don't have a problem, and therefore anyone pointing out that problems do actually exist or trying to change the status quo is a threat to me.'" Niles shrugged. "But they do their bullying anonymously, with words and cyber attacks, not physically. Any hints otherwise is just them talking big."

"Yeah, well, one guy—or a group of them—could take it into his head to up the ante." Tim frowned thoughtfully.

Niles groaned, rubbing his temples. "See, you're doing it. Assuming it's a gamer."

Tim sighed. "Niles, I'm acknowledging that it *could be* a gamer. It could also be some random stranger who got the drop on the young women in the parking lot. The difference between those two theories is that one leaves me a possible connection to investigate, and honestly, the crimes don't seem random. Stranger-on-stranger crime is much less common than crimes where the victims know or have some connection to their attackers. So I *need* to know the sort of people these young women would have associated with."

"Fine. Okay." Niles scrubbed his fingers through his hair. "Just . . . don't get tunnel vision where gamers are concerned, okay? Especially not based on all the crap people have thrown out about gaming and its effects on our culture."

"I know how to do my job." Tim fought to suppress a frown. "You can trust me to give everyone a fair shake."

"Can I? You were never very open-minded back when we were in school." Niles pressed his lips together and shook himself. "Forget it. What sort of cosplay did they do?"

Tim blinked at the change of subject but forced himself not to be diverted into discussing personal business that had no place here. "There are different kinds?"

"I mean the characters."

Tim was interrupted when the waitress approached to take their orders. He tried not to flinch when Niles ordered two meals packaged to go.

"One was a sort of femme fatale," Tim answered when the waitress was gone. "The other was sort of an alien or nonhuman creature, we think, judging from the leftover face paint. No one working the crime scenes recognized a specific character or costume."

"Okay, well, that narrows it down to, oh, at least a couple hundred archetypical characters," Niles said wryly, refilling his glass. But then something tightened in the corners of his eyes and his face went a little gray, putting Tim on alert. "Um, one of the girls wouldn't happen to have been wearing brown leather, was she?"

Tim straightened, then leaned farther across the table, pitching his voice low. "Yes, actually. Do you know who she was portraying?"

Niles closed his eyes, his lips moving silently. When he opened them, they were bright with tears. Tim felt an answering knot of unease form in his stomach. "If it's who I'm thinking of, she was playing Issis Lowe. And her companion, the alien, was a character named Gairi. I saw them that day. Talked to them. Me and Rosie and Jordan, at the autograph signing."

"Did you get their names?"

Niles nodded. "Yeah, but off the top of my head, I couldn't—"

"Charity Anspach and Lakshmi Agrawal?"

"Oh God. That's them." Niles blew out a shuddering breath. He hung his head for a moment, then wiped his eyes and looked up. "They're really dead?"

Tim nodded and reached across the table to squeeze Niles's hand, hesitating at the last moment. He cleared his throat. "Look, I'm going to need you, your brother, and your boss to come down to the precinct and give us statements on your contact with the victims that day."

"All right." Niles's voice was little more than a whisper. "I'll call Rosie and Jordie. Just let me take the food home to my guest, and then I'll come down to the precinct."

"Okay, I'll call Payne, have her meet us down there." He stood, digging his phone out of his breast pocket while Niles stared at the table. Tim could almost see his mind trying to throw up its defenses, shutting out the ugly image of what those young women had suffered. Things like that had no place in Niles's universe. Tim had always adored him for that dewy-eyed worldview, but it was heartbreaking to see Niles when he couldn't protect himself from the harsh realities of life.

"Niles?" He had to repeat himself before Niles looked up. He didn't like how hard Niles was taking this. What sort of connection had he had to those girls? "Just one thing: the characters the girls were playing . . . where were they from?"

"*My* game." Niles's mouth quivered, and he drew a deep breath, meeting Tim's eyes dead-on. "Issis and Gairi are my characters. I wrote them."

CHAPTER 10

R osie looked up from the spreadsheet she was working on at the coffee table when her phone rang with Niles's ringtone. She swiped the screen to answer, leaning back on the sofa, away from her laptop. "Hey, I thought you had a date tonight. What's up?"

"Rosie . . ." Niles cleared his throat, and his voice was raspy. She sat upright, stiff and tense in an instant. "Rosie, those girls from the convention? Issis and Gairi? They're . . . they're dead."

"What?" The breath shot from her lungs, leaving her chest aching.

"The girl in Forest Park they found this week—"

"Oh my God." She closed her eyes, trying not to think of those bright, eager young women dead. Her pulse pounded in her ears, making it hard to hear Niles's next words.

"The police want us to come down to the precinct, give a statement about when we saw them that day."

"Of course." She was standing, reaching for her coat and shoes before she even finished nodding. "Are you okay?"

Niles's shuddering breath rattled the speaker of her phone with a staticky sound. "I don't know. I mean, I guess I'm fine compared to those women, but God . . . Am I crazy for feeling a personal connection to this?"

"They were playing characters you created, Niles. Of course you feel you had a connection to them. I feel it too. You know how I identify with Issis." That much was true, though it was Charity's bravery in the face of being harassed at the convention that now haunted her. "It'll be okay, honey. Call Jordan. He'll take care of you. I'll meet you down at the precinct."

———

NILES HAD to take a deep breath before he turned the knob to enter his own house. The odor of the food he'd bought was now vaguely nauseating. Hell. He didn't want to face Daniel still reeling like this.

Daniel was on the sofa, where he'd been when Niles had left, playing a first-person shooter on Niles's Xbox. He smiled when Niles walked in and paused the game. "Hey there, how— Are you okay?"

Niles tried to return the smile, but he couldn't manage it. "I'll be fine. Look, there's been a change of plans. I need to go down to the police precinct and talk to them awhile longer." Damn it. He owed Daniel some sort of explanation, though Tim had cautioned him against sharing details with anyone else. He sighed and ran his hand through his hair. "*The LEET News* might be interested to know that the murder victims that have been in the news here in Portland this week were gamers."

There. That should be safe. The murders were already on the news. Maybe *LEET* could do a memorial for them or something. Honor them specifically as members of the gaming community. Maybe Third Wave could find out what charities the girls supported and make a donation in their names.

"Are you kidding me?" Daniel, eyes wide, came to his feet as

Niles set the bag of takeout on the counter. "Can you tell me anything else?"

"I don't . . . I don't know. I don't know what is public information and what's being kept under wraps for the police investigation, so let's just assume there's nothing else I can say." He scrubbed his hands down his face. "I'm sorry about this. Just— Make yourself at home. You're welcome to anything in the kitchen, any of the games. I don't know when I'll be home. I'm sorry."

"Hey." Daniel crossed the kitchen and reached for Niles, stroking his hands down Niles's arms before pulling him into a soothing hug. "It's okay. This is important. I get it. You do what you need to do. You've got an awesome game library. I'm good here."

"Thanks." He leaned his head against Daniel's shoulder, accepting the embrace. "I don't know how long I'll be. Don't wait up if you need some sleep."

———

Rosie watched Detective Payne jotting down notes. "What can you tell us about the guys who were making advances on Charity at the convention?"

"Assault."

"What?"

"Assault. The word you're looking for is *assault*." She raised and lowered her shoulders, craning her neck from one side to the other to try to get rid of some of the tension. "On at least one occasion, a man touched her sexually without her consent. When you say *making advances*, you make it sound like she was the target of some harmless flirting."

The detective narrowed her eyes for a moment—the expression thoughtful and considering, rather than annoyed. "Point taken. What can you tell us about the guys who *assaulted* Charity at the convention?"

"Which time?" The response came out more caustically than she had intended, but it felt like the walls were closing in on her, despite the wide-open space around the detective's desk. At another desk, Jordan sat with Detective Wyatt, who was writing down notes based on Jordie's statement just as his partner was doing with Rosie. She caught his eye and jerked her head minutely in the direction of the chairs on the outskirts of the large, chaotic room. Niles sat there with his elbows on his knees, his hands clasped together, and his head bowed almost prayerfully. She hadn't seen him this upset since the day two years ago when she'd told him about the tumor in her skull.

"Ms. Candelaria?" Detective Payne prompted, and Rosie tore her attention back to the interview.

"Sorry," she murmured, clamping down on her irritation. Niles looked devastated by the news that those young women were dead, but anger was boiling under the surface of Rosie's composure, vibrating the lid she was trying to keep on it. "I'm taking my temper out on you, and I don't mean to. I saw several incidents while Charity and Lakshmi stood in line when people wanted them to pose for pictures. The one where Jordan interfered was the most obvious, but I noticed several moments where Charity looked uncomfortable enough to make me suspect someone was being inappropriate with her."

"Ms. Candelaria—"

"You can call me Rosie, Detective."

"All right. I'm Angie." The detective took a deep breath and met her eyes evenly. "Rosie, I'm not interested in downplaying the way those young women were treated that day at the convention. You were right to call me on my sugarcoated word choice. So if you think I'm trying to blame the victims or whatever, that's not how I operate. Okay?"

"Okay." Rosie inhaled and exhaled several times, deep and

slow. "I'm not pissed at you. I'm pissed that someone killed them."

Angie frowned. "Sounds personal. You just met them that day, right?"

"Yeah, but—" Rosie grimaced. "They stood out. I've actually been thinking about them a lot this week, particularly Charity Anspach. She was bright, and happy, and brave. She stood up for herself, you know. Not just against the guys who groped her, but even with Jordan. She told him to back off and let her handle it."

"Really?" Angie tapped her pen on her pad, frowning even more deeply. "That doesn't fit the description everyone else has given of a quiet, shy girl who never bothered anyone."

"Why not? Quiet and shy doesn't mean spineless. Especially if she was making a deliberate effort not to let that sort of thing slide, to confront misogyny when she came across it."

"True, that," Angie conceded. "So tell me about the guys. The specific guys from the incident you witnessed where Jordan intervened or about anyone else you saw with her that day."

Unfortunately, the guys at the convention had all bled together into a faceless mass. After giving the world's most useless eyewitness report, Rosie asked, "Can you tell me if you have any leads?"

"Not really." Angie put down her pen with a sigh. "I can't discuss the case in any detail. Right now we're just trying to get a picture of who Charity and Lakshmi associated with. Their social lives were all online, maybe to do with those games, but we don't have their computers or phones to begin working through that."

Rosie tapped her fingers restlessly on the table, nodding. "If they had subscriptions to multiplayer online games, like *World of Warcraft*, it would show up on their bank statements, unless they bought prepaid time cards. And if they were into other games like *PF3*, where the gameplay isn't multiplayer, there might still be purchases for DLCs. That's short for download-able content, which is basically a bonus pack that can contain gear and weapons or even whole new story modules. Third Wave will cooperate fully if you need any of the records from our fan forums, but other gaming sites might not be as helpful."

Angie nodded and made more notes. "All right, I'll look into that. Thank you, Rosie."

They came to their feet, Angie gesturing with an arm for Rosie to precede her to the edge of the room and the chairs where both Niles and Jordan were now waiting. Detective Wyatt was standing there not saying anything to them, looking awkward.

Niles rose at her approach and she slipped an arm around him, rubbing a hand up and down his back, then she turned to face Angie. "I'm sorry we didn't see much. If there's anything else we can do to help, please call us."

The detectives nodded and escorted them out of the precinct into the dark and dreary drizzle. Once they had gone back inside, she hugged Niles fully, and he clung to her. "You okay, honey?"

"I'll be fine." After a moment, he shuddered and drew back, and she let him go. "I need to get back to my guest."

"Want me to come with you?" Jordan asked, but Niles shook his head.

"No. I'll see you in the morning."

They started to follow as Niles walked down the street, but he whirled on them and huffed. "I promise you, I can get to my car unassisted."

"Someone left a threatening note at your house earlier this week," Jordan said gruffly. "Shut up and let us walk you to your car."

He stared at them a moment as if he were going to fight, and then that look of wounded disillusionment was back in his soft eyes and his shoulders slumped. "Right. Okay."

As they fell in step together again, this time with Rosie and Jordan flanking Niles, Jordan remarked, "I was thinking that we should try to find out the girls' favorite charities and organize a donation drive in their names."

Damn, she should have thought of that. As she chided herself, Niles stumbled and stopped, turning to look at his brother.

"What?" Jordan shifted uncomfortably. "I'm not completely heartless."

"No, you're not." Niles continued to stare at him, a gentle smile just pulling at the edges of his mouth. "That's a great idea, Jordie. I love it."

CHAPTER 11

T he downpour from the showerhead spattered Niles's face as he tipped his head back, letting the torrent wash his guilt and confusion away. He sighed, then went still when a cool draft brushed his body, followed by warm skin that grew slick against his under the steaming water.

"Hey," he murmured, pushing aside all his ambivalence to make his voice warm and welcoming. Whatever issues he had, he wasn't going to treat Daniel awkwardly. He could beat himself up over it later, but there was no reason to make Daniel feel like they'd done something wrong.

"Morning," Daniel greeted. Evidence of how good his morning was starting off was prodding the back of Niles's thighs, and Niles felt an answering tug of arousal despite everything. His body didn't seem to much care about his emotional turmoil, and Niles turned to wrap his arms around Daniel and hug him instead, willing his cock to cool it. He'd spent enough time last night using Daniel to erase the image of Charity Anspach and Lakshmi Agrawal out of his head. He wasn't going to do it again this morning.

Daniel pulled away slightly, tipping his head back to look up at Niles. "I don't have to be at the train station for another hour and a half."

"Sounds nice, but I'm about to be late to my first meeting of the morning." Niles stepped back, letting Daniel have the spray. "I'm sorry."

"What for?" Daniel wiped away the water sluicing down his face, cracking an eye open to peer at Niles.

Niles rubbed at the grout between the tiles with his thumb. "I, um, I feel like I owe you an apology. I had a lot on my mind last night, and I feel like I sort of tried to get away from it by being with you. I'm not usually like that."

"I wasn't complaining." Daniel smirked, then shrugged, reaching for the shampoo. "Though if you're telling me you're normally some sweet, submissive bottom, I'm intrigued and would like to know more."

Thank God for the steam and the heat disguising his blush. Niles looked away, then offered Daniel a smile. "I did have a good time, even if the evening didn't turn out to be what I think either of us was planning on. Thanks for staying."

Daniel rinsed the suds out of his hair, then turned and planted his hands on the tile wall at either side of Niles's shoulders, trapping him against it. He closed in for a kiss, and Niles allowed it, sinking into it, sliding down the slick wall until they were the same height. He let Daniel own the kiss with no hint of the aggression that had driven him the night before, though his interest was becoming quite literally palpable. And Daniel was more than glad to palpate.

"*Fuck.*" Niles hissed and let his head tip back as Daniel stroked him, catching his bottom lip between his teeth and letting it slide out a little puffier than it had been before.

Daniel sipped a stream of water off his Adam's apple. "Sure you can't be late for that meeting?"

"Oh God, don't tempt me." It took Niles a moment to gather himself enough to open his eyes and straighten up. "Unfortunately, I need to get a move on. There's just too much to do before I leave for the Bay Area tonight."

"Okay." Daniel backed off, turning off the shower. "Can I give you a call if I'm ever back in Portland? Assuming you get this other stuff worked out, I mean. Maybe we can try this again without the exes and protesters and police."

"Please do," Niles said, quelling the urge to blush or apologize again, and slipped back into the bedroom to get ready for the day.

"Can I give you a ride to the train station before I go to work?" he asked when they were both dressed and finishing off the remnants of their toast. His messenger bag sat by the door, and he picked it up and slung it over his shoulder.

"Nah, it's fine. Drop me off at a coffee shop along the way, and I can take the bus. You're running late, and I have plenty of time."

"Okay." Niles paused, irritated with his own uncertainty and frustration. "I don't do this much, sorry. I'm a little out of practice, especially with being in such a rush and everything so crazy. If I had more time I'd have cooked you breakfast, but—"

"It's fine. I'm a big boy. We're cool." Daniel stepped up for another kiss. "I'll email you an advance copy of the article when I have it written, probably next week. Enjoy the Bay Area."

"Right." Niles tried to meet Daniel's eyes and offer him a smile, but he couldn't. Fuck it all. He turned away. "Thanks, Daniel. For everything."

———

AFTER DROPPING Daniel off at the coffee shop, Niles spent the rest of the drive to Third Wave's studios gripping his steering wheel in annoyance. He couldn't even pinpoint what bothered him most: that he'd used Daniel or that he'd been that urgently in need of forgetfulness for a while. He felt guilty and for no reason that made sense.

Without the escapism Daniel provided, Charity and Lakshmi were now fully in the front of Niles's mind. He turned on the radio, listening for any news of the murders, but it was all weather and financial and world news instead. The previous night's events were taking on a surreal quality. Had they really been at a convention with two girls who were now dead? The thought didn't compute. He couldn't—wouldn't—imagine those beautiful, smiling young women being the victims of the sort of violence Tim had described. Besides, brushes with things like that were the territory of protagonists in books and movies and games, not guys like him who just wrote the story.

Sighing and desperate to think about something other than the image of them being dead, he hit the button on his car stereo to connect to his phone's Bluetooth and located the number of the company phone assigned to the writing staff intern.

"Patrick? Hey, it's Niles. Can you do me a favor on your way in to work? Do you have your car today? I saw your brother picking you up last night— Yeah, okay, great. Listen, that reporter we had at the studios the past couple days needs a ride to the train station . . ."

———

JORDAN QUASHED a surge of unease beneath his heel as he watched Niles pack his computer and some printouts to take with him to the convention in San Francisco. He wasn't comfortable with Niles going alone, but there was no need for them both to be there and Jordan had a lot on his plate at the moment with the PR push leading up to the *PF3* release and managing the response to the protests this last week.

It was the murders; that was what had him so jumpy. There was no other rational cause for his vague sense something being wrong. Niles hadn't mentioned any additional physical notes left at his house, and the texts and emails had quieted down as the week drew to a close. Niles had reported the note, and if Jordan wasn't certain he wanted Timothy Wyatt working his way back into his brother's life, at least he was fairly confident that Tim would take the situation seriously and deal with it if things got worse.

And yet that gut instinct that his brother was in trouble —"twinscience," Niles had once called it, like "prescience" or "omniscience"—wouldn't be quiet. The twin telepathy thing was the kind of mystical crap Jordan scoffed at. At best, it was far more clichéd than he ever wanted to be accused of being, but Niles was a believer, and at moments like these, Jordan could almost buy into it.

Niles's head snapped up. "Will you quit scowling over there? You're making me nervous, and damn it all, I'm already enough of a psychological disaster zone today."

"Feeling that good, huh?" Jordan smirked. "That columnist from *LEET* must not have been very impressive."

"No, Daniel was great. It's just all this other shit." Niles shrugged, which was as good as a confirmation, since Jordan knew he didn't kiss and tell.

Niles jabbed in an extension on the speakerphone, which was answered by one of his writing staff. "Avery, where's the final draft of the slave camp scene dialogue for me to approve? I was supposed to have it this afternoon."

Jordan leaned against the wall, watching his brother as he tried to pinpoint what was nagging at him. It wasn't the trip to San Francisco, but *everything* was off, and pretending it wasn't there wasn't going to make it stop bothering him. They needed to stick together now.

"Damn. I'll have them to you right away," Avery answered, his voice echoing on the speakerphone. "Idiot interns."

"Can we not refer to our interns that way?" Niles snapped.

"Patrick was supposed to deliver them to have a final proofing pass done and get them formatted, then email them to you this morning, but he never came in today."

"Patrick Rutledge?" Niles's brows drew down, and that thrum of anxious tension in Jordan's gut amped up another notch. "I knew he was going to be late this morning—I asked him to run an errand for me on his way to the office—but he should have come in after."

"Like I said, idiot interns." Jordan watched Niles's mouth tighten at the dismissive insult. "Anyway, I've emailed the file. Sorry it won't have received the final proofing pass."

"Okay, thanks. See you Monday." Niles turned off the speaker-phone, still frowning. "Damn. Didn't think Patrick was the sort of kid to flake out on us like that."

He dialed a number on his phone—Patrick, presumably—and then frowned even more sharply when he obviously went to voice mail.

"He's new, right?" Jordan asked.

Niles gave him a stare. "I'd think you'd remember him, considering you had him running your errands at the convention last weekend. I better see if he ever bothered to pick up Daniel like I asked him to. Maybe there was a problem with the car." Niles grabbed his cell off the desk and dialed, listening with a glower before he left a message. "Hey, Daniel, just wanted to see how your train trip went and make sure you got to the station all right this morning. I had a really good time, so thanks again. Give me a call, and I'll look forward to seeing your article."

He hung up the phone and braced his fists on the desk. "Damn it. Now your mood has caught on, and I'm even tenser. And today was already going *so* well."

Jordan grimaced. "*Now* you're nervous. Better than moping, I guess. I've been pacing the floor all day while you've been lost in your head, ignoring me."

"You pace the floor when you've had too much sugar and when you haven't gotten laid in the last forty-eight hours. And I'm just trying to push the elephant to the corner of the room so I can finish whatever else I need to get done before I go." Niles rubbed the back of his skull.

Jordan's eyes narrowed. "You have a headache?"

"Hm?" Niles dropped his hand from his head, staring at it as if surprised that it had been up there. "Um, yeah, I guess. We've got voice actors flying in and the studio booked for next week, and the scripts aren't where they're supposed to be. I really don't want to *not* have our shit together when we've got Angela Bassett and Darryl Stephens in the studio to read Issis and Gairi."

"I don't think you should go to California."

"Whoa, non sequitur much?" Niles stopped dithering and blinked at him. "What reason would I give not to go? This convention is important."

"I don't know, but I'm pretty sure we should stick together for the time being. You're still upset about those girls being murdered, whoever took the trouble to hand deliver a harassing letter to you is still out there, and I'm half a second away from channeling classic lines by Han Solo."

"Careful, you're on the verge of ranking yourself among us geeks." Niles made an attempt at a smile, then grimaced and shook his head. His eyes had darted away from Jordan's, which didn't help Jordan's uneasy feeling in the least. Niles slung his messenger bag over his shoulder with a lot more force than necessary. "This is ridiculous. I need to get to PDX. Do me a favor and swing by my house on your way home later? I don't remember if I set the alarm or not."

Jordan's stomach gave another anxious twist, but he nodded. "Yeah, I'll do that."

Niles stopped in front of Jordan on his way to the door, opening his mouth as if he was going to say something, then clapping Jordan on the shoulder and leaving without another word.

When Niles was gone, Jordan returned to his office, trying to settle in to contact bloggers and magazines who were interested in the content of Niles's appearances that weekend at the convention to confirm interview times. He debated going out to a club that night; getting laid would take his mind off matters nicely, but he didn't really care to be diverted. He wanted to sit and fixate on this nagging feeling until he pinned the problem down and took care of it.

Irritable and edgy, he kept himself busy for hours after Niles had left for the airport, until he finally decided 10 p.m. was plenty late to work on a Thursday night. He slapped his computer closed, stuffed it in its case, and muttered goodnight to the security guard in the front lobby before heading for Niles's house to check the alarm as he'd promised.

The porch light was off, so he pulled his keys out to let himself in, only to find it was unlocked. Mail was scattered on the floor inside the door from where it had been dropped through the slot, and in the dim light filtering in from the street in the unlit foyer, Jordan's eyes zeroed in on an envelope right on top of the messy pile that didn't appear to have a stamp or postal mark. He bent over to gather up the mail, scrutinizing the envelope as he fumbled along the wall for the light switch.

The antique fixture above the door flared on, and in the blind instant when his eyes adjusted, agony erupted in the back of his skull. With his vision awash in a red-and-black swirl of pain, he dropped to his knees, and heard the shushing sounds as the mail scattered across the floor again. Then he pitched forward and heard nothing.

CHAPTER 12

Niles's messenger bag swung against his hip as he jogged, and each jolting step sent a flash of pain through his skull, where a vicious headache had burst into being just as his plane had been touching down at SFO. When he'd landed back in Portland, he'd had to take a cab to the hospital from the airport, because the pain had been too bad for him to consider driving.

He spotted Rosie at the end of the hospital corridor, leaning forward with her elbows braced on her knees. She was staring down at the gray tile as she rubbed her hands together in an absent, almost mechanical gesture. He'd already been trying to book a flight home, after finding Jordan wasn't answering his phone, when she had called to tell him what had happened.

She pushed to her feet as Niles approached and hugged him tightly. "How is he?" he panted, closing his eyes against the nausea the headache was causing. The Tylenol he'd bought at the airport gift shop hadn't touched the damn thing.

"Concussed. They did a CT, and there didn't seem to be any bleeding in his skull. He regained consciousness on the way to the hospital, but they gave him something for the pain and now he's out again."

"What the fuck happened?"

"Someone hit him in the head with a rock." Her mouth tightened, her eyes grim. "The police think they were after you."

"*What?*"

"He was attacked on the front porch of your house." Niles spun when another voice joined the conversation, to see Tim Wyatt approaching. A glance at Rosie showed she was unsurprised with his appearance, so obviously he'd been there for a while, perhaps had already spoken to her. "Your neighbors were just getting home around midnight from a party, and they noticed your door was open and your lights were on. They saw a shape blocking the door but they couldn't make it out so the wife decided to see if you were home and found him there. I got a call because I had let dispatch know to alert me if anything comes in involving your name or address."

Niles sank down onto one of the molded plastic chairs, rubbing his head again. "Do you have any idea who it was?"

Tim dug a plastic evidence bag out of his pocket. Inside, Niles could make out an envelope with his name on it. "No, but they left you some fan mail."

Niles reached for it and stopped himself, remembering what Tim had said about not handling the letters. "What's it say?"

"It says, 'You were warned.' Same font, ink tone, and grade of paper as last time."

"Jesus." Rosie rubbed his shoulder as Niles scoured his hands down his bristly face. He'd landed in San Francisco too late to turn around and catch the next flight back, so he'd spent the night trying to sleep in a chair in the airport while his head pounded mercilessly. Coupled with the lack of sleep when Daniel had stayed with him, it meant he had only a handful of hours of rest under his belt over the last two days. He'd also been in the same clothes for a full day now.

"Jordie's head still hurts," Niles said, rubbing the back of his head. "I think the meds are wearing off. Can they give him something for the pain?" He turned a questioning look at Rosie, and she blinked at him once, then stood.

"Sure. I'll go talk to a nurse, see if that's all right."

"They might need to wait for him to wake up before they give him anything else," Tim suggested, taking another chair a couple of seats down from Niles.

"Figures. They need him to regain consciousness before they can knock him out." He slumped in the chair, rubbing his eyes again.

Rosie shrugged. "Can't hurt to ask. I'm sure Detective Wyatt has questions for you. Why don't you do that down in the cafeteria and get some coffee? I'll call you if he wakes up, or if they say you can take him home."

Niles hovered on the verge of protesting, but common sense won out and he nodded, following Tim down to the cafeteria.

"Did you find anything else? Any clues?" he asked once they were ensconced at a table with cups of questionable coffee in their hands.

Tim shook his head. "No. I'm not holding out hope for fingerprints on the letter, since the assailant appeared to use gloves to handle the rock. It's November, of course, so it could very well be that whoever did this was wearing gloves due to the weather rather than any particular attempt to avoid detection, and if that's the case, might have taken them off at some point. We're printing your doorknob, mail slot, around the doorframe, porch railing, and so forth, so we'll need your prints and Jordan's and whoever else has visited your house recently. For elimination."

"Um, that might be tough on one front. My guest from the other night has gone back to Seattle now." He was too fucking tired to be concerned if Tim was dismayed by that bit of information, but Tim just nodded slowly, his expression neutral.

"What time did he leave?"

"Who?"

"Your guest."

"Oh, um, his train departed around midmorning yesterday."

"Any chance he might have missed it?" Tim asked, pulling his phone out and tapping in notes.

Niles frowned. "Not that I can think of. Why?"

"I'm asking if he might have been at your house when Jordan came by."

"What? You think *Daniel* hung around to bash in my brother's skull?"

"Well, he would have been hanging around to bash in your skull, actually." The throbbing in Niles's head amped up another notch as he opened his mouth to let Tim know exactly what he thought of that idea. Tim held up a hand, forestalling the tirade. "I'm just covering all the bases."

"Fine." Niles gave him a resentful look, crossing his arms. "He'd have no reason to believe I would be coming home. He knew I was heading to the airport straight from work. Besides, I dropped him off at a coffee shop on my way to work and had my intern give him a lift to the train station. Is this a jealousy thing? Really?"

Tim sighed, putting away his phone. "No, Niles, really. I'm just trying to narrow down the possibilities."

"Then no, Tim. No, there was no reason for him to stick around. We said good-bye, he said he'd call me if he was ever in Portland again, and that was it. He was a good guy, a straight shooter."

Tim nodded, though he didn't look entirely convinced. "You work with proprietary information, don't you? Was there anything in your house that someone might have been after?"

"What, you mean like industrial espionage?" Niles frowned. He closed his eyes, hoping to block out any distractions and help himself focus, but all it made him do was want to sleep. "Daniel works for a respected trade magazine. He wouldn't jeopardize their rep doing anything shady, and besides, I gave him all the scoop he could want. As far as anyone else is concerned, I don't keep anything like that at my house. It's all on my work computer or my laptop, which I always carry with me." He patted his messenger bag.

"Niles. Look at me." Tim's voice was a little blunter, a little firmer than before, compelling Niles to meet his eyes. "I swear to you, I'm not trying to lynch your one-night stand. If anything comes up that looks like he might have something to do with this, I'll be handing this case off to another detective because I'd have a clear conflict of interest."

Niles ducked his head at the intensity of Tim's gaze. "Really?"

"Yeah. In fact, I should have done so already since I'm a homicide detective and this is a stalking and menacing case. My captain is letting me follow it for now, but I need to tread lightly. So, don't worry about defending him to me, okay?" Tim leaned back, easing off the heavy stare. "Just answer the questions, and this will all go faster. Leave the detective work to me; it's what your tax dollars are paying me to do. Now, can we get through this so you can focus on taking care of you and your brother? Okay?"

"Right. Sure." Niles closed his eyes again for a long moment, then forced them open before he nodded off.

Tim's mouth twitched. "You really do look like hell."

"Yeah, you try spending the night in an airport, see how sprightly you look." Niles took a long drink of his coffee, inhaling the smoky aroma. His headache was easing up slightly, at least.

"Do you still think this is related to your work?" Tim asked after a moment, watching him closely.

"What else could it be?"

"We just had two girls murdered after a convention you were at. You tell me."

Niles shook his head adamantly. "You can't think there's a connection."

"There's nothing to indicate one just yet, no, but the rate of violence happening against people who attended that convention means I should at least keep the idea open as one avenue of inquiry." Tim's eyebrows lifted until Niles settled down again. "So tell me why you still think this is connected to your work."

"Because right now we're besieged with people unhappy with what we're doing." Niles ran a hand through his hair, pushing it back violently. He could hear himself speaking quickly, the words pouring out. "I mean, you've got the dude-bros in one corner protesting any potential shift in a status quo that favors them. In another, you have the anti-gaming lobby that wants to blame video games for the violence in our culture in a country where you've got people giving their kids assault rifles for their birthdays. In yet another, you've got the family-values yahoos afraid that playing a game with a queer character in it will turn their kid into a fag. I mean, Jesus, the fucking Guiding Light Fellowship was outside our offices the other day to remind us that every time God lets a soldier in Afghanistan die, it's all our fault." Niles slid down in his chair in a tired slump. "I need a scorecard to keep track of all of them nowadays."

"What about other relationships? Any bad breakups?"

"Well, there's Anthony, but he's harmless."

Tim smirked. "Famous last words. Tell me about Anthony."

"Anthony Joyner. I was seeing him for a couple months this fall, but it wasn't working out. He still calls and texts me a lot, thinks maybe we can try to get back together, but he's never been the slightest bit menacing. Just . . . clingy."

Tim turned on his phone again. "Where does he live? Work? What does he do?"

"He's a sound engineer at the studio where we record our voice actors. I met him early last year when the actors were in town doing the voice work for *PF3*. It's over off Hawthorne. He lives in John's Landing."

"Well, give me his phone number, and I can at least get an alibi to rule him out." Niles rattled it off, and Tim gave him an approving nod for his cooperation. "Okay, now, tell me about these protesters. Have there been any particular ones who have stood out, been more aggressive than the others, tried to escalate matters?"

Hunched in his chair and aching with the need for sleep and something stronger than Tylenol to knock out the residual headache, Niles answered Tim's questions until Rosie called to let them know Jordan was awake.

———

"NILES? Y'OKAY?" were his first words, and Niles laughed softly, shaking his head. He brushed a gelled and matted hank of hair back from Jordan's face.

"I'm fine, Jordie. Tim's here, though. He needs to ask you some questions."

"'ll kick his ass again," Jordan slurred. Niles heard Rosie laugh behind him.

On the other side of the bed, Tim snorted. "No, not about that," he clarified. "You got bashed in the head with a rock at Niles's house, Jordan. Remember?"

Jordan blinked, his eyes flicking back and forth between them. "Um. No?" He looked at Niles as if for confirmation.

Niles gave Tim a shrug and a wry smile. "Guess that answers that." He squeezed his brother's shoulder. "Hang tight, Jordie. I'll see if they'll release you or if they need to keep you awhile longer. Rosie, you think you can give us a ride back to Jordie's place? I don't have my car."

"I'll do that," Tim said before Rosie could answer. Niles flashed him a look, and he offered an apologetic smile. "I'd like to check Jordan's place, make sure no one is waiting for either of you there."

A protest died unborn on Niles's tongue. "Right. Okay. Looks like you can get some rest, Rosie. I'll be back soon."

It took a few more wearying hours to get Jordan released from the hospital, and then only once they were assured someone would be staying with him. Once they reached his condo and had finished waiting outside while Tim checked the apartment, Niles escorted his shuffling brother to bed. When he came back out to the living room, Tim was on the balcony talking on his phone. A glance at the clock told Niles it wasn't even noon yet, so he decided to forego the beer he wished he could have and helped himself to the orange juice in Jordan's fridge instead.

He was seated on the sofa, sipping it thoughtfully, when Tim came back inside, his medium-weight microfiber jacket beaded with small drops of water from the misting rain.

"That was Payne." He sank onto the sofa beside Niles. "I asked her to follow up with your ex."

"Okay. I thought of something else that might have . . . provoked someone."

"Oh?"

Niles cleared his throat. "Yeah. The other night, as I was leaving work with Daniel after you and I arranged to meet, we drove past those Guiding Light douche bags and, um, decided to give them something to really protest."

He wasn't sure how Tim would take that bit of information, but Tim grinned. "Way to go. But I take it they weren't thrilled?"

"We were gay and breathing. Of course they weren't thrilled. The kiss was just salt in the wound."

"Was there anyone who seemed particularly upset by the display?"

Niles shrugged. "You know, I didn't really check. I didn't care how they reacted. I was just sending them a big *fuck you*."

Tim looked down at his hands. "You always were so comfortable with who you were. I used to envy you that. I think that's why I got so mean when I broke things off."

"I guess that makes sense, in a way." Niles rubbed his palms up and down the denim covering his knees. "I wasn't always, you know. Of the two of us, Jordie was the brave one, the confident one. We came out to each other before anyone else, of course, but I wasn't going to come out to him at all. I'd thought I was alone in being gay, and he . . ." He chuckled, shaking his head. "It never occurred to him that I *wasn't* gay. He took it as a given that if he was, I would be too. No question about it. So he blurted it out to me like it was no big deal, assuming that I had the same confidence in him that he had in me, that I *just knew*. Weird. It was the only time in our lives that I ever doubted anything about him, even for an instant. After that, though, it didn't matter what anyone thought of us. Of me. As long as he was there alongside me, I didn't care who else objected."

"You're lucky." Tim turned sideways on the sofa to face him more fully. "If I'd had that sort of support system, maybe I would have handled things differently."

"Yeah, well, I wasn't as sympathetic as I could have been to what you were facing. Coming out was so easy for me, and once I knew Jordie was gay too, I was so secure that the people who mattered most to me wouldn't care. I couldn't really appreciate how much harder it must be for other people." Niles sighed and looked away. "Sorry. I'm being rude. You want some juice? Water? I can make a pot of coffee."

"Coffee would be great, thanks. I got the call about your brother around three o'clock this morning."

"Sure." Niles pushed himself up off the sofa, grateful for the excuse to put some distance between them. "So, how did your family take it? When it finally all went down?"

"My wife was both furious and not surprised, if that makes any sense." Tim chuckled without much humor. "She said she'd known since I'd come back from college that something was off. She'd assumed I'd met another girl there and felt guilty about it. Then when the truth came out, so to speak, she was livid that I'd been lying to her for so long. As divorces go, it wasn't terribly acrimonious, but it wasn't a joyride, either, and now we're awkwardly amicable exes."

"Could be worse." Niles fell silent while the electric coffee grinder burred. "Any kids?"

"No, thank God. Though, really, I should thank her for that. I was pushing for it. I think maybe I believed that if we had kids, I would forget everything else, forget you, and everything would finally feel right in my life. I'd focus on them and that would be all that mattered. But like I said, Kayleigh knew something was off and kept telling me she didn't think we were ready yet. Pretty smart of her, in the end."

"What about the rest of your family?" He was proud of himself for sounding so calm and steady. Tim's fear of coming out to his family was what had broken his heart and left him devastated, after all. Maybe ten years had actually been enough to relieve some of the sting, though even thinking about it, his chest felt tight.

"As awful as this is to say, my dad's illness was probably a good thing on that front. No one had time to get hysterical when I was outed, because we had other things to worry about. And by the time Dad had passed away and we'd stopped mourning, it had just sort of settled in." Tim shrugged, and Niles turned on the coffeemaker and returned to the sofa, cursing Jordan for having a sectional instead of a chair where he could actually sit across the room from Tim. He would have stayed standing at the breakfast bar if he weren't so exhausted that his knees felt weak. "My mom and brother don't actually talk about it. It's a little *Don't ask, don't tell*. They never inquire about whether I'm dating anyone or anything like that, which is something I'll have to deal with someday when I want to bring someone home for the holidays, but for now, it's okay with me to just leave things like that."

Niles nodded, biting his lip against the urge to ask why Tim had been in town for seven years and never called him. Awkward silence fell, disrupted only by the burbling of the coffeemaker in the background.

Finally, Tim spoke again as Niles poured the coffee. "So you and this reporter—"

"No, it's not anything." Niles flicked him a quick look before dedicatedly studying his coffee. "I don't know what you think I've been doing all these years, but it wasn't pining for you."

"I didn't think you had been." Tim cleared his throat and ventured a few more desultory questions about who might wish Niles harm, but by the time they were midway through their first cups, they'd lapsed back into silence. Niles thought Tim looked as exhausted as he felt.

"I should go," Tim muttered finally, pushing himself up. "I'll have more questions later, and I'll need to talk to Jordan, of course, once the drugs wear off, but right now we're both too tired to come up with anything useful."

Niles nodded, slumping into the sofa. "Yeah. I need a shower and some sleep in the worst possible way. I'm going to hang out here with Jordie today until he's in the clear, then I'll be at home the rest of the weekend. One good thing about missing this convention: it gives me some free time I hadn't planned on having."

"Okay." Tim's mouth tipped up in a rueful smile, as though he were on the verge of pursuing that opening. And that was what it was, Niles realized. He was making a point of letting Tim know he was available. But Tim just reached for his jacket. "Tell Jordan I'll call later, when he's feeling better."

"Sure. Thanks, Tim. For everything." He escorted Tim to the door and locked it behind him. He was too tired for even his brain to spin wildly, trying to make sense of everything that had happened, the way it normally would have. If he let himself sit and think too long, he was probably going to end up freaking out over the fact that he might have lost his brother. Instead, he grabbed a change of clothes out of the suitcase he'd dragged with him from the airport and headed for the shower.

"'S Tim gone?" Jordan slurred when Niles climbed into bed beside him, feeling somewhat more human for his shower and the clean shorts and T-shirt, if not any less exhausted. He borrowed one of the hydrocodone the doctor had prescribed for Jordan's pain to knock out his own residual headache.

"Yeah. He's going to need to speak to you when you come down off the meds."

"'Kay. Sorry 'bout your trip."

"*Pfft.* I'm sorry I went when you were telling me you had a bad feeling about me going. Clearly, I should have listened."

"Eh, don't do that." Jordan burrowed deeper under the covers, and Niles huddled beside him, feeling the wooziness of the meds starting to kick in. "'S better you went."

"Why's that?"

"'Cuz if you hadn't, it would have been you getting hit."

Niles was still trying to parse how that realization made him feel when Jordan's quiet snores lulled him to sleep.

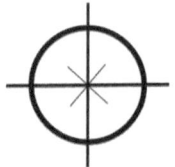

CHAPTER 13

"Niles, can you come in here, please?"

"Sure thing, Rosie."

Rosie hung up her phone, staring at the images on her computer. She gnawed her lip a moment, then turned away from her laptop to open the files on the large-screened gaming rigs set up against the far wall in her office.

"Jesus, what are those?" She turned to look at Niles where he stood in the doorway, his eyes troubled.

Their *PF3* characters stared back at them in multiple series of comic-style drawings. The last panel of each series showed eyes wide with horror, faces eternally caught in the rictus of a gruesome death. The drawing of Issis was the worst of the lot, her final pose so blatantly sexualized that it felt like a deliberate taunt from the artist, as if making a statement about Third Wave's anti-male-gaze approach to rendering female characters. Or maybe mocking them, now that news of Charity's and Lakshmi's deaths had gotten out into the gaming community. After the shit people had said when Rosie'd had her brain tumor, it wouldn't surprise her. There was no limit to how low these guys would sink to make themselves feel big.

"Fan art," she said. "Jordan emailed me the link." At her insistence, Jordan was working from home this week, even though it had been three days since the attack and he said his head was fine. "He found them on one of the fan site message boards—not ours, unfortunately, so we have no way to trace the account. The thread was titled, 'How PF3 SHOULD Be Played.'"

"Well . . ." Niles swallowed audibly, and Rosie nodded in sympathy. The images were definitely disturbing. The style of the art looked familiar, also, though she couldn't place it. "Someone is in violation of the NDA."

"Yeah." She'd been so thrown by the level of personalized violence in the sketches that it had taken her a while to notice the little details that marked the artist as having access to the content of the beta release. Beta participants were bound to a nondisclosure agreement, but that wasn't the worst of the issues with this series of drawings. "We could get legal on it, send a cease and desist based on that, but you know it will turn into a censorship firestorm."

"True, that." Niles moved closer, his eyes intent on the monitor. He reached for the mouse and began scrolling through the images. "What is this, exactly? These aren't scenes from the game."

"Well, they could have been, in a manner of speaking." Rosie took the mouse from him and navigated to one particular image. "See? This is the scene where Issis is waiting for her contact in the park. The thugs are about to get the drop on her and hit her with a board when the PC shows up and alerts her to the attack."

That scene was proving to be controversial among beta participants; in it, the player character was too far away to prevent the attack and Issis Lowe dealt with her attackers on her own, quickly and easily taking them down. Players felt the PC should have saved her. They also didn't appreciate that Issis reamed the PC out afterward for interfering with her meeting.

Depending on if the PC agreed that Issis could take care of herself, the scene could spell the end to any hope of the sexual relationship between Issis and the PC evolving into an actual romance.

"Only in this series of sketches, the attack happens, but the PC never arrives," Niles observed, paging through them one after the other. "God, this is just—" He fell silent, clicking through each collection of panels one by one. "Some days I wonder what sort of people call themselves fans if this is what they want to see."

Rosie let him take it in, watching Niles try to plug it into his worldview that one of their fans had drawn these. She could practically see the "Does not compute" alarm going off in his brain, followed by a cascade of attempts to rationalize rather than accept.

"It just turns into an orgy of gratuitous violence." He shook his head as though denying it. "Here it's the same with Marc's crisis storyline. The PC never shows up, so he dies. And Sang's. Grace, Halliday, and Chino, too. All the companion characters. It branches off from a point where they're in danger and proceeds as though the PC doesn't exist."

Rosie nodded. All that was bad, but the implications from the final series of sketches actually *hurt*. "Now check out the ones with Gairi," she urged, still trying to pick her own way between betrayal and disbelief.

Niles paged forward and promptly shot to his feet. "What the *fuck*? How did they get that?"

"Now you see why I'm not all that worried about the beta content."

"This is from the DLC. *None* of this has been made public yet!"

The last series of sketches began by depicting Gairi's enslavement during his return to his home planet, giving loving detail to violence that was only implied in the game itself, such as Gairi being whipped by the slavers. The images focused on his back as the lash shredded his tunic and cut into the skin below, then continued to show his recapture by his mother's people and, eventually, the moment where he's to be thrown off the cliff into a river, the same moment when the player character would normally arrive and save him.

The last image was of Gairi floating facedown in the river. As though the viewer were in the water beneath him, his dead eyes stared at them, open and unseeing. Again, if not for the fact that the series of sketches included all the other characters, it might have seemed a pointed mockery of Charity's and Lakshmi's deaths.

"Either whoever did these works for us or we have a leak." Rosie sighed, hugging herself to rub the gooseflesh off her arms.

Niles shook his head adamantly. "No one who works for us would do this!"

Rosie could understand his resistance to the idea. There was something about the way the violent scenes were depicted that spoke of a deep-seated malice she was unwilling to believe anyone in her company held toward their brainchildren. "Would someone who works for us leak these sorts of story details?"

"I did." Niles's face was pinched and pale, and Rosie pulled out a chair, pushing him down into it as she did a double take.

"What?"

"Off the record, with Daniel Fortesen last week." Niles's shoulders shifted, as though he was trying not to squirm. "He asked me what was in store for Gairi, and I told him. But he's a professional. He wouldn't—"

"Give him a call, find out who has access to his notes." It was probably ridiculous to feel so violated by images of one's characters being gratuitously murdered in such grotesque ways, but Rosie couldn't help feeling creeped out by it. And if the nauseated twist of Niles's mouth was anything to go by, he was too. They were still reeling from the news of Charity's and Lakshmi's murders. If felt personal. Threatening, even. Which it wasn't, of course. It hadn't been sent to them directly. It was just fan art, posted to a forum that wasn't even run by Third Wave by someone who would likely never know anyone at the gaming studio had ever seen it.

Perhaps it felt personal because she and Niles had invested so much of themselves in the characters. Or perhaps it was the lingering unease of the hand delivered notes Niles had gotten and the attack on Jordan. There was no reason to assume a connection between the two, but taken altogether, it had her feeling besieged.

As she pondered why this felt so overwhelming, the light around the edges of everything in the room started to take on a distinctly sparkly, glaring quality, punctuated by floating blobs of shadow. Niles's normally subtle cologne became suffocatingly strong.

Fuck. Rosie dropped into her desk chair and pulled open a drawer, grabbing her migraine meds.

"What about that kid interning for the art department? Did he ever turn up?"

"Patrick. He was in the writing department, and no, he never did. He just stopped coming in. He's not answering his phone, either. I've been trying to reach him."

"Have someone call his school, find out if he's still showing up for classes. If he's the one who leaked the DLC material, I'm going to have his ass."

"You'll have to get in line." Niles strode out of her office, his phone already to his ear and his movements jerky with irritation. She was almost glad for it, and for her own anger. Since the news of the murders and Jordan having gotten bashed with a rock last week, she and Niles had both been keeping their heads down, as though afraid that they—or anyone who worked for them—might be next. It wasn't a good mindset for a company whose raison d'être was to overthrow the dominant paradigm and give a voice to a sector that was so frequently muted. They needed to get louder with each attempt to silence them.

Grimacing one last time at the image of Gairi drowned in the river, she turned off the monitors and went back to work.

———

NILES POURED a shot of crème de menthe into a steaming mug of cocoa and carried it to the desk in his den, listening again to the small creaks and thumps of the house. The sounds came part and parcel of living in a late-nineteenth-century house. He'd fallen in love with it the moment he'd seen it, but he'd never thought he'd be able to live here working for an upstart game studio with a social-justice mission. Only the unforeseen success of the first Phoenix Force title had made it possible. He'd bought it and made it his, renovated and decorated and turned it not just into a historic house, but a real home.

Now he didn't dare turn on music to listen to while he worked for fear he might not hear if someone tried to get in. All he could do was wonder what might have happened to his brother if the neighbors hadn't checked on the house. What if the attacker came back?

Was this how Rosie had felt when the trolls had posted those images of her house?

Sipping his drink, trying to let the alcohol and mint soothe him, Niles stared at his computer and tried to get his thoughts back in order. He was writing the preliminary outline for what would be the second *PF3* DLC, the one featuring Marc. Issis's story would be the third. Niles didn't write the dialogue for any other *PF3* characters besides Gairi, but he was still the lead writer for the *Phoenix Force* franchise and coming up with the framework for the story was his purview.

A knock at the door froze him just as he set his hands on the keyboard. He breathed through the automatic leap of his heart into his throat. He grabbed his mug of hot chocolate to toss into the face of anyone who might attack him and called through the door, "Who is it?"

"Niles? It's Tim. Are you busy?"

Groaning, Niles slumped against the wall, drawing a couple of deep breaths before he unlocked the dead bolt and unhooked the chain. Tim stood in the block of yellowish light thrown by the fixture over the door, bundled against the chilly rain in a leather bomber jacket and jeans. Obviously off duty, then.

"You okay?" Tim's brow furrowed as he stepped inside, closing the door behind him. Niles managed to push himself away from the wall, but his heart was still racing.

"Yeah, just jumpy." He grimaced, leading the way into the living room. "What's up? Can I get you something to drink?"

"I just wanted to see how you were doing. If there have been any more problems? And yeah, thanks. Got a beer?"

"I'm doing all right, I guess. Only drama today has been that a reporter and an intern, either of whom might have leaked spoiler details about an upcoming release, have both fallen off the face of the earth and aren't returning anyone's calls." Niles ducked into the kitchen to grab a bottle of Widmer Hefeweizen out of the fridge and handed it to Tim as he passed. Niles set his cocoa on the coffee table and dropped onto the sofa with a frown. "Have a seat."

"That's a big deal, these . . . spoilers?" Tim asked, ignoring the chair across from Niles in favor of the sofa beside him.

"Sort of. You really want to control the flow of information about upcoming titles as much as you can. If the audience knows the story in advance, they might not want to play. You want them to be surprised. Or sometimes, if it's something really good, you want to arrange an 'accidental' leak a few days before it hits the shelves. So yeah, the spoilers aren't good. Frankly, I feel pretty betrayed."

"Why's that?"

"Because the intern was in my writing department and the reporter got the details from me, in confidence."

"Ah. That reporter."

"Yeah. That one."

The silence that followed grew more and more awkward.

"But that's not why I came. I swung by to check on you."

"You're off the clock," Niles said stupidly.

"I can't be concerned about you off the clock? Your brother was attacked on your doorstep a few days ago. I've got patrol cars driving past periodically, but I wanted to check in also. Have there been any other incidences?"

Niles shook his head. "It's been quiet."

"Good. You'll let me know if that changes?" Tim stared at him hard until Niles sighed and nodded.

Awkward silence again.

"So, you seem like you've gotten married to your work since college." It was a clumsy segue on Tim's part, but it was better than sitting there staring at each other.

Niles chuffed a soft laugh. "I pretty much have. You're a cop, you should get how that goes."

"What is it about the job that makes it worth it?" Tim cocked his head to the side, watching Niles in an intent way that felt far too familiar.

Niles shrugged. "Part of it's personal loyalty. Rosena Candelaria is brilliant. She's an amazing person to work for, and her vision is so powerful and so easy to believe in, you can't help but throw yourself behind her wholeheartedly, you know?" Tim nodded as Niles paused to sip his cocoa, shifting to face Tim better. "When I got in with Third Wave, it was just a start-up that no one thought would go anywhere. Where would a gaming company producing hardcore titles intended to appeal to women and queer gamers possibly go in such a market, right?"

"But you proved them wrong."

"Fuck yeah, we did. *Phoenix Force* even ended up winning at the Spike TV Video Game Awards, which are all about the testosterone, because Rosie's smart. She knew there were plenty of men out there who wanted more intelligent, more engaging material, where the focus was on the gameplay and the story. So we make a game that is first and foremost engaging and entertaining and challenging, yes. But along the way, we make sure to eliminate the factors that have made the genre so unfriendly to women, queer, and POC gamers. The majority of the male gaming audience doesn't *care* about all that, if the gameplay is good."

Tim's smile seemed less forced now. "You're really proud of what you've done. That's why you work so hard."

"Yeah." Niles returned his cocoa to the coffee table and leaned his head on the back of the sofa. "This is where change begins. In a culture's art. Whatever snooty intellectuals might say, video games *are* art. So are comic books and anime and television. The Coalition for Responsible Media isn't wrong. When it comes down to it, we *are* after the hearts and minds of the kids."

"I never thought of it that way." Tim's look was soft, almost intimate. It reminded Niles too much of similar looks he'd received after far too many amazing fucks in too-narrow dorm-room beds. "I don't think many people do. It's fascinating to see how much you love it, something that most people dismiss as being trivial. For you, it's a crusade."

"Well, I'm not sure I'd go that far, but I'm not going to downplay the importance of reversing the media trends that have helped oppress us. Gaming is the fastest growing form of entertainment on the market today. We need to have a strong foothold there."

"Is the culture behind it all really that bad?" Tim asked. "I mean, you showed me those texts, but ..."

"Those were the tip of the iceberg. Here." Niles grabbed his laptop and opened it, scanning through his libraries for a particular folder. "These are screencaps of the tweets and text messages Rosie gets every single day."

Niles watched Tim grow steadily paler as he read the messages:

I'll rape u and keep ur head in my freezer if u don't leave my games the fuck alone.

Who let this feminazi dyke out of the kitchen?

Reporting u to INS so they'll send ur fat ass back to Mexico.

Tim blinked and turned a disbelieving stare to Niles. "This is for real?"

"She has thousands of those. Maybe tens of thousands." Niles opened another directory. "And it's not just text. These are audio files of voice mails she's received after someone posted her home phone number online."

Tim grimaced and clicked the first one.

"I'm warning you, you need to resign. Shut Third Wave down and don't ever pick up another controller again. I'm coming after you. I'm going to murder you. Not just you. Your whole fucking family. I'm going to slice your tits off with a box cutter and nail them to my wall while you watch. I'm going to . . ."

Tim swallowed hard and stopped the playback. "Jesus." He blew out a deep breath and wiped his mouth. "I don't get how anyone could act like this about a game."

Niles shrugged. "Cross online anonymity with a threat to cis-het white male privilege and this is what you get. We came across some fan art today that was so creepy I can't even make myself look at it again. And watch this." He set the laptop on the table and stood to retrieve the remote and controller for his Xbox. "Here, choose a game. One of the first-person shooters. Any one."

Tim chose *Front Lines*, and Niles started a new game and created an avatar, naming it GaymerTW. He logged into the multiplayer chat, turned up the speakers, and entered the game, beginning to chase after an opponent. For a few seconds, no one took notice of him, chattering about the gameplay, but then someone scoffed.

"GaymerTW—What are you, some sort of fag?"

"Oh, Jesus, we've got a fag in here."

"Hey, Gaymer, you gonna play or you too busy sucking a dick?"

Niles noticed his avatar taking damage and checked around to see who was targeting him. "Look." He pointed out the name to Tim. "I'm about to be killed by my own teammate."

"Ha-ha, check it out, gonna frag the queer," someone shouted. "Yep, he's dead. The fag's goin' ta hell!"

"Not cool, dude," Niles murmured into the microphone. "Come on, we're all just here to play the game, okay?"

"Not my fault you're goin' ta hell, cocksucker. Someone wipe him out again."

It was a nonstop stream of invective until Niles had no more lives left and quit the match, with self-congratulatory hoots about making the pussy run away echoing over the speakers.

"So, this is what it is like for women and queers in gaming spaces when they don't hide the fact that they're women or queer. And as you can see from Rosie's messages, there's plenty of racism to go around too." Niles smiled sadly.

Tim propped an elbow on the back of the couch, resting his chin on his forearm. "Until that, I was enjoying seeing you talk about it. You light up, you know. So beautiful."

Niles snorted, trying to ignore the nervous *thud* in his chest. "So much for waiting for me to call you. Is that why you came here?"

"No. I really did come to check up on you. I was worried." Tim reached for his beer again, his eyes shuttering, becoming more guarded. "You just make it so easy."

"To what? Flirt?" He shot for cynical, imbuing his voice with disdain, but he wasn't sure it translated.

"Yeah, that's a safe place to start." Tim's smile held more than a dollop of regret. "I was a scared kid, Niles. I can't apologize enough. What's it going to take to convince you it wouldn't happen again?"

"I believe you mean it." Niles shrugged, looking away. "I just don't know if I'm capable of letting go of baggage like that. And you've had seven years to contact me and apologize. Obviously it wasn't a priority."

"That's not true." Tim shook his head emphatically, setting his beer back down on the coffee table. "I thought about you all the time."

"Then why?"

Tim went oddly still, as though he were fighting the urge to squirm. "I didn't think you'd want to hear it."

That . . . was actually a pretty good point. There was a time when Niles wouldn't have wanted to hear what Tim had to say for himself, no matter how remorseful he might have been. Niles looked down into his mug, where the cocoa had grown cool, a scum of chocolate forming on the top. Sighing, he set it aside. He should ask Tim to leave. There was nothing good that could come of his being there. But Niles couldn't seem to make himself say the words.

"So tell me more about your game," Tim urged, sparing them another laden silence as he finished off his beer. "You've told me about the company, but what about the games themselves? What are they about?"

"Well, why don't I show you?" He pushed himself up off the sofa and crossed to the desk, undocking his laptop and carrying it back to the coffee table. He set it in front of Tim and plugged in the wireless mouse.

"I'll pull up *PF3*." Sitting this close to Tim, a spicy cologne— something vaguely reminiscent of cinnamon, but not so sweet— mingled with the yeasty tang of beer. The scent distracted him for a moment, making him stutter as he showed Tim the character-creation screen.

"We have default PCs you can use, male or female and from a number of different races and backgrounds. Your background often determines how non-player characters react to you in the game. You might encounter enhanced acceptance from some NPCs and uncooperative bigotry from others. You won't get the same reception from a wealthy socialite if you're the uneducated son of an asteroid miner than if you were the cultured daughter of an alien ambassador."

He moved away from the computer to let Tim take over, experimenting with creating an avatar. Niles had to look away from the way the red-gold hairs on his forearms seemed to gleam in the lamplight. Goddamn it. Tim had always had this effect on him, ever since the day they paired up in chemistry class. For a while there in his idiotic youth, he'd thought it was love at first sight.

Now he knew better. Lust at first sight. Apparently however much he didn't think getting involved again with Tim was a good idea, his hormones were still tuned in to those memories.

He cleared his throat and stared at the computer resolutely. "You can see we have a lot of options for the player character's physical appearance. Not just face and hair and skin color, either. It costs more to produce, but it was important to Rosie that we include realistic physiques, something beyond the idealized muscle-bound barbarian and super-stacked warrior princess. But anyway, let's go ahead and load up one of my saved games so you can get right into meeting the NPCs."

Niles scooted forward again, reaching for the computer before he realized just how close it would press him against Tim's side. He felt Tim's breath against his ear, ruffling the ends of his hair where it brushed his neck.

"You smell just as good as I remember."

Niles shuddered, his fingers fumbling to grasp the mouse and navigate to the character-selection screen and then to pick an avatar at a stage in the game where he had been introduced to all the companion NPCs. "I thought you weren't going to—"

"Change of plans. I'm *definitely* going to." Tim shifted, planting one knee into the sofa cushions behind Niles where he bent over to reach the laptop. He thrust his hands under the edge of Niles's shirt. His fingers spread, staking a presumptuous claim to Niles's skin. Niles bolted upright, and then Tim's lips were against his neck, warm and moist and open, sucking just below his ear.

"Tim—"

"Show me the game," Tim breathed against his skin, teeth grazing up and down his neck. Tim's hands rounded Niles's ribs, his fingers seeking the hard dots of Niles's nipples. The portion of Niles's brain that wasn't sure this was a good idea whimpered, but its protestations were getting weaker with each passing second. It had been shunted over into the passenger seat, desperately clutching the Oh-Jesus handle while his libido steered them at breakneck speed down a one-way street that would dead-end with Tim between his thighs.

A quick jerk of the wheel and Niles turned, twisting to catch Tim's mouth as it dove in for another pass at his neck. A flurry of movement ended in a jolt, and then he was on his back, Tim pressing him down into the sofa. His hands fisted in the shoulders of Tim's shirt as their lips ground together, Tim's tongue thrusting deep into Niles's mouth.

"Oh God." Niles wasn't quite sure which of them groaned the words, but it probably didn't matter. Tim's thigh was between his legs, snugged up nice and tight against the crotch of his jeans, rubbing against his dick and nuts, and Tim's hand was in his hair, taking over the kiss with a brand of aggression Niles remembered far, far too well. He tasted like beer and something salty he must have snacked on before coming over, and Niles seized the moment when Tim withdrew for a panting breath, and he ran his tongue along Tim's lips to sample that flavor further. Hot puffs of breath exploded against Niles's mouth, and he gripped Tim tighter, licking a wet trail down the stubbled column of his neck.

"Niles . . ." Tim pulled him back by the hair for another kiss, rocking that thigh against his crotch again, tempting Niles to grip it between his own and just start dry humping. His hands moved from Tim's shoulders to his back, where he grabbed twin handfuls of Tim's T-shirt and rucked it up to his armpits. And then there was skin. Acres of pale, freckled flesh covering that broad back and wrapping around massive shoulders. He felt warm and hard and *so fucking good*. Niles's misgivings didn't have a chance when pitted against the feel of Tim's body on his.

When Tim broke away again, there was a growl riding the undertone of his words. "If you don't plan on us fucking tonight, better let me know now."

At some point when Niles wasn't paying attention, his reservations had been evicted from riding shotgun and were now bound and gagged in the trunk. He peeled Tim's shirt over his head, panting, "Bedroom," because those two syllables were all he could manage to convey where they'd find the condoms and lube.

Wild-eyed, Tim pushed his weight off Niles to let him up.

It was three o'clock in the morning, and Niles lay looking up at the ceiling as Tim snored softly beside him. His body ached in all the best ways, and he should have been worn out because Tim was as enthusiastic a lover as he had been back in college—and considerably more skilled these days—but his mind refused to rest.

It was a horrible idea to get involved with Tim again. Forget their history, between the harassment and the shock of the murders, Niles was in no shape to be making good decisions and he knew it. He didn't want to use Tim the way he had Daniel, for the sake of escapism and just to feel something other than dread and grief.

Suppressing a sigh, he eased himself out from under the covers—and Tim's arm—stepping into a pair of sweats before padding barefoot down the stairs.

His laptop sat on the coffee table still, the screensaver swirling before Niles's eyes. He grimaced at it, as if it were the computer's fault he'd slept with Tim.

Well, if he couldn't sleep, he might as well work. He pulled it onto his lap and pressed the touchpad. The save-game screen, complete with its lineup of companion characters, confronted him, and he found himself staring at it, zeroing in on Issis and Gairi. God, how could he even continue to work on them without thinking about Charity and Lakshmi?

"Can't sleep?"

Niles jumped, nearly fumbling the laptop. "Jesus *fuck*! How did you make it down the stairs without them creaking?" He pressed a hand to his chest, which ached with the racing of his heart and the surge of adrenaline.

When he'd calmed down, Tim was leaning over the back of the sofa behind him, staring at the characters on the laptop screen. He reached out as if he was going to brush his fingers over the images of Issis and Gairi.

"How are things going with the case?" Niles asked, his throat tight.

"Right now we're trying to track down the guys who may have harassed the girls at the convention. It's slowgoing. Most of them were from out of state, and the rest have alibis."

"You know what's creepy?" Niles looked at the screen once more. "I didn't realize it until listening to the news yesterday, because I've been trying to avoid knowing too many details about the murders—I don't want that in my head—but Lakshmi's body washed up in the river. And in the DLC we're in production on, the one that has had spoilers leaked, Gairi has a moment when he nearly dies when someone almost throws him into a river."

Tim went still. "What?"

The reaction made Niles's adrenaline surge again, reducing him to a nervous stammer. "Well, he's taken captive by slavers, see, and the guy who rescues him has a grudge and is about to throw him into the river—"

"What about Charity— I mean, Issis?" Tim's posture was tense now, his voice sharp and demanding. "Is she bludgeoned?"

"Almost." Oh God. This sinking feeling in his stomach was going to make him sick. "She's a mercenary, and there's a scene where she meets with some buyers on a tech deal, where they plan to double-cross her, but the PC interrupts the attack."

"Fuck." Tim jerked his phone out of his breast pocket and dialed. "Payne? It's the game. Someone is recreating the game the victims were cosplaying for."

For a moment, the world blurred around the edges and his hands grew tingly. So this was what it felt like to nearly faint. "Oh no. God, no."

CHAPTER 14

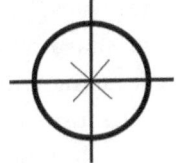

W*ell, that didn't take long.*

Jordan arrived at the studios around 6 a.m. to find Niles leaning over the back of Tim Wyatt's chair, walking him through *Phoenix Force 3* on one of the gaming rigs they used to test code. He shook his head with wry amusement.

Niles glanced up and no doubt accurately read his expression. "Not a word," he warned.

His brother was pale and drawn, which pissed him off because Niles had just started to get his feet under him after the shocks of the last week. Jordan frowned and looked at Rosie, who was propping up the wall, her arms folded over her chest, her mouth in a grim line, letting Niles do most of the talking. Detective Payne still hadn't arrived, but then, they were all early.

"I noticed our friends from the Coalition for Responsible Media are back, setting up out front," he murmured to Rosie, taking up station beside her and watching Niles and Tim. "Tell me they haven't gotten wind of this."

"Not yet, but it's only a matter of time." Rosie grimaced. "I don't want anything in our handling of this to even hint at opportunism. Our hearts and prayers are with the victims' families, and we are assisting the police in whatever way necessary. That's it. End of story."

Jordan bristled. "Come on, Rosie. I may be a marketing guy but even I'm not that sleazy."

"Sorry." She shot him a contrite look.

Jordan leaned close to her ear, whispering, "Is there any talk that this person might be after Niles?"

"No." Her denial was so sharp and sudden that Tim and Niles jerked around to look at the two of them. Rosie offered them a wan smile. "Sorry. Excuse us." She grabbed Jordan's elbow and led him down the hall to her office, closing the door behind them and hissing, "Why would you even *think* such a thing?"

"After the threats you and Niles have been receiving, how could I *not*?" Rosie narrowed her eyes at him, but Jordan glared right back. He rubbed the back of his skull, where a scab still formed a crust under his hair from the rock's impact. "Someone tried to bash my brother in the head, if you recall. Charity and Lakshmi were dressed as the two most controversial characters in *PF3*, who you both have used to make statements about sexual politics and racial and queer issues, *and* you and Niles spoke to the victims within hours of their disappearances. And now it's obvious that whoever did it has access to spoiler details about the game, including the upcoming DLC, and Patrick Rutledge and Daniel Fortesen—both of whom are fairly close to Niles—aren't answering their phones."

She immediately looked stricken. "Oh Jesus."

"I know." He sank into the chair across the desk from her, casting a yearning eye at the empty coffeemaker on her filing cabinet. "Have you shown the cops those drawings yet?"

"No, why would I— Oh God, the spoilers." She buried her face in her hands, her shoulders rising and falling as she drew several breaths. "I've barely slept since Thursday. I keep thinking about Charity and Lakshmi. And when I do sleep, I dream about them. I should have realized—" She stalked over to her computer and with a few clicks, began printing off the series of drawings he'd discovered on one of the fan-run forums that was known to host a lot of Third Wave critics.

Jordan sighed as the images printed. "You know, I'd be a lot less happy about my brother fucking Tim Wyatt again if not for the fact that it means he'll be spending his off-work time with a cop."

"What? Huh?" Rosie spluttered. "Niles and Detective Wyatt? When did that happen?"

"Back in college. It wasn't pretty."

"As if things weren't interesting enough." She grabbed the printouts and he followed as she stalked back down to the lab, where Detective Payne had arrived and was asking questions about the game.

"Good morning, Angie," she said, shaking the detective's hand. "Jordan just brought to my attention something you two should see. Do you think we could all go sit down in the conference room and talk?"

He watched the solicitous way Tim hovered over Niles as they made the transition, grateful that he at least realized just how hard Niles was taking this. When they were seated, Rosie slid the printouts across the table to the detectives.

"Jordan found those yesterday on a nonaffiliated fan forum. As you can see, whoever drew them had access to spoilers about the game, particularly the details of the DLC currently in production, which whoever killed Lakshmi Agrawal would have to know as well, if her death was imitating the game."

Detective Payne's gaze sharpened, and she snatched up the pages, scanning through the comic-style panels. Niles's expression was still pinched, but as she passed them to her partner, he added, "There are panels of the other characters dying, as well. I'm not sure how relevant that is."

"Who had access to these spoilers?" Tim asked.

"Everyone who works here, obviously." Rosie's mouth was pulled into a tight line, even as she spoke. "Some other people associated with our production, like the recording studio where our voice actors do their dialogue. And—" she flicked a glance at Niles "—a columnist from *The LEET News* who Niles did an interview with last Thursday."

"*The LEET News*?" Detective Payne looked dubious. "What kind of publication is that?"

"It's a trade rag." Rosie shrugged wryly. "The name is an outdated bit of gaming jargon. Don't ask."

"If those spoilers were leaked on the internet, thousands of people could have them now," Niles said too quickly, leaning forward with an anxious expression. "It doesn't have to be one of our people or someone we know."

"Niles, honey, these spoilers weren't made public," Rosie said with gentle certainty. "They would have been all over the internet, and we haven't found a thing."

"If the columnist didn't have the details until Thursday, that's too late," Tim pointed out. "Our perp knew a week earlier, before Lakshmi Agrawal was killed."

Detective Payne nodded slowly. "Whoever did these drawings has a personal connection to whoever had access to the spoilers. Same for the murderer."

Niles eyes widened. "You think the *artist* is the killer?"

Tim shook his head. "It's too early to say. We just need to follow the connection. If we track down the source of these spoilers, we'll know more."

"We've had an intern stop coming in." Jordan gave Niles an apologetic glance when he opened his mouth to protest. "Patrick Rutledge. He worked on the writing staff, so he would have known the details of the game. I'm not saying he spread them intentionally, but if he confided these details to someone and then it got out that there was a leak, he seems like the kind of kid who might hide from that rather than own up to it."

"We'll check into it," Detective Payne said. "Tell me which site you found these on. Wyatt, can you tell Cyber to work on getting a warrant for their user records? I'm going to sit down and familiarize myself with this game. I want to play it through, beginning to end, see what other details we might find in there. The whole thing."

"There's ninety-eight hours of gameplay to get through the core storyline, and about twenty more if you do all the side missions," Rosie warned.

"Guess you better get started, Payne," Tim gloated with a smirk. "Better you than me. Niles has showed me enough this morning to make it clear that I don't get video games, so I'll be hanging out with Bryan in Cyber if you need me."

———

"Go. Home." Niles's frustration with his brother was reaching the boiling point, but Jordan remained stubbornly seated behind his desk. "Seriously, Jordie. Go home and take one of your pills. You're not supposed to be working this week."

"No way. This has the potential to be a PR disaster. I need to be on top of it."

"You need to recover from getting bashed in the head!"

"I need to be with my brother!" Jordan snapped, and Niles jumped. Jordan *never* spoke sharply to him. Ever.

He rose from his desk and crossed the room to Niles. "Someone's trying to hurt you," he said gently, gripping Niles's shoulders. Niles closed his eyes. He kept losing track of the fact that he was the likely object of the attack on Jordan. The idea that someone would target him violently seemed unreal, and Jordan being injured was all *too* real. "Maybe the person who hurt Charity and Lakshmi, or maybe not, but we need to stick together right now, okay?"

"Okay." He wrapped his arms around Jordan's waist and

hugged tightly, breathing in his brother's scent. He just let himself feel the moment, feel *Jordan*. Familiar. Safe. *Home.* "I don't know what to do," he whispered plaintively. "Not about Tim, not about Daniel, not about Patrick, not about the murders. I don't know what to do, Jordie."

"You'll be okay. Why don't you come stay with me until the police get to the bottom of this?" He could hear what Jordan wasn't saying as if he'd spoken it anyway. Jordan's building had a lobby, a security door, cameras in the elevators.

"I can't—" He buried his head in the crook of Jordan's neck, blushing. "Tim."

"Oh, gee, if you stay in my apartment, you won't be able to fuck the guy who broke your heart. What a shame."

Niles huffed a watery chuckle. "I'll think about it, okay?"

"Okay."

Niles continued to hold on to Jordan, and Jordan let him. He always knew when Niles was regressing to their preschool days when he wouldn't sleep unless he was wrapped around his brother. Sometimes Niles needed that connection. Jordan, too, he knew, but Jordan had other ways of expressing it.

He was considering pulling away when Rosie came dashing into the office. "Turn on the TV. We've got a problem."

Jordan jerked back, reaching for the remote, while Rosie caught her breath.

"The news has a story that Patrick Rutledge's stepfather has filed a missing person's report. And someone on the forums has drawn a connection between that and the murders being linked to Third Wave."

"Rosie, Eliza is right. You cannot talk to him."

Rosie glared at Jordan as she paced her office after Eliza Muldrake of Stanton, Cobb, and Muldrake, Third Wave's lawyer on retainer and an old college friend of Rosie's, had left. Niles sat beside him with his head bowed. He hadn't said a word since she had brought them the news of Patrick's disappearance.

"I don't care what she said! That kid is one of my employees. One of our people!" Fuck, her head hurt. She was taking her fear and pain out on Jordan, but she couldn't seem to stop herself. "If he's been hurt on our watch, working for us, I want to know that he's all right and I want to know what the fuck happened!"

"We've got two dead girls and now a missing intern associated with Third Wave. If you interfere with the investigation, it will look like you're trying to cover our asses, or *something*."

She planted her fist on the desk, looming over it. "I don't *care*. I just want to be sure he's okay. What does Daniel Fortesen have to say about this?" she demanded, jumping mental tracks.

"No one at *LEET* has heard from him since the day he supposedly left Portland. He sent the managing editor a text saying he was staying here longer than planned, but he's missed the deadline for submitting his article and hasn't checked in with anyone." She saw Jordan slide a concerned look over to Niles, who seemed to shrink even further in on himself. "Niles, it isn't your fault."

"Isn't it?" Niles's voice was barely audible, and his eyes were bleak when he finally lifted them. "I asked Patrick to give Daniel a lift to the train station that morning. I just can't believe—" He swallowed and looked down at his hands again where they rubbed nervously on his knees. "Everyone around me is getting hurt."

"We don't know they're hurt," Jordan said, massaging his shoulders reassuringly. "For all we know, they eloped together."

Niles shot to his feet. "I need to go. I'm supposed to be at the studio. They're starting to record Gairi's dialog for the DLC today."

"We have a director for a reason, Niles. You don't need to do that. Why don't you go home?" Rosie caught his shoulder, making him face her. "Or we can all go out for a drink. Try to calm down a little and figure this all out?"

"Figure what out?" His muscles quivered under her hand before he shook her off. "That someone is after me, and everyone I care about is collateral damage? Thanks, I got that."

He stormed out, slamming the door behind him as he went. Rosie stared at it a long moment, then startled at the *smack* when Jordan's palm hit her desk.

"*Fuck*." His voice was muffled and heavy with dismay. "Give him time to cool off, then I'll talk to him. He's just thrown."

"Yeah," she muttered wearily, dropping into the chair behind her desk once more. "Who isn't these days? I need a fucking bourbon and it's not even noon yet."

Jordan flipped his wrist and looked at his watch, then shoved himself to his feet. "Close enough. I'm buying."

CHAPTER 15

The blank email form on his laptop was the only light in the house as Niles sat in front of it, filling his glass from the bottle of vodka sitting on his desk. It seemed to mock him for the dozens of half-formed thoughts he wanted to send to Daniel—on the off chance that he was still getting emails—that he couldn't seem to find the words for. In another window, he could see the accumulation of unread tweets with the hashtag #3rdWaveFail, but he didn't have the heart to scroll through them anymore. Quips that this was what was bound to happen when they let a woman out of the kitchen and put her in charge of a video game studio were the prevailing theme.

He'd turned off the TV a half hour ago. On the evening news, Emmerich Corbin, the disbarred lawyer who headed up the Coalition for Responsible Media's anti–video game crusade, and Joyce Draheim, a congresswoman from Kentucky known for her homophobic platform, had been taking turns blaming video game violence and marriage equality for what had happened to Charity and Lakshmi, and now, presumably, Patrick. In Niles's inbox was an email forwarded from human resources, which they'd received from Portland State University, where Patrick went, and messages from several other colleges where they hired interns, withdrawing from Third Wave's internship program, citing safety concerns.

And then there was the message from the CEO of Electronic Entertainment Unlimited, Third Wave's parent company and distributor, scheduling a meeting Monday to discuss delaying the release of *PF3* until the negative publicity died down. They also mentioned the possibility of shelving the Gairi DLC for the time being in order to focus on "less controversial" characters from the franchise.

It was all falling apart.

Stop being so dramatic. That wasn't quite an accurate summation of the situation, and he knew it. Third Wave's activist fans were defending them and feminist groups were throwing their support behind them, as well. But he was having a hard time seeing that upside, especially when their supporters were being derided as fringe ideologues.

The only thing their lawyer had permitted was a short press release stating that their sympathies were with Charity's and Lakshmi's families and that they were hoping for Patrick to be found alive and well, and that they would cooperate in every way to see the culprit brought to justice.

It was the beginning of the end. Rosie wasn't ready to see it yet, but Niles could. EEU would start taking a heavier hand in overseeing the production of Third Wave's titles until they were conformist, noncontroversial, and lacking anything that might be considered a socially progressive narrative. Third Wave would become just another voice in the chorus of cookie-cutter game studios making titles filled with shallow, queer stereotypes, ham-handed attempts at ethnic diversity, and images of sexualized violence intended to appeal to the male gaze.

A creak that didn't quite sound like the house settling came from somewhere near the door and jerked Niles out of his thoughts. He set his vodka aside, closed his eyes, and listened. A small metallic squeak, the soft *swish* of paper hitting the floor, and then the *click* of the mail slot closing brought him out of his chair. The mail had already been delivered before he'd gotten home that evening. He rushed to the door, his pulse pounding in his ears as footsteps scurried over the wooden porch and thundered down the front steps.

Niles ripped open the front door in time to see someone in a dark jacket and stocking cap disappear around the tall hedges bordering his tiny front yard.

"Hey!" The figure broke into a jog at his shout, rushing down the sidewalk. He looked down at his own bare feet; he'd never catch up if he decided to give chase, and the concrete was cold and wet. "Fuck."

Disgusted, he turned to study the letter he'd stepped over in his rush to get to the door. His name and address were printed on the envelope, but there was no stamp or postmark. Again. Rather than pick it up, Niles pulled his phone out of his pocket and dialed.

"Tim? It's Niles."

"Hey, I was just about to call you. Payne told me things went to shit this morning after I left. I wanted to check on you."

"Someone just put another envelope through my mail slot. Same as the others."

"Have you opened it?"

Niles stared down at the envelope. "No. I haven't even touched it. It's right here on my floor where it fell. I caught a glimpse of whoever left it, but only from the back. They ran off before I could get a good look."

"Okay. Leave it there, and I'll be right over."

Niles stood in the open doorway, letting the chilly November air cool the flush that had come with the adrenaline rush. He looked out at the darkened street, where the asphalt glistened wetly under the yellow-orange glow of the streetlights. Was whoever had delivered the letter still out there, waiting to break his skull open like he'd tried to do to Jordan? He knew he should go inside and shut the door, but instead, he watched the break in the hedges that opened from the sidewalk into his yard, waiting for the unknown person to appear, ready to confront him or her, tired of being passive before the nonstop onslaught of harassment and intimidation. People like that were the ones too cowardly to show their faces or even put their names to their threats and opinions, yet Niles was the one helpless and afraid, with even the security of his own home violated.

He glared at the walkway, daring it to produce the culprit until his nerves had calmed and he began to shiver in the cold wind. Feeling foolish, he turned to go back inside, and promptly screamed when a voice called his name from behind him.

"Niles?"

"Jesus!" He spun, his heart in his throat, nearly nauseated with the sudden tension in his stomach. "Anthony! What are you doing here?"

Anthony stood in the open gate between the hedges, clutching the front of his khaki microfiber jacket, nearly as startled as Niles himself. "Christ, you scared me. Are you okay?"

"You're the one who came up behind me! How long have you been there?"

His brow beetled. "I just parked down the street a moment ago. What's wrong?"

"Really?" Niles strode to the edge of the porch, looking down the steps at him. "So you weren't here five minutes ago dropping an envelope in my mail slot?"

"What?" Anthony gawked at him. "I just got off work. I came to check on you. What's wrong, baby? You just seemed so stressed out when you were at the recording studio today, and then I heard something on the news about an intern . . .?"

Niles raked his hair back from his face, growling softly. "Nothing. It's nothing you need to worry about. I'm not up for visitors right now, so you need to go."

"Go? I just got here. Can I at least come in for a drink? I thought we could talk."

"No. No, we don't need to talk." Niles positioned himself to block the stairs as Anthony began to mount the steps. "We need to just go our separate ways. There's no reason for you to call me, and you certainly don't need to stop by my house. Believe me, Anthony, you probably don't want to be associated with me right now."

"Look, whatever went wrong in our relationship, I'm sure we can work on it." Anthony laid his hand on the railing only an inch away from Niles's. "I really care about you—"

"God! This. *This*, Anthony! *This* is what went wrong. *You.* Not being able to take no for an answer when I told you I needed you to back off. Calling too often, coming by uninvited and unannounced, needing to know every single thing I was doing and when and where and with whom. Getting upset when I spent time with my *brother* instead of you—" He broke off, clenching his fists at his sides. "Okay, listen. I've had a shitty day. I can't deal with this. Just leave and don't come back."

Beneath his dark mop of hair, Anthony's pale face started to get that pinched, irritated look he'd worn far too often before Niles had broken up with him. "Are you seeing someone else? Is that what this is about?"

"I told you last time we spoke, what I do isn't any of your business." Past Anthony's shoulder, Tim came striding up the walkway to the steps. "Good-bye, Anthony."

"Everything okay?" Tim asked, glancing up at Niles. Anthony jumped and whirled around, then gave Niles an accusing glare.

"Not up for visitors, huh?"

"Still not any of your business." Niles refused to reassure Anthony that Tim was a cop there for a completely nonpersonal reason.

"Fine. Fine." Anthony threw his hands up, pushing roughly

past Tim. When he reached the hedges, he turned back to face Niles. "You know, I could really be there for you, really help you with all you have to deal with if you'd give me half a chance, but whatever. You do what you're going to do. Someday you'll wish you'd taken the time for me."

Niles stripped his rain-spotted glasses off and covered his eyes with his other hand until he felt Tim touch his shoulder. When he dared to open them again, Anthony was gone and only Tim remained, his face grave.

"You all right?" Tim's other hand came to rest on Niles's other shoulder, stroking up and down his arms, his touch all-encompassing and warm through his now-damp shirt.

"Yeah." Niles pulled away. "I definitely know how to pick 'em, don't I? Clearly, I'm a *stellar* judge of character."

Tim let his hands drop to his sides. "Ouch."

"No, I didn't mean— Shit." He thrust his hand through his hair again, and it came away wet where the drizzling mist had beaded into droplets. Christ, was it only this morning he'd thought he might end the day taking Tim out to dinner and back to bed again? "Sorry."

"It's okay." Tim flapped his hand dismissively and dug into his pockets, pulling out a pair of nitrile gloves. "I probably deserve at least a few more digs before I'm done with my penance. Where's the letter?"

"Right there on the floor." Niles gestured to the envelope, stark white against the vintage hardwood. Tim lifted it and drew a pocketknife out of his jacket, carefully slitting the envelope, pulling out two plain sheets of printer paper.

FINAL WAVE.

The words were printed in a large, bold font. Niles stared at it while Tim looked at the second sheet, then held it out to show him. On it was a series of sketches of a man being crushed, mowed down by a futuristic vehicle.

"More of those drawings. That's Halliday, isn't it?" Tim asked, glancing at it again. "From the game."

"Yeah, except it isn't quite right. Halliday is a POC character, and this guy is white." Niles drew as close as he dared without touching the page. "Jesus, the game hasn't even been released and the fans are already whitewashing the characters. Come inside, into the kitchen. The light is brightest in there."

He led the way and flipped on the overhead light. Tim laid the drawing on the counter, and Niles stared at it. "Well, I guess that answers that. Our artist with the spoiler details—or someone associated with him—is my secret admirer. I need to grab my computer. I'll be right back."

By the time he returned to the kitchen, he had opened up the series of JPEG attachments in a slideshow and skipped to the Halliday ones. "They are. They're the same. Except Halliday wasn't whitewashed to begin with. The artist either redid them or someone downloaded them and edited it."

"Tell me more about these scenes. What's going on here?" Tim tabbed through the slides.

"Someone took a pivotal crisis scene for each companion character and drew it as it would have transpired if the player character hadn't somehow influenced events by intervening or making certain choices. Halliday gets crushed by an out-of-control ground-car because the PC was greedy and didn't choose to set aside the funds to maintain their vehicles properly. An attack on Issis that should have been interrupted results in her being bludgeoned to death. Gairi gets thrown into a river and drowns . . ."

Tim's phone rang, and he withdrew it from his pocket. "Payne? . . . Yeah, I'm at Niles's house . . . He received another threat, and it appears to be connected to whoever did those drawings of the characters . . ."

As Tim spoke with his partner, Niles returned to the images of Halliday on the computer, comparing them to the ones that had been pushed through his mail slot. Each line was identical until he got to the face. He focused on the features themselves, rather than just the skin, and jumped back from the counter. "Shit!"

"What? What is it?" Tim pulled the phone away from his ear.

Niles pointed weakly to the paper on the counter. "It's Daniel."

CHAPTER 16

J ordan looked at his brother across the conference room
table. Once again, they were waiting for Detective Payne to
arrive, but this time the wait was much grimmer. Tim sat
beside Niles, while near the head of the table, Rosie and Eliza
murmured back and forth to one another. This late-night
meeting—or what would be a meeting once Detective Payne
arrived—had already prompted one vociferous argument when
Eliza had asked Tim to leave the room and suggested that Niles
might want to consult a criminal attorney.

"What? What for?" He'd demanded as Jordan had tensed,
prepared to launch into his own outraged tirade. Rosie had
watched grimly.

"Because right now you were one of the last people, if not *the*
last, to have contact with two murder victims and at least one
missing person."

"Are you saying they might try to accuse Niles of something?" Jordan had stepped in behind his brother, resting his
hands on Niles's shoulders, which seemed bowed under the
weight of all that had happened in the past few days. Niles had
taken the news of the murders like a body blow, and now he

seemed to be reeling again. "Why him? Why not Rosie, or me, or any of the other thousands of attendees at the convention? We saw those young women too."

"But you weren't intimate with Daniel Fortesen. If you're right and that drawing means Fortesen could be dead, it might just start to look like too many people around Niles are dropping like flies, and that's going to make someone ask why." Her expression was sympathetic, but unyielding.

"Tim already cleared my alibi for Lakshmi's and Charity's murders." Niles didn't lift his eyes as he spoke, his voice subdued.

"All right." Eliza pulled out a chair and dug a legal pad out of her briefcase, taking notes. "And what about the day Patrick Rutledge and Daniel Fortesen disappeared?"

"Niles was here at work from morning until early evening," Rosie supplied. "I don't think he even left for lunch."

"I didn't." Niles clasped his hands on the table in front of him. "There would be records of me buying a coffee at the shop where I dropped off Daniel, and I believe he made a purchase too, so the last time I saw him was in public. I went to work, and then I left from here to go straight to the airport."

"Okay, good." Eliza made more notes and gave him an encouraging smile. "This is all very good. You were places that can be easily verified, places with cameras or electronic records or witnesses. Odds are good you have nothing to worry about, though I would still encourage you to be careful how much time you spend with Detective Wyatt." She made a face. "His job is to find someone he can charge for these crimes. You don't know what sort of things you could say that he might interpret wrongly."

"He wouldn't do that," Niles protested, shaking his head.

Eliza arched her pencil-thin eyebrows at him. "Are you sure? Are you sure if it comes down to it, he's not going to try to make his case at your expense?"

"I don't—" Jordan's hands tightened on Niles's shoulders as he shrugged helplessly.

"My brother is a victim here," Jordan said firmly. "He's being menaced by someone who seems to know something about these murders. Detective Wyatt's job is to protect him too."

"Well, let's make sure the detectives see it that way, shall we?"

Jordan was jerked out of his memory when Detective Payne came bustling into the room, carrying a small stack of files. "Sorry I'm late," she said and leaned down to confer quietly with Tim. He gave her a startled look and cleared his throat as she handed him a file.

"Is this Fortesen?" Tim asked, sliding a picture from the top of the folder toward Niles.

Niles drew in a sharp breath and swallowed hard. Jordon thought for a moment it looked like he might vomit. "Maybe? Hard to tell with all that, um, damage to his face. But I think he was wearing that jacket when I met him. What happened?"

Tim's mouth tightened as he thumbed quickly through the pages in the folder, skimming. "Hit and run. There was no ID on the body, so we've had him in the morgue as a John Doe since Friday. We're waiting on dental records from Seattle."

"Jesus," Rosie muttered, covering her mouth. "They really are putting their own ending on outtakes from the game."

"You said he was killed Friday?" Eliza asked sharply.

Tim nodded as Detective Payne sat down. "Yeah, the afternoon he supposedly left Portland."

"I've got the computer forensics guys going after the identity of whoever posted these to your web boards." Payne started spreading out the series of drawings on the conference table. "Look, we don't use this term lightly, and we're not making it public yet, but this is starting to shape up like a serial case. According to these sketches, there are four more characters whose deaths are depicted. We need to go through them and see if we can match them up to any open homicides, and if not, we need to figure out who the perp—or perps—is going after next."

Tim tapped the plastic bag on the table in front of him, with the latest hand-delivered letter inside it. "'Final wave.' What does that mean?"

"It's a gaming term." Rosie leaned forward. "You might have noticed when we were introducing you to the game that combat generally happens in waves of mobs—enemies. The usual formula is three waves. You defeat one, another spawns, you defeat it, another spawns. The last wave is generally the most difficult, and if there's an elite—meaning more difficult than usual—mob, that's where it's going to be, when your power and ammunition and whatever else you might rely on has been depleted."

Niles frowned, drawing Jordan's eye. "What is it?"

"The notes. They've all been from the games until now."

"They have?" Tim blinked at him. "Why didn't you mention that?"

"I didn't realize until now. 'Watch yourself.' It's what one of the companion characters says in *PF1* when the PC is in danger of tripping a booby trap. And 'You were warned' comes from *PF2*, something one of the boss mobs yells during combat."

Detective Payne wrote that down. "Does anyone say 'Final wave' in one of the games?"

Niles shook his head. "No. Like Rosie said, it's just a generic gaming term."

"Could it also be a reference to your company name?" Tim asked.

Rosie nodded. "Possibly. The company name is a bit of a play on words. It refers to the common mechanics of game combat, yes, but also to third wave feminist theory."

"So this could be a statement on gender politics, as well." Tim gestured to the letter again.

"We've known that all along," Niles interjected quietly.

"We've always known the harassment was about Third Wave's philosophy. We just didn't know it was linked to murders."

Fear for his brother constricted Jordan's lungs, making his breath tight and shallow. "If it is a reference to the company name, it's a threat. He sees himself as facing off, getting ready for combat," he observed.

"So let's go over the other characters. Sang." Payne spread out the series of sketches. "What's his story?"

Niles drew a breath. "He's the doctor. Alien. His species's culture is vaguely analogous with early-century Chinese culture. He comes into the story as a political dissident seeking asylum. In these sketches, the player character doesn't grant it, so he's killed by assassins, who make it look like a suicide. They hang him."

"All right." Detective Payne pulled out a laptop from her bag and began entering data. They all fell silent, watching her, until she looked up. "Okay, here. Keilana Savanh. Lived in Beaverton. She's Laotian, not Chinese—what are the odds we're dealing with a white perp who thinks all Asian cultures are interchangeable?—admitted to St. V's and subsequently died after allegedly hanging herself in her closet. Her family is contesting the ruling of death by suicide and has requested an investigation. They say she'd never do that, that she was happy and had far too much to live for."

Tim nodded. "Wanna bet she was a gamer or a cosplayer?"

"Doesn't say." Detective Payne stared at the computer a while longer. "There are no reports of men matching that pattern."

"Doesn't matter," Rosie said dismissively. "Lakshmi was cosplaying a male character. In gaming, the character is an avatar; it can be a woman or a man controlling it."

"Okay." Tim nodded slowly, looking at Niles's laptop, which was open to the companion-selection screen of *PF3*. "So that's Issis, Gairi, Sang, and Halliday. Which leaves us with . . ."

"Marc, Grace, and Chino." Niles shuffled through the printouts of the sketches. "This is Marc. He's young, barely more than a teenager. He's also not a full-fledged companion. He's the foster brother of the player character, a student, and it's his abduction by terrorists that propels the PC on his or her quest. Unlike the other companions, there's no crisis moment where a choice or action by the PC can change the fate of the character. Marc is kidnapped, no matter what. You recover him later in the game, but you rarely have the option of having him on your team the way you do the other companions."

"Abduction?" Eliza piped up for the first time since she'd apparently decided no one was threatening her clients with legal action. "You mean like Patrick Rutledge?"

"Oh God." Rosie's breath hitched.

"So Patrick's Marc." Niles frowned at the sketches, particularly the one where the terrorists set Marc on fire.

"And that makes the first two waves." Detective Payne took the sketches of the various characters and divided them into rows. She pointed to the pictures of Issis and Gairi in the first stack. "Charity and Lakshmi the weekend before last, and Keilana, Daniel, and Patrick—possibly—this past weekend."

Tim rapped his fingers on the surface of the table. "If not for Rutledge, I'd point out that the victims have all been women or queer men."

Jordan glanced at Niles and Rosie, both of whom appeared to be biting their tongues. Of course they weren't going to say anything, but fuck it, this was a police investigation. "Patrick's gay. He was with us for a while that night at the club, in fact."

"He's not out to his family or, presumably, his friends," Niles hurriedly added. "Please respect that when you question him or people he knows."

"So that pattern is consistent." Tim spread out the sketches of Chino and Grace and glanced at Niles. "That leaves us with the final wave. Now is Niles Grace or Chino, and who is the last person?"

Payne looked from the drawings to Niles and Rosie. "After the player character, Grace is the leader of the company."

Rosie blinked. "Me? You think I might be a target?"

Jordan laughed, though it was bitter. Nothing about this was a damn bit funny. "Rosie, when haven't you been a target?"

"But he's been leaving the notes for Niles."

"Because you have a doorman and security. He can't get to you, and if he sent them via email, they would just get lost in the thousands of other threats we file and ignore. He wanted our attention, and the emails and texts aren't the way to get it."

"You're the boss," Niles said, staring at Rosie. He had a quaver in his voice that Jordan didn't like, as if he were moments from falling apart. "To get to the boss, you have to go through his or her lieutenants, right?"

Detective Payne nodded grimly. "It has to be you both. Chino is her right-hand man and best friend."

They shifted awkwardly in their chairs. Jordan cleared his throat, covering a smile. "Slightly more than that by the end of *PF3*."

"Well, I think we've already established this guy isn't going for literalism." Niles reached for the sketches. Like the others, they were sorted by the character they depicted. "The thing with Chino and Grace is that their crisis moments come together, shortly after they escalate their friendship. Unless the PC makes a very specific set of choices throughout the game—a few of which are rather ethically ambiguous—you lose one or the other of them. The only other alternative is that, if the PC plays it just so, she'll have the choice of sacrificing herself instead of Chino or Grace. See?"

Jordan watched Niles shuffle the sketches around as they spoke, his attention more on his brother than on the discussion. He arranged them like puzzle pieces until they came together to form a set of panels in sequential order. What had looked like separate death sequences for Chino and Grace were actually a single series of events, with the perspective moving back and forth between the characters, culminating in an ending that did *not* happen within the game, namely both Chino and Grace dying.

Tim rose and stood leaning over Niles's shoulder to take in the entire tableau, and Detective Payne joined him. "So, they're going to try to take the two of you out together."

"Maybe." Payne frowned. "They may be trying to put their own ending on scenes from the game, but like Niles said, we know their methods aren't literal. They had to have taken Charity and Lakshmi together, after all, and that isn't depicted in the sketches. Their crisis moments aren't together. Hell, they're not even in the same game. Marc's and Halliday's aren't together, either, for that matter."

Rosie chewed the inside of her cheek. "I'm going to hire more security. If they want to go after both of us, here is the obvious place."

"Good idea. We'll be having units doing frequent drive-bys of your residences and this building, as well," Tim said.

They continued talking about security arrangements and risk factors, but something niggled at the back of Jordan's mind. He drummed his fingers on the table, trying to shape the nagging sense of unease into a coherent thought until he felt Niles's eyes fix on him from across the room.

"What is it, Jordie?"

"Why did he try to crush my skull?" Jordan blurted, bringing the chatter to a halt.

"What?"

"If you're the final wave, why did he go after you—mistakenly clobbering me in the process—this weekend when he went after Patrick and Daniel?"

Niles's brow furrowed. "Maybe he wasn't coming after me, yet. Maybe he wanted to deliver the note, and he thought you'd seen him or would see him?"

"But he'd already delivered the note. It was in the house, below the mail slot. Why would he stick around after that, if he wasn't lying in wait?"

"I don't know." Niles rubbed his forehead wearily. "The dude —or these dudes—is killing people based on a video game. I don't think logic has much to do with his thought processes."

"I wouldn't be so quick to dismiss them," Payne cautioned. "There's always a logic to the way these people work. It's just not necessarily a logic we understand, or that's readily apparent. Don't write them off."

Niles nodded and slumped in his chair a little more, chastened.

Tim frowned, looking back and forth between Rosie and Niles. "I notice the three of you are defaulting to this being a male perp. Now, statistically speaking, that's probably correct, but we have been trying to stay open to the possibilities. Still, from people with your politics, it makes me wonder if you know something about the perp that we don't."

Rosie shook her head, her mouth twisting in a bitter smile. "We're not being sexist. Look at the drawings of Issis and Grace. See how sexualized and powerless their death poses are? I've seen a lot of art in my day, and done a lot of study into feminist media criticism, and I can tell you, this is male gaze stuff. Women don't draw women like that."

"And the drawings were from a fan site with a lot of traffic from cis-male gamers who don't like Third Wave's position on women in gaming," Jordan added. "And you said it yourself earlier, there's a good chance this is a statement on Third Wave's gender politics."

"From the height and build, the person I saw running from my house after leaving the note tonight was probably male, and it's always been cis men who have threatened us," Niles agreed, then bowed his head, covering his face with his hands. "Sorry. I just— I need to get home. I'm exhausted. And thinking of

Patrick and Daniel, and that Rosie and I are probably next . . . I can't. I just need to go home, now. Please."

"You shouldn't be alone." Tim pushed his chair back, but his expression was conflicted as he looked back and forth between Detective Payne and Niles. "I need to stay here, keep working on this, but—"

"I'll take you back to my condo." Jordan stood, watching Niles's face with concern. It was obvious the events of the last two days were catching up and crashing in on him. He looked overwhelmed, almost in shock. Jordan wasn't sure he wanted Tim Wyatt and all the complicated shit that came with him around Niles just now, even if Wyatt did carry a gun. "Third floor, closer neighbors, cameras in the lobby. It'll be safer there than your house."

Wyatt looked at Niles as he nodded and gathered his computer and jacket. "When we're done here, I'll come check on you at Jordan's place."

"Just make sure Rosie gets home safe, would you?" Niles murmured, neither approving nor refusing the idea of Tim coming by.

"We'll take care of that," Detective Payne assured him as Rosie stood and hugged Niles tightly.

"Don't worry about me. We're not gonna let this bastard stop us, okay?"

"Okay." Niles kissed her cheek and bowed his head again, subdued as he accompanied Jordan out the door.

CHAPTER 17

It was nearly 2 a.m. when Detectives Wyatt and Payne left Third Wave's studios with a list of every beta participant for *PF3* and the names of everyone who might have access to the story script for the upcoming DLC. Rosie sighed and rubbed her eyes. The identities would be cross-checked against the IP information of the most vitriolic critics of Third Wave's politics to find out who was in the Portland area and would have the sort of access to commit the crimes in question.

"What are you thinking?" Eliza asked, stacking her papers and slipping them neatly into her briefcase. She'd offered to give Rosie a ride home and see her safely inside her house. As a lawyer who in her spare time had made a fair number of men angry taking divorce cases for abused women pro bono, she had a concealed-carry permit, put in monthly sessions at the shooting range, and had periodic lessons to hone her skills.

"That this could be it for us." Rosie rubbed her eyes again, leaning back away from the conference table. "EEU might decide to shut us down if they think we've attracted too much negative publicity. They're run by corporate men, and they've never been comfortable with Third Wave's in-your-face politics."

"Then you'll start a new studio, and you'll find a new distributor. Come here, sugar." Eliza pulled Rosie into her lap, laying an arm across her shoulders and kissing her temple gently. She let herself relax into the hug. She and Eliza had been friends—and occasionally more—since college, back when Eliza Muldrake had still been Elijah Muldrake. Their personalities were too strong to ever make a relationship work, but just then she was willing to take any reassurance that came her way.

"Will it be worth it?" She wrapped her arms around Eliza's waist and leaned her head on the soft swell of her breast, yielding to the rare moment of self-doubt. "Have I put my employees in danger?"

Eliza stroked her close-cropped hair, kissing the top of her head. "Niles knew what he was signing on for. He believes in what you're doing. Hell, he's just as passionate about it as you are, if that's even possible."

"Patrick Rutledge didn't."

"No. He didn't. Innocents are always the ones to suffer when terrorists attack. And make no mistake—that's what this is. If it's true that this is targeted at Third Wave's politics and philosophy, then this person or these people are using fear and intimidation and violence to silence a message they don't want the world to hear. That's the definition of terrorism." Eliza leaned back, moving away to meet Rosie's eyes.

"I'm getting burned out," she confessed, giving words to the thought that had been there since before all this had begun.

"Oh, sugar, of course you are. You've been through hell the past couple years. First the tumor and now this?" Eliza hugged her tightly. "You know we all get to the point where we wonder if it's worth it anymore."

"What am I going to do? How can I lead a company with a mission statement like ours if I'm just phoning it in?"

"It's okay to dial down the intensity for a while. Not to give up, but just to give yourself some breathing room until you find your passion for it again."

Rosie closed her eyes and didn't let herself ask if that would save anyone else from being killed.

————

TIM FIDGETED with nervous energy as he knocked on Jordan River's condo door. He hadn't been particularly comfortable with the stare Jordan had been giving him at their meeting, but he was damned if he was going to let that keep him from checking in on Niles. When Jordan answered the door, he did so without uttering a greeting, staring at Tim with his arm braced against the doorframe, denying him entrance.

"I wouldn't recommend slugging me again," he said after a long standoff.

"I wouldn't recommend giving me reason to." Jordan smiled tightly and stepped aside, finally permitting him to enter. "Look, maybe you don't get this about Niles, but he refuses to believe anything bad about anyone. He's a modern-day fucking Pollyanna. It's why he was with you to begin with when I—and everyone else he knew—told him you were absolutely not going to leave the closet for him. So he might be able to forgive you, but I don't forget that easily."

Tim remained by the door, closing it behind him but not coming any farther inside. The staring contest was reaching the point of absurdity, but he didn't think buckling before Jordan was going to win him any points, however much remorse he might feel for what he'd done to Niles back then.

"I respect that you want to look out for him, but Niles is a grown man. I've made my apologies to him. I owe that to him. But not to you."

Jordan's eyes narrowed. "I'm the one who picks up the

fucking pieces when things don't end up as rosy as he hopes they will."

"Yeah, I get that. But there's not a goddamn thing I can do here that's going to convince you that this time you won't have to. So what is it you expect from me, Jordan?"

Another moment of heavy staring, and finally Jordan broke eye contact. He appeared frustrated. Like he wanted to do more but couldn't. "Not a damn thing," he sighed. "Niles is resting. I'll go wake him up."

"You don't need to," Tim said quickly, thinking how drawn Niles had been at the meeting earlier. "I just wanted to check in, make sure the two of you didn't have any trouble getting home. It's not necessary to disturb him if he's tired."

"He'd think it was necessary." Jordan folded his arms across his chest. Tim couldn't blame him for feeling helpless. This probably wasn't even about what Tim had done in the past, so much as it was just a general sense of being on alert. Jordan was probably feeling particularly protective of his brother right now, seeing as how someone appeared to be threatening his life. "And he's not tired, he's in shock."

"*He* can speak for himself." Tim glanced past Jordan's shoulder as he turned to meet Niles's censuring stare. He was tousled and groggy, and there was something hollow in his eyes. Heartsickness. It had been there since the moment he'd realized that people actually were dying because of the work he'd spent the last seven years doing.

As Tim and Jordan watched, Niles drew himself up, packed all that away somewhere deep. "Rosie made it home all right?" he asked, gazing past Jordan to Tim.

He nodded. "The lawyer, Ms. Muldrake, drove her home. I had a unit follow them. She got there safely, and there's a doorman and security guard in the lobby. Her building is tight."

"I'm trying to convince Niles to stay here." Jordan gave Tim a challenging look. "Since you need a key card to get into the elevator."

"Not a bad idea," Tim said mildly. "If he decides to stay at home, though, like I said, we'll have units checking on them both."

Niles ran a hand through his hair, scratching his scalp and chest simultaneously. He didn't even glance at his twin. "Stop posturing, Jordie. Hackles down, alpha dog mode disengaged. Whatever. Go to bed. I'll be okay."

Jordan sighed and deflated. Tim couldn't imagine that Jordan thought he was all that much danger to Niles's well-being. He just couldn't menace the actual threat.

"You heading home or staying?" Jordan asked his brother.

Niles never took his eyes off Tim. "Going home."

"Okay." Jordan slipped past Niles, brushing a hand along his upper arm in passing and glancing back over his shoulder. His warning glare at Tim wasn't even so much *Don't do anything to hurt him* as it was *Don't let anything happen to him*. Tim nodded once in brusque agreement, and Jordan went into the bedroom and closed the door.

Niles was pressed against him in a second, his lips hot and soft and welcoming. He felt good in Tim's arms. Right. He'd always felt that way, since the first day Tim had met those pale gray-green eyes across the lab table. That had been the day he'd started to realize the occasional flickers of attraction he'd felt toward some of his male classmates—and the difficulty he had convincing himself that he was attracted to girls—actually meant what he feared it had. It would just be years until he was forced to admit it.

What is this, really? A do-over? A chance at redemption?

He didn't know, and the gravitational pull of Niles drew him in so strongly it was almost impossible to step back and analyze. Not with those soft moans in his ear and that willing body aligned so eagerly—almost urgently—with his. He could feel the rising pressure of Niles's cock against his thigh, and the warmth of Niles's fingers slipping into his waistband at the base of his spine, and it made it so easy to dismiss everything else.

But it was different now. They weren't simply smitten college kids. Niles was in danger, and Tim had a job to do, and if he even deserved this second chance to begin with, maybe he needed to ask himself where he thought he was going with it.

"Niles, wait." Tim tried to put a little strength in the protest, but in the end, he didn't have the conviction, and it came off as more of a plea. "We need to—"

"Not tonight, Tim, please?" Niles pressed his forehead to Tim's shoulder, hiding his face. He was shaking, Tim realized, and he tightened his arms around him. "Just . . . please. Take me home?"

This wasn't about Tim at all. He almost groaned at the realization. No wonder Jordan was trying to warn him off. This was about Niles trying to escape, trying to forget. Trying to bury too many confusing and painful thoughts. Fuck. He really did need to slow this down, maybe stop it. Niles would cling to anyone tonight, and Tim couldn't—*shouldn't*—take advantage of that neediness to try to get back something he'd stupidly given up.

But then Niles shivered again, and there was fuck-all Tim could deny him.

"Sure, baby," he murmured, kissing the top of Niles's head. He reached for Niles's jacket hanging on the coat rack. "Let's go."

BLUNT FINGERS THRUSTING AND SPREADING. The scrape of teeth down his throat. Low, growling moans in his ear.

Niles lost himself in it, in the familiarity of Tim's touch— even after so many years—and the earthy, spicy scent of his skin and aftershave. He was using sex to run away from reality, but he just couldn't manage to care. He'd practically thrown Tim to the floor the moment they made it into the house, devouring him despite Tim's halfhearted suggestions about getting to the bed first, until he remembered that the last guy he'd gotten so aggressive with had wound up dead the next day. It had been enough to slow him down.

But then, once Tim was half-inside him and rocking his way toward balls-deep, all the wrongness around them brought his libido to a screeching halt.

"Stopstop*stop*." Niles bucked Tim off his back, rolling to look up at the bedroom ceiling as he caught his breath. Every nerve in his body was screaming to keep going, but his brain kept feeding him images of Daniel's bruised and mangled face. He ground the heels of his hands into his eyes, trying to rub the visions away.

"What? Are you serious?" Disbelief and strained arousal sharpened Tim's tone, and then he managed to pull it back. "What is it? What's wrong?" He fell off to the side, concern masking any sexual frustration admirably as he propped himself up to stare at Niles.

"What if he goes after you?"

"*That's* what you're thinking about right now?" Tim groaned and slipped the condom from his still-rigid dick, tossing it in the bedside trash while Niles sat up and wrapped his arms around his knees.

"Well, why else did he go after Daniel? Why choose *him* to be Halliday instead of some random stranger? He had nothing to do with this, not until he came down here to interview me and decided to stay an extra night." The tight, anxious feeling that had been twisting in Niles's chest since he'd found out Daniel was dead swelled, threatened to cut off his breath. "I got him killed."

"*No*, Niles." Tim shook his head emphatically. "No. Don't do this to yourself. You didn't get Fortesen killed. You didn't get your intern abducted. And if this guy does come after me, he'll find it a hell of a lot harder to get to me than he did anyone else. I can take care of myself, and I'm not unprepared."

Niles's eyes burned as he turned his head, his gaze tracking toward Tim. "I just don't understand this. Any of it. How can someone want to silence someone else this badly? Over a fucking game?"

"What the fuck does it matter?" Tim flung up a hand. "Unbalanced people are always finding something they're willing to kill for, to keep others from having it, or changing it, or being part of it. Particularly when they congregate and egg each other on to more extreme measures. So, why not a fucking game? People have killed reporters, photographers, novelists, painters, singers and songwriters, actors and scriptwriters and playwrights in order to stop the message they were putting out. Why *not* video game creators too?"

Video games were the fastest-growing form of mass entertainment—Niles knew that. He'd even told Tim that. Knowing it, knowing the impact swaying video game culture could have on society in general, why was it so unthinkable that privilege-protecting reactionaries would resort to violence? Was he—despite his lip service—as guilty as the rest of society of deriding the actual significance of games?

How could he be so naive as to think he could use his artistic medium as a vehicle for change without people reacting the way they always had to such vehicles?

He gave Tim a disillusioned look. "It's just— It's supposed to be *fun*. It's supposed to make people feel *good*, not—" Niles broke off, shaking his head in disgust. Weak, that's what such thinking was. At best it made him irretrievably gullible, and at worst it made him a hypocrite. He couldn't have it both ways. Either he was doing important work and could expect to be treated the way people who did such work always had, or he was just supplying mindless entertainment to a generation of drones incapable of critical thinking.

He sighed and stared up at the ceiling, willing answers to fall from it. "Never mind."

Tim drew back the covers they had twisted and rumpled and slipped into the bed. "C'mere."

"I'm sorry." Niles managed a chagrined smile, but Tim waved the apology off. He drew Niles into his arms and pulled the blankets up over them.

"Don't worry about it." He pressed a kiss to Niles's temple. "I get it, y'know? It's kind of surreal, isn't it?"

"What, the idea that someone out there is taking aim at me? *Me*? I mean, I'm just some gamer geek writing stories about animated characters for a living."

"Yeah, that." His arms tightened around Niles. "He won't get to you. I'm not going to let that happen. And with us, you take all the time you need. We're rushing this, I know. *I'm* rushing it. But we've got time to deal with it later."

What if we don't? Niles wanted to ask, but he'd been maudlin enough already.

The room grew silent and still, except for the omnipresent sounds of the old house and the occasional gust of breeze outside. Tim was still awake; his fingers tracked up and down Niles's back in soothing strokes. He could do it, he realized with a sigh. He could fall in love with Tim Wyatt again. Maybe he'd never even really fallen out of love with him. Whether or not it was a good idea, whether or not he could trust Tim again, didn't seem all that important right now. Tim's nude body was warm, the arms around him firm and sheltering, and that was really all that mattered. Was he using Tim? Maybe. But that didn't mean all the old feelings weren't still there and in very real danger of being resurrected.

It was ridiculous to feel disloyal for thinking about Tim right now, when Daniel was dead. But then, there was a bitter symmetry to it too, wasn't there? He'd used Daniel to escape thoughts of Tim, and now it was the other way around.

He lifted his head as a thought occurred to him. "If Patrick and Daniel are both victims, they can't have been the ones to leak the spoilers."

"What about the rest of the writing staff?" Tim pressed.

"Everyone would have access to the information if they really wanted it, but only the writers involved with the *Phoenix Force* titles would be intimately acquainted with it, and none of them would say a word."

Tim licked his lips, nodding slowly. "Tell me something. You said your ex worked at the studio where you recorded dialogue. Would he have access to it?"

"*Anthony?*"

"Answer the question, Niles."

"No, this is ridiculous!" Rolling away, Niles flung the covers back and got out of bed, hunting for his clothes and jerking them on.

Tim sat up, running a hand through his hair. "Baby, sooner or later you're going to have to accept that someone did this, and it's probably someone you know. How else would they have privileged information about a game that hasn't been released to the public yet? That's how we're going to crack this. Who has access to those sorts of details?"

"Anyone could know about the beta, providing someone breaks their NDA." Niles pressed the heel of his hand to his forehead, where a headache was beginning to blossom between his brows. "But not everyone knew about the DLC. But why would you even think of Anthony?"

"Jealous lover? Please. It's the oldest story in the book. He has motive to wish you—or the people you're intimate with—harm. One of the bodies on the ground is a guy you slept with."

"I certainly didn't sleep with Lakshmi, or Charity, or that other girl, Keilana!"

"You spoke to at least two of them. Were you kind? Did you smile? When you were with him, was he jealous of the time you spent at work? Did he resent your relationship with your brother?"

Tim looked unmoved by Niles's glare, so he spun on his heel and left the room. Tim followed him, thundering down the stairs without even bothering to get dressed. "You don't know the sorts of things that can go through the heads of stalkers when they see the target of their fixation do even the most innocuous of things with other people. Even a friendly word can seem like a threat to someone that unbalanced."

"Well, obviously you *would* know! Funny how your potential suspect is someone who could be considered a threat for my affections!"

"You think I haven't been asking myself that?" Tim crossed his arms over his bare chest, leaning in the archway between the living room and the dining room as Niles opened his liquor cabinet and dragged out the vodka. "Hell, I probably shouldn't be with you at all, and the odds of me having to recuse myself from this case are mounting by the minute. So you can be damn sure that each time it occurs to me that the perp might be someone you fucked, I ask myself what evidence I'm basing that theory on. Now answer the question. How much could Anthony have known about the Gairi DLC?"

The vodka scorched its way down his throat as Niles threw back a shot, then poured another. "All of it, all right? *Fuck.* He listened as I brainstormed the damn thing. It was pillow talk. Happy now?"

"No. Not really." Tim stomped over to the breakfast bar and thunked his elbows down on it, scrubbing his face with his hands and hanging his head for a moment. "In the morning, I'll be explaining to my captain why I'm taking myself off the case and letting Payne know we need to take a good look at Anthony."

Niles set the vodka and glass on the table. They felt too heavy to hold any longer. "Shit. I'm sorry." It hadn't occurred to him until Tim gave him that resigned look how important the case had been for Tim. "Fine. I believe you. I can't really believe it could be Patrick or Anthony or anyone I know, but I believe you."

Tim shrugged. "That's something, at least."

"Okay, look. If you need to stop seeing me so you can work the case—"

"No." Tim shook his head before Niles could finish the thought.

"You don't need to choose me over the case just to prove something. I get it."

"That's not it." Tim's rueful smile was gentle and sweet, and Niles found himself drawn toward it like a lodestone. "I would have had to do this even if I'd never touched you again, just because of our history. It wouldn't be enough to get a strong case thrown out, but it could muddy the waters."

"I'm sorry anyway." Niles stopped, near enough to see goose-flesh on Tim's skin. He still stood there nude, and they hadn't bothered with a fire or turning up the heat in their rush to get to bed.

"It's worth it." Tim reached out, hooking a hand around the back of Niles's neck and pulling him close. "Can we go back to bed now?"

"Yeah." Suddenly, nothing sounded better than falling asleep beside Tim and putting this whole day behind them. He took Tim's hand and led him to the stairs. "Let's go."

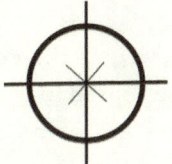

CHAPTER 18

T he atmosphere in the studio felt different when Niles came in to work the next day. Jordan had tried to urge Rosie to close the office, but Niles had protested. He needed to work. He needed things to be normal again. In the end, Rosie had sent out a mass email to all their employees, giving them the option of working from home until the investigation ended and they were sure no one else associated with Third Wave would be harmed.

Unsurprisingly, considering the dedication of the people Rosie pulled to herself, most people had shown up, their attitudes almost defiant. But everyone was tense, and the sense of relaxed camaraderie they usually enjoyed seemed to have disappeared overnight. The art department, writing staff, programming and design people, all did their work—grim, quiet, speaking only when necessary, and then only in hushed tones.

Niles was supposed to be preparing notes for a preproduction meeting for the DLC that would follow Gairi's, but he found himself staring at the concept art pinned to the wall across from his desk. Issis, Gairi, Halliday, Marc—they were all there, all the characters he'd helped bring to pixelated life, whose words and voices he'd crafted. But now his mind's eye kept superimposing other faces over the familiar characters. He saw Lakshmi Agrawal's sweet, quiet smile eclipsed by a sickly gray pallor as they pulled her from the river still wearing her Gairi costume. He saw fiercely brave Charity Anspach falling under a hail of bludgeoning blows, Daniel crushed by a car, Patrick abducted and terrified . . .

He had, quite literally, written their death scenes.

How the hell was he supposed to ever write again?

Unable to focus, he left his office, heading down to Rosie's where she had set Detective Payne up on one of the gaming rigs, away from the bustle of coders working in the lab. He met Jordan in the hall, apparently on his way to consult with Rosie about something. He caught his brother's eyes, but he couldn't think of anything to say besides to tell him to back off Tim, so he pressed his lips together and said nothing.

Tim was in Rosie's office too, looking as bewildered as ever as Detective Payne carried on a murmured discussion with him about each bit of dialogue, each choice made in the game. She was the one playing, controlling the player character, but Tim was taking notes.

"Seriously?" Rosie groaned at her computer screen.

"What is it?" Detective Payne paused the game and turned in her chair.

"Oh, this picture." She gestured to her screen, and Detective Payne rose and crossed the office to look. "The new Wonder Woman in the upcoming *Superman v Batman* movie."

Detective Payne made a derisive sound. "Needs to be a sistah."

"I know, right?" Rosie held up her hand and bumped fists with her.

Tim shuddered. "Did you just feel that?"

"I think that is what the geeks would call a great disturbance in the Force," Jordan murmured.

Niles shrugged, feeling a touch of amusement for the first time in days. "Well, if it's any consolation, on the day of their coronation as joint Planetary Imperators, we can tell people we were there the moment the Unholy Alliance was forged."

Rosie was giving Detective Payne a rundown of the controversy over whether or not casting the Israeli actress was considered POC representation or not when Tim spoke up again.

"Let me ask you a question, Niles. I know you love your work, and you've spoken a lot about the potential outreach factor, but, still—*video games*? Why make your stand there? Why not just find something else to do for recreation, and fight the good fight someplace a little less, well, fringe?"

Rosie clearly overheard because she cut off her discussion with Detective Payne, and Niles met her eyes as she asked casually, "Angie, Rosa Parks should have just found somewhere else to sit, right? I mean, a bus seat doesn't really matter."

Detective Payne rolled her eyes in response, and Tim held up his hands. "Whoa, that's not— We're talking about *video games*, not the next great civil rights frontier."

Jordan moaned softly, muttering to Niles, "When he starts digging, he brings the backhoe, doesn't he?"

Rosie came to her feet, and Niles gave Tim a sympathetic look. No way was he going to get in the middle of this.

"Tell me. What do you think the next great civil rights frontier looks like?" Rosie asked, drawing herself up. She didn't fold her arms over her chest or look defensive or confrontational. Instead, her posture was open, conversational but authoritative. He'd seen her do it before, and something about her presence compelled people to listen, which was why she was such an amazing public speaker. "The face of prejudice in the twenty-first century is not a guy in a pointy white hood. It's hundreds of thousands of little ways our culture sets people who aren't white, able-bodied, cis-het males to the side and says, 'You're different, and therefore you can't have what we have.' You can't have the

same access to healthcare, to jobs, to education, to bodily auton-
omy, to protection under the law, to tax and inheritance laws. To
basic human dignity."

He watched Tim's reaction, but Tim didn't say anything. You
didn't interrupt Rosie when she was in this zone. Her intensity
was electrifying, and you just shut up and listened.

"Two years ago, while I was in the hospital having a baseball-
sized tumor removed from my skull, I had people posting
images of my house online, daring someone to rape or kill me,
wishing death on me. Why? Because I have this audacious idea
that people who aren't white, straight cis-men should see positive reflections of themselves in media and common recreational
activities." Her eyes flashed with a fire that Niles hadn't seen in
her since— God, he didn't remember when. "One of the last
interactions Charity Anspach had on this planet was with a guy
who called her a crazy bitch for saying that he shouldn't grope
her without her consent. And our culture supports that. In
hundreds of little ways, it tells him that he's right and she was
unreasonable. And if you found that guy today and told him she
was dead, I'll bet you cash money that the first thing he'd do is
hop online and start mouthing off about how she deserved it."

She lifted her chin, and the stare she fixed Tim with became
a little challenging. "So, what do you think? Should I go do
something more important, something *less fringe*? Because sure,
I could teach women's studies, but is that guy going to sit his ass
down in my lecture hall and walk out thinking, 'Wow, I've been a
real douchenozzle, maybe I should knock it off'? Or do I need to
go into the spaces he thinks are his, and get up in his face, and
challenge him, and say, 'This is not okay, this is not okay, this. Is.
Not. Okay,' until he finally gets it?"

She fell silent, but she held Tim pinned with her gaze until
he bowed his head. "I'm sorry. That was a completely stupid
thing for me to say," he murmured.

Rosie's mouth curved into a wistful smile. "Apology noted. I suppose I should thank you. You just made me remember why I do this."

She sat down, turning her attention back to her computer. "You guys have about ninety hours of gameplay left. I'll let you get back to that."

Detective Payne nodded once and returned to the computer against the far wall, gesturing for Tim to start taking notes again, and Niles slipped quietly back to his office.

A QUICK RAP on the frame of his open door later that morning brought Niles's head snapping up to see his brother standing there, looking sober.

"What is it?"

Jordan took that as an invitation and came all the way in, shutting the door behind him. "You haven't spoken to me today."

"I've been busy." Niles gestured to his laptop, though the characters on the screen might as well have been gibberish for all the sense he'd been able to make of them all morning.

"You're pissed at me."

"No. Yes." He sighed and pushed a hand through his hair, sweeping it back from his face.

Jordan moved around to the other side of Niles's desk, and perched on the edge of it, facing his brother, his expression still solemn.

"You need to get off Tim's back," Niles said.

"Okay." Jordan shrugged easily. "Anything else?"

"Where did this idea that I can't take care of myself come from?"

Jordan's eyebrows inched upward. "From the fact that you *don't*, bro," he said simply, as though it should be self-evident.

"Excuse me?"

"You don't, Niles, and you never have. You live with your

head in the clouds half the time, off building fantasy worlds where you forget to eat and sleep. I've seen you mourn fictional characters like they're real people. And that's great. It's who you are. You know I'd never change you. You *know* that."

Warmth spread though Niles's chest. Sometimes it was easy to lose sight of why Jordan was the closest person in the world to him and always would be. And it wasn't just a matter of identical DNA; Jordan *got* him without ever disapproving or judging.

"You're not wrong," he conceded. "But that's got nothing to do with Tim."

"Sure it does. You forget to protect yourself the same way you forget to feed yourself. Or maybe it's more deliberate than that. Thirty-two years and I still can't figure out if you just forget to be suspicious, or if you refuse to because you find that trusting takes less effort. Whatever it is, you always want to give people the benefit of the doubt, which leaves you wide open. That's not a complaint." Jordan held up a hand, forestalling Niles's protest. "Sometimes I really envy you that, the way you look at the world with such optimism and trust. It must be nice. But it makes you vulnerable, and right now, someone is trying to slip past that vulnerability and hurt you. You can't ask me not to react to that. I couldn't, even if I wanted to."

"So what you're saying is, this isn't about Tim at all. He just makes a convenient punching bag."

Jordan shrugged. "It's not like I don't owe him."

Niles snorted a soft laugh. "If anyone owes him a few cheap shots, it's me. But I'm not going to do that. And I can't really figure out whether or not this thing with him is going to work if the two of you keep posturing at each other. So back down. Let me handle it."

"I already agreed to that part." Jordan swung his foot from where his leg was hitched up on the desk, nudging Niles's knee and pushing his chair back. "Let's get some lunch."

Niles considered refusing, but the words on his computer

made no more sense than they had before Jordan had arrived. He shut his laptop and stood, stretching until a series of pops zipped up his spine. "Sure. Anywhere is better than here right now."

There was an armed security guard stationed in the front lobby near the receptionist, a sight that made Niles grimace. No wonder the studio felt different now: everyone was working knowing a man with a gun was sitting outside the office waiting for trouble to arrive, while a similarly armed woman patrolled the building and grounds. Next week there would be metal detectors installed and a fence erected around the employee parking lot, with a key-card-controlled gate.

"Let it go, Niles," Jordan murmured, clapping him on the shoulder as he came to a standstill and looked around the lobby as if he'd never seen the place before. "This is what has to happen. Right now we need you and Rosie safe."

"I don't like it."

Jordan sighed and gave the guard—who had no doubt over-heard Niles's remarks—an apologetic smile, then opened the door to let them out into the gray afternoon. "I know you don't. But Rosie's going to do what she has to do in order to protect you and herself and everyone else here."

"Yeah, but—"

"No buts," Tim interjected, and Niles spun to see him standing beside the door, evidently lying in wait. "Hey. Payne and I are taking a break from combing through the game—she needs to go conduct some interviews—so I thought I'd ask if you wanted to get lunch, but it looks like you two already have plans."

"You can come with us," Jordan offered before Niles could even open his mouth. He turned to flash his brother a grateful smile over his shoulder.

"Unless 'lunch' is code for a nooner," Jordan added. "Then I'm out of here."

Niles chuckled. "No, I'm pretty sure we're all talking about food. Let's go."

"So, how's the investigation going?" Jordan asked Tim as Niles fell into step between them.

"I asked my captain to take me off the case, but he just made Payne the lead detective and told me to tread very lightly and stay away from anything to do with Niles's ex. Which is why I'm taking notes for her today and why she's going to interview Anthony Joyner without me."

And just like that, Tim and Jordan were chatting like they hadn't been bristling and snarling at each other twelve hours ago. Niles shook his head and let them talk without interruption. Trying to make sense of it would be useless.

———

JORDAN HAD LEFT twenty minutes ago to get back to work— something about a conference call—but Tim was willing to bet that he was offering Niles and Tim some alone time before lunch was over. Which Tim fully intended to take advantage of, at least until Payne called. With a rueful smile, Niles murmured something about going to get the car, which they'd been forced to park a couple blocks away, while Tim stepped around the corner of the pub to talk with Payne under the sheltering eaves.

"*Niles?*"

Tim jerked at the vaguely familiar voice calling out Niles's name with a note of desperation. He managed to place the voice just as Niles's sharp response floated around the building toward him.

"What do you want, Anthony?"

"I want to know what the hell is going on!" came the angry reply. "The police came by—"

"You *there*, Wyatt?" Payne's question was impatient enough to suggest she'd already asked a couple of times.

"I'm here, Payne." He pitched his voice low. "So is Anthony Joyner. I can hear him talking to Niles now. He sounds upset."

"Shit. Where are you?"

"Outside the Lucky Labrador on Quimby."

"I'm sending a car and am on my way." The phone beeped the disconnect signal before Tim could respond. Reaching inside his jacket to unsnap his holster, he peered around the corner of the building to see Niles's ex blocking his way. He had to hold tight if he could, until Payne or the patrol got there. If he joined in, it would likely escalate the matter.

"How the hell did you even know I was here?" Niles demanded.

"The GPS tracker on your phone." Joyner said it casually, as though stalking his ex's whereabouts was a completely rational thing to do. "Niles, why do the police think I know anything about some girls being killed after a convention?"

"That's between you and the police, Anthony. I really can't talk to you about it." Niles attempted to walk past him, but Joyner sidestepped to block his way again. "Anthony, just let me pass. Now."

"They all but insinuated that I killed some guy you had a date with a couple weeks ago!"

"Well, did you?" Niles shot the question back so quickly it was almost reflexive, and Tim winced. *So much for not talking to him about it.*

"How can you ask me that?" Joyner was nearly shouting now. Passersby were turning to stare at them. One big guy decked out in spandex and Gore-Tex stopped and got off his bike. He propped it against a light post and attempted to intervene.

"Hey, everything okay here—"

"Back off!" Joyner screamed, his rain-dampened hair straggling down his furiously red face. He took an aggressive step toward the cyclist, and there went any chance Tim had of staying out of the scene.

Tim strode out from his vantage point and closed the distance between them, his hands held out in a placating gesture. "Hey, whoa, let's take a deep breath and calm down," he said, trying to keep his voice firm but nonconfrontational. "Can you back up, give Niles and the bystander some room to breathe?"

"You again! Who the fuck *is* this guy, Niles?" Joyner's frantic eyes flew back and forth between him and Niles.

Niles raised his hands, mirroring Tim's conciliatory posture. "Anthony, settle down. This is Tim Wyatt. He's a detective and a friend. He's been trying to help—"

"Oh, so this is a setup!" Joyner dragged his hands through his hair, making it spike wildly. The bicyclist had the sense to move out of the way, and Tim took a step back as Niles's ex turned his anger toward him. He kept his smile pasted on and his posture open, even though Joyner's aggression was hitting all his protective and self-preservation instincts. But trying to defuse the situation was his only option. Drawing his weapon wasn't even a consideration as long as Joyner appeared unarmed. "Is this how you get rid of the competition? Frame them for a crime they didn't commit?"

Niles groaned. "Jesus, Anthony, don't be so dramatic." The weary, scornful tone behind the mutter was so unlike Niles that it distracted Tim for a split second.

"Nobody is framing you, Joyner. We just want to find out who killed those people."

"*Fuck you!* This is your fault!" Tim tried to step back as Joyner charged him, but Joyner was too close. He rammed into Tim, sending him stumbling off the curb between two parked cars. Tim took Joyner with him as he tried to catch one of Joyner's wildly swinging arms. When he got a hold, he twisted it into a wristlock behind Joyner's back. Before Tim could shove him forward over the hood of one of the cars, however, Joyner managed to get his feet up on the bumper and push back off it, making Tim stagger backward, out from between the cars and into the street. Without Tim blocking his momentum, Joyner tumbled after him.

Niles's alarmed shout, the screech of tires, Joyner's pained cry, and the snap of breaking bones all mingled with a flood of pain *everywhere*. He was on the pavement with no recollection of landing, the traces of gas and oil on the street riding on top of the puddles in an iridescent film right before his eyes. Somewhere nearby, Joyner was groaning, and he could hear sirens in the distance. Mostly, though, he could hear Niles.

"Tim— Oh shit! Jesus, Tim!" He was close. Those knees that hit the wet asphalt right by Tim's face, did they belong to Niles? It hurt too much to try to move his head to find out.

"Don't move him, sir! Wait for the paramedics. I need to check on the other guy." That voice wasn't familiar. The cyclist?

His entire body ached and stung, but the pain seemed to be concentrated in his left shoulder and upper chest, sending throbbing rings of agony through his body as if that spot was the epicenter of a one-man earthquake. He tried to find the breath to reassure Niles, but it hurt too damn much to inhale.

The shining pavement, the wet denim covering Niles's knees, the buzz of gathering gawkers all mingled in a gray blur that stole vision and time, and when Tim managed to focus again, Payne's authoritative voice was cutting through the cacophony, snapping orders, instructing someone to push back the crowd. Another wash of gray, and then Tim was on his back staring up at the sky, and there was a paramedic hovering over him trying to get him to answer questions.

"Jordan," he finally managed to whisper, though it felt like red-hot bands of agony were constricting his ribs, making speech impossible.

"What?" Niles's short laugh was sharp with astonished disbelief. "You want *Jordie*?"

His thoughts blurred together like the scenery, all one big

confusing muddle with fear at the center. Someone needed to stick by Niles until they found out who was gunning for him, in case it wasn't Joyner after all. "Look after you."

That laugh sounded more like a sob. "Goddamn it, Tim."

Then there was a lurch, another gray tidal wave of pain knocking loose his tenuous hold on awareness. Trying to draw a deep breath and control the pain only seemed to make it worse. When he opened his eyes again, the leaden sky had been replaced by the organized chaos that always seemed to line the inside of an ambulance, and Niles was gone.

CHAPTER 19

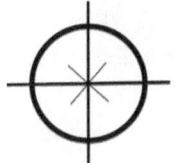

Niles was pale and visibly shaken when Jordan caught sight of him in the emergency waiting room. He clutched his jacket around him as though he was freezing, and he trembled when he threw himself into Jordan's hug.

"Hey, what's the news? How's Tim?" he murmured in Niles's ear, rubbing his back briskly.

"They're still doing neurological tests." Niles sank down into the ugly and uncomfortable chairs again, and Jordan followed suit, keeping his arm around his brother. "Three cracked ribs, broken collarbone, a dislocated shoulder . . . He's probably going to need reconstructive surgery on his ear because the skid across the pavement almost tore it off too, and they need to assess the extent of the head injury. They think it's just a mild concussion, but you know they have to do scans and, and . . ." Niles's brow furrowed, a confused look coming over his face as if he had no idea what he'd been talking about. "Uh, scans and shit, you know?"

"Yeah, I know." Jordan kissed Niles's temple, holding him close. "What about Anthony?"

"Um . . ." Niles shook his head, the effort to change tracks and think of something else clear in his expression. "A car went right over his leg, snapped both bones below the knee. The impact also broke his arm, and there might be some spinal damage. At least that's what I overheard. No one will tell me anything about him."

"Shit." He rested his forehead against Niles's, the images behind his eyelids those of Niles being the one thrown across the pavement, crushed under a car. If it had been, Anthony would be a dead man right now. "You're okay?"

Niles snorted as Jordan drew back to look him up and down, assuring himself of Niles's well-being. "I'm fine. No one touched me. Anthony was just upset, you know. I don't think he was trying to hurt anyone. He just was *afraid* because the police were questioning him—" Niles's voice cracked, and Jordan pulled him into another tight hug. "It wasn't him, Jordie. It wasn't! Our relationship may have gone to shit, but I know him well enough that I don't believe he could have faked being that confused. He didn't harm anyone. He doesn't *deserve* any of this."

"Shh. No one deserves this." Jordan swayed, rocking Niles. "It was just an accident. It has nothing to do with anyone deserving anything. Okay?"

A pair of feet in fluorescent-accented shoes disrupted the stretch of tile Jordan was staring at, and he followed them up legs encased in tight spandex biking pants to an almost unreasonably tall man, who blinked in surprise at the sight of him.

"Um, I brought coffee, for Niles." He held out a cup, and Jordan released Niles to allow him to take it.

"Thanks, Rhett," Niles murmured, sitting up straighter. He took a long drink, then seemed to remember himself. "Jordie, this is Everett Abrams, he stopped to help just before the accident. Rhett, this is my brother, Jordan."

A brisk handshake and a polite greeting later, Jordan's hand was still tingling from the contact and the cyclist was shifting impatiently from foot to foot, looking between them. "Niles, man, I hate to run out on you, but now that your brother is here, I really need to get to work. You guys gonna be okay?"

Niles nodded, clutching his coffee. "Sure, Rhett. Thanks for helping. Sorry for disrupting your day."

"Hey, don't worry about that." Abrams waved his hand negligently. "I was happy to help. Not that I did much, really. Um, look, I already gave Detective Payne and the officers who showed up at the accident my statement and contact information, but here, just in case anyone else needs it . . ." He dug into a zipped pocket of his Gore-Tex jacket and pulled out a business card. His eyes flicked between them for a second before he clearly decided Niles wasn't in any state of mind to keep track of minutiae, and offered it to Jordan. "Just give me a call if there's anything I can do."

"Thanks," Jordan said soberly, holding his gaze while Niles echoed the sentiment. Abrams lingered a moment longer, then spun on his heel and left.

Once he was gone, Niles curled up against Jordan again—as much as the waiting room chairs would allow, at least—and sipped his coffee in anxious silence. Rapid footfalls on the linoleum tile grabbed their attention, and they looked up to see Detective Payne striding toward them, cutting through the slowly growing crowd of uniforms as Tim's comrades arrived to show their support and get updates.

"How is he?" Niles demanded, springing to his feet.

"He's okay." Her normally blunt voice was soft as she sat down. "Sedated for now. He was in a lot of pain, but they don't think there's going to be any significant neurological trauma." She snorted. "I coulda told 'em that. My daddy had a chopping block in his butcher shop softer than Wyatt's head."

Her joke had its apparently intentional effect and drew a smile from Niles. Her teeth flashed in a wide grin before she grew serious again. "There won't be any charges against Anthony Joyner. Well, aside from assaulting a cop."

Niles nodded his acceptance of that. "He's been cleared."

"Yeah. He had some airtight alibis for the times when Charity Anspach, Lakshmi Agrawal, and Daniel Fortesen were all killed. Namely, you."

"*Me?*" Niles squawked. Jordan's shoulders tightened, matching the tension rising in his brother's body.

"You." Detective Payne paused to open an energy drink and chugged half of it down. "He was keeping pretty close tabs on you, Niles. That's why he was reluctant to answer my questions when I interviewed him this morning; he had something to hide, just not what we thought it might be. You could call it stalking, and you wouldn't be wrong, but receipts, GPS tracking of your phone, even some pictures he took of you leaving the convention and going to the club the next night confirm that he wasn't with any of our victims around the time they died."

"So all this was for nothing," Niles said, ire gathering beneath his deceptively weary tone. "Anthony was pushed into a panic, and Tim is injured. They both could have died, and it hasn't accomplished a damn thing."

Jordan gripped his brother's shoulder and squeezed. "Niles, you can't blame them for investigating a likely lead—"

"No, but maybe someone should fucking listen to me when I say I know what someone I've been close to is and isn't capable of. I *told* Tim it wasn't Anthony." Niles jerked away from Jordan's grasp and stood, glaring back and forth between them both. "You like to act like I'm some naive little lamb, Jordie, but I'm not stupid. There'd be a couple less people in the hospital right now if someone would credit my fucking judgment for once."

There was a flash of something that looked an awful lot like guilt in Niles's eyes before he spun and stalked away. Jordan sighed, slumping in his chair for a moment before pushing himself up to follow. "Excuse me, Detective."

———

WELL, *did you?*

The insinuation he'd snapped at Anthony earlier, the moment of suspicion and doubt, kept replaying in his mind. Maybe Anthony wouldn't have gone off on Tim if Niles hadn't all but accused him.

He drew a deep breath in the chilly mist outside the ER entrance, scrubbing his face with his hands. Even in his jacket, he was shivering; the temperature was dropping pretty quickly, and there was talk of the possibility of the snow level falling to five hundred feet, which meant the areas of high elevation in Portland could get hit. He'd have to stock up on supplies just in case, since his house rested just on the edge of where downtown Portland began to rise into the West Hills.

He felt Jordan standing at his shoulder before he even registered the *swoosh* of the doors opening behind him.

"I accused him, you know," Niles volunteered before his brother could demand an explanation. "I was starting to buy into all the suspicion and mistrust."

"That's not a bad thing, Niles. It might not be Anthony, but someone *is* threatening you. It doesn't make you a bad person to be a little wary right now."

He closed his eyes, shaking his head. He couldn't make them see without sounding irredeemably gullible himself. "Don't you get it? Didn't you feel it at the office today? How everything is *different*? A couple days ago we were all together, working toward a goal we all believed in, trying to *accomplish* something. And now everyone is side-eyeing everyone else, we've got people with guns in the office, and all the camaraderie is gone. That's not what I helped Rosie build. That's not the world I want to live in."

"It's the only world we've got right now, bro." Jordan's arms came around him, and he turned to hug his brother tightly. Jordan was right, of course. The atmosphere at work was the last thing he should be worrying about, but everything else was just too immense to consider. "We'll stop whoever is doing this, whoever is hurting people, and then you can help Rosie pick up the pieces of what's left and build that world you want again."

Niles sighed and buried his face in his brother's shoulder. "You were wrong, Jordie."

"Not that I doubt it, but which specific instance are we talking about?"

"When you said trusting takes less effort. It's not easy." He drew back to look into Jordan's eyes. "Every day I have to remind myself that I'm not going to be that guy who thinks the worst about everyone he comes across. If you think that doesn't take effort, you're wrong."

Jordan didn't answer. He just stared at Niles for a long moment, then acknowledged the point with a nod and pulled him back into another strong hug. And Niles let him.

———

"You know, I had a thought." Rosie looked over her shoulder toward the bank of gaming rigs on the other side of her office. It was ridiculously late, but Angie had asked Rosie if she could come straight from the hospital. She seemed determined to make as much progress as she could through the *PF3* beta.

"What's that?" Angie sounded distracted, but Rosie had worked with gamers for well over a decade and was used to conversing with people whose minds were at least halfway in another world.

"You said you still haven't found Charity's and Lakshmi's computers or phones, no trace of their social circle. You've been looking for posts about their cosplay on the Third Wave and Phoenix Force beta forums and other fan sites. But maybe we need to go more meta than that."

Angie's left hand flicked the ESC key to pause the game, and she swiveled around in her chair. "I'm listening."

"Well, there's no way those ladies didn't show off their

cosplay. Trust me on this. If they went to all that trouble to create those incredible costumes, they were going to put the pictures up. They just didn't do it in the usual places."

"So where do you recommend we look?"

"Charity was a women's studies major, right? Particularly focused on modern media. Was Lakshmi in any classes with her? Or Keilana Savanh?"

Angie shook her head. "Lakshmi was enrolled at University of Portland, not PSU, and Keilana was going to PCC with the intention of transferring to the nursing program at OHSU. We thought there might be some connection there, because Charity was a nurse's aide, but we haven't found it yet. We don't even know how Charity and Lakshmi met, because their families have no clue. And we can't find a connection between them and Keilana at all."

"Her computer and phone were missing too?"

"No, but she'd wiped them before she killed herself, apparently using some sort of data-eating virus, and did a pretty good job of it. Our techs have managed to recover some of the data, but nothing we've found useful yet. No links to your game or forums. She did appear to have one anime interest in common with Charity, but neither of them seem to have been active in it for a couple years, and we haven't found any sign of them interacting through those fan circles." Angie frowned, looking disgusted. "I just do not get how three young women can go so completely unnoticed that no one knows what they did."

"How does a prenursing student know how to wipe a computer and phone that thoroughly?"

"Yeah, we've already asked ourselves that question down at the precinct. Aside from her parents' claim that she wouldn't kill herself, it's the best indication we've got that her death isn't a cut-and-dried suicide."

"Okay. So, what if their connection wasn't a game or a fandom, but a cause?" Rosie drew a knee up to her chest, planting her foot on the seat of her chair. "When Anita Sarkeesian of Feminist Frequency began a Kickstarter campaign to do a series of web documentaries about female tropes in video games, the backlash was tremendous and hugely toxic. A lot of that, tragic as it is to say, is the cost of doing business as a woman in the gaming industry. I've gotten the same treatment, and so has every other female writer or producer of games that I know of."

Angie nodded. "Okay, sounds bad, but what's that got to do with our four dead bodies?"

"Well, it gets especially vitriolic when a woman makes a specific goal public, particularly one that threatens the male-privileged status quo. There's nothing they won't sink to in order to shut up a woman shining a spotlight in the dark and creepy corners of the genre."

Angie blinked slowly. "You think Charity had a project."

"Yeah." Rosie wiped her hands on her thighs, trying to bring her pulse down. It had been a long time since the almost pro forma harassment that came with being a woman in gaming had caused her anxiety attacks, but this was all bringing it back up. "Convention harassment has been big news in geek circles lately. That day at the convention, I *saw* Charity being harassed. What if she was working on a paper for one of her classes? What if the cosplay wasn't a product of her involvement in fandom so much as it was some undercover reporting?"

"Her adviser never mentioned anything like that, but then her adviser might not have known. Maybe she hadn't told anyone what her thesis was gonna be." Angie's eyes took on the same smoldering determination that Rosie felt burning in her own chest. Part of her felt bad for unloading on Detective Wyatt that morning, but somehow it had helped her find her drive again.

Angie whipped out her phone and dialed. "Bryan, it's Payne. I need you to start searching for message boards and sites dealing specifically with women in gaming and convention harassment. I want you to look for anyone seeking volunteers for projects or papers on the subject of cosplay and harassment. Then I need you to trace those posts back and see if they lead to one of our victims."

Rosie closed her eyes and rested her forehead on her knee as she listened to the detective's rapid-fire dialog with her computer forensics tech. The aching knot behind her ribs that had been there since the day she learned of the murders began to loosen. Those beautiful young women weren't going to die without justice. Whether or not Third Wave Studios and *PF3* were going to survive the turmoil and bad publicity—and suddenly keen scrutiny of their parent company—she couldn't say. Hell, *she* might not even survive the whole thing. But at least they would have justice.

CHAPTER 20

The phone on his desk beeped, and Niles swore, hating his life. Most of the day had been a waste. He couldn't focus on his work because he still couldn't shake his awareness of the presence of armed guards on the premises. Every couple of hours he'd see a patrol car pull into the parking lot through his office window, and a uniformed cop would go to the lobby to check in with the hired security stationed there.

It was fucking unreal. Sooner or later, reason was going to set in and they would realize they'd all made a mistake, that he and Rosie weren't the targets of a killer after all. Patrick would show up alive and well and with some crazy story about how, one night, he enthusiastically embraced his sexuality and spent the week in Vegas with male escorts watching drag revues.

Niles had just finally managed to get a good rhythm going on the next DLC script, and now he was going to have to find his concentration all over again thanks to the damn phone. Which would make it that much longer until he could leave and go check on Tim, who was—according to his text messages—climbing the walls on the third day of his hospital stay.

"What is it, Thad?" he asked the receptionist after turning on the speakerphone with a sharp punch of his finger.

"Hey, there are a couple guys up in the lobby here who say they've come to collect Patrick's stuff from his desk. Should I let them in?"

"What?" A quick glance at his clock answered Niles's question before he had a chance to ask it. It was almost a quarter after five; the guard stationed in the lobby would have gone home for the day, and the night guard was probably doing rounds, which was how they'd handled the shift change the past couple days since Rosie had hired them. For that matter, Thad should already have left by now. "Jesus Christ. Are they already declaring him presumed dead?"

"I've been keeping an eye on the news. They say the search is still ongoing."

"Is his family giving up on him?" That thought felt like a knife to the chest, but then just about any thought of Patrick these days felt that way.

"I . . . don't know." There was a heavy, saddened note in Thad's voice. "Should I ask these guys to come back?"

"No." He closed his eyes, pinching the bridge of his nose. "His family has to be worried sick about him. If collecting his stuff from his desk is what they need to do to deal with it, I'm not going to make this any harder on them than it already is. I'll be there in a minute to let them in."

In accordance with the new office security policies—at least those in place until the metal detectors could be installed—Thad had kept the visitors standing outside until their entrance could be approved, so Niles got a good look at them through the glass doors. He recognized Patrick's stepbrother from the convention and the few other glimpses he'd caught. The other guy, though, wasn't familiar. He was dressed in a trench coat with a fedora pulled low over his brow like some sort of film noir tribute. If not for the fact that these guys were no doubt having a hard time with Patrick's disappearance, Niles might have looked askance at that particular fashion choice.

The stepbrother was shifting nervously from foot-to-foot outside the door. The fedora-wearing one, however, looked suitably grim.

"Shit," Niles whispered and closed his eyes against the dread. He didn't want to do this. He drew a bracing breath and pushed open the door to let them inside. "Come in, gentlemen. You're Patrick's brother, right? I'm Niles River. I'm Patrick's supervisor."

"We know who you are," the other guy said as the stepbrother entered. "He's Charlie Pryce, and I'm Mike. I'm Charlie's cousin and leader of the Soldiers of Justice guild."

Niles blinked. He felt the need to introduce himself by his guild title? "Um, I see. I just want to say how sorry I am for what your family must be dealing with. All of us here are hoping Patrick will still come home safely."

"Right," fedora-wearing Mike scoffed and stuffed his hand in his pocket. Niles tensed. The dude was making him jumpy. He was acting angry, rather than worried. "It's because of you people that he's gone. Charlie's dad wants us to get his stuff, and when and if Patrick comes back, we're going to make sure he never has anything to do with your company again."

Niles flinched, the accusation spearing him right where his own self-doubt had already gnawed a weak spot. It was their fault Patrick was missing, and that four other people were dead.

"I'm sorry," he murmured, unable to look at them. "If there's anything else I can do to help—"

"Just show us to his desk," Mike said.

"Of course. Thad, let Rosie know I'm going to help them collect Patrick's stuff, then head on home if you want. It's late. I'll handle this."

"Um, Niles, can I . . .?" Thad jerked his head to the side. "Can I talk to you a moment?"

"Sure. Excuse me, gentlemen." He followed Thad through the security door to the inner office and let it close behind them, the electronic latch engaging. "What is it?"

Thad shifted nervously. "I just— Rosie and the security guys gave me a procedure I'm supposed to follow to the letter now when we have visitors in the building. I'm not supposed to let them in until the guard clears them."

"They're the family of a victim. I don't want to give them a hard time. They're going through enough."

"Yeah, I don't, either, but I'm supposed to follow the security procedure. Maybe if the guard were here—"

"Is she still out on her rounds?"

"Yeah, but she should be back soon, and if the cops are on schedule, they should be checking in in another half hour or so."

"Right. Damn. That doesn't help us just now."

"I can call her cell, tell her we need her back here."

Niles blew his breath out in a long, slow sigh, scrubbing a hand through his hair. "I don't want to put you in a bad position, Thad. I get that you have a job to do. So tell you what, you give her a call, and we'll seat them in the visitor's conference room off the lobby while I box up Patrick's stuff and bring it out. Just . . . do what you can to make sure they feel welcome, okay?"

"Sure, Niles." Thad nodded readily, relief evident on his face. Niles straightened his shoulders and opened the door to return to the lobby.

Mike and Charlie came to their feet from where they'd been sprawled in the lobby chairs as he approached. "I'm sorry, only authorized visitors are allowed back in the studio. It's for security reasons; we have to make sure all our people are safe. I'm sure you understand that. If you want to make yourselves comfortable, I'll go pack up everything from Patrick's desk and bring it to you."

"How do we know you'll bring it all?" Mike asked.

Niles glanced at Patrick's stepbrother, who had yet to speak up, but he had his hands stuffed in his pockets and his eyes on his cousin. It was clear to see who was alpha in that dynamic. "You can go through the box, let me know if anything is missing."

Mike's tone sharpened, became a little more belligerent. "I don't see why we just can't go back there."

"If it were up to me, I'd be happy to let you, but after what's happened to Patrick and the fact that we have other people here who have been threatened, we've had to institute security procedures." He opened the door to the conference room and turned on the light, gesturing them inside. "I'm very sorry. I'll be back shortly."

The two exchanged unhappy glances, and then brushed past him. Charlie flung himself into a chair with a disgusted sigh. Niles reminded himself of the incredible stress Patrick's family must be under and left the conference room, leaving the door partially ajar.

"Did you get ahold of the guard?" he asked as he passed Thad's desk, where he was shutting down his computer.

"Yeah, she was checking out a noise in the warehouse. She'll be back in a moment."

Niles nodded. "Okay. See if they want something to drink. They're going through an ordeal right now."

"Will do."

"Thanks." Niles tried to muster a grateful smile, but the best he could manage was a grimace. Sighing, he dug his key card out of his pocket and swiped it to go back into the studio.

———

"Hey, Rosie?"

Rosie looked up to see Niles standing in her doorway, his expression somber. "What's up?"

"Patrick's family is here. They want to collect his stuff from his desk."

"Ah, Jesus." She scratched her scalp, closing her eyes for a moment at the sharp surge of grief. "Has it really gotten to that point?"

"They could still find him alive . . ." Niles said, a wistful, hopeful note in his voice. "Couldn't they?"

She opened her eyes and smiled gently at him. Her poor, wounded, idealistic best friend. "How do you want me to answer that? Realistically or encouragingly?"

His shoulders slumped. "Never mind. They're in the visitor conference room if you want to go out and say something to them, but they're a bit hostile. They blame us for what happened to Patrick. I can sorta see where they're coming from."

"Hey, no. None of that." She rose and rounded her desk to hug him quickly. "We're not responsible for the actions of the person or people doing this. Don't blame yourself."

"Right. Yeah." Niles's mouth twisted bitterly. "I guess I'll go pack up Patrick's things. Thad's taking care of them, and the security guard knows they're here."

"All right. I think if I try to say anything to them, it will just make things worse, so I'm going to stay out of it. Come see me when you're done."

She stared at the door a moment after Niles left, frowning. Of course, they should have expected someone to come clear out Patrick's desk, but this was going to hit Niles hard, and Jordan had left early for a meeting with some suits from the PR department at Electronic Entertainment Unlimited, who were all still frantically trying to strategize spin control.

Hell, maybe Niles was right that everything they'd worked to build was slipping away. If it was, Rosie didn't have the first idea how to stop it. It was hard to even worry all that much about her own safety when she could see the possibility of the work she'd poured her heart and soul into crumbling.

Or maybe it was that she'd been living with insubstantial threats so long that real ones didn't *feel* real. She knew Niles struggled with that too. There was a disconnect, a place where they had conditioned themselves to ignore the hostility as background noise, and even knowing people had died didn't quite cut through that sense of unreality.

Her cell rang, and Angie Payne's name and number flashed on the screen. She picked it up, shaking off the morbid thoughts. "Hey, Angie, what's up?"

"We found our girls," Angie said. "You were right. Charity and Lakshmi hung out on some obscure feminist media criticism blog where they talked about Charity's project. They were recruiting volunteers to attend conventions in other cities and add their stories to the study. And that's where they met Keilana Savanh."

"So there was a connection." Rosie blew out a slow breath.

Angie sighed. "Yes and no. It still looks like Keilana committed suicide, but the posts on the blog indicate that she'd been the target of a bunch of harassment from some former gaming companions of hers for nearly a year. Apparently they had some boys-only guild in one of the multiplayer games, and when they found out she was a woman behind the avatar, they came after her. Nonstop emails and texts, same sort of shit you've been showing me for days."

"Ahh, the song of my people," Rosie said bitterly.

"We think that might be the source of the virus that wiped her computer, not any attempt on her part to clean it before she killed herself. We're tracking that down, to see if there's a connection between her harassers and Charity or Lakshmi. We don't have any answers yet, but this brings us a step closer, and we wouldn't have looked for it if not for your insight, so thank you."

That was a badly needed shot of validation at just the right moment. Too bad she couldn't do something similar for Niles.

"You're welcome." She turned the phone on speakerphone and began digging through her emails as she spoke. "I don't know shit about criminal justice, but I can say without ego that if you need more information on feminist theory and how it pertains to these young women and their activities, I can answer any questions, anytime, and I can point you to a lot of other sources as well."

"I'll keep that in mind. Our techs say we're also close to possibly recovering something off Keilana's computer, so we're holding out hope for a lead there. Meanwhile, I still need to come by the studios to finish my play-through."

"You still think there might be something pertinent in there?"

"Not really, but, girl, I'll be damned if I've sunk that much time into some game and don't finish it." There was an amused note of self-deprecation in Angie's voice, and Rosie found herself laughing for the first time in days.

"This is how it starts, Detective. I'm going to be here late, as usual. Just come by whenever you're off duty. I'll let the security guard know to let you in."

"I'll be by later," Angie replied and disconnected the call.

Tucking her phone away, Rosie focused on her email again. She frowned to see a broadcast message titled "Recent Events" from one of the accounting staff. What the hell was she doing sending a message to the whole company? Damn it, if that email was about Patrick and the murders and it had been sent to everyone, Rosie was going to have her ass.

The moment she clicked on it, her virus software went crazy, trying to isolate and scrub the code and apparently having a hard time with it. She quickly turned off her laptop manually, bypassing the shutdown process, before it could do any more damage.

"Fuck," she muttered, crossing to the bank of gaming rigs on the wall and shutting them down. She snatched her phone off her desk, hitting the speed dial for their IT manager at home as she rushed out into the open floor of cubicles outside her office to begin making sure all the computers were shut down.

CHAPTER 21

Niles growled as he set the box of Patrick's belongings on the reception counter, staring with disbelief at the empty conference room where he'd left Patrick's stepbrother and Cousin Fedora.

"You've got to be kidding me."

"Problem?" He turned to see the night security guard—what was her name, Reina? Rena?—come in from the blustery night.

"Did you see our visitors take off?"

"I was back checking that the warehouse was secure. I had to finish up after I got Thad's call."

Niles sighed. "Yeah. Do me a favor and hang out here in case they come back for this box of stuff. It belongs to the intern who's missing, and his stepbrother and cousin are here to collect it. One of them's wearing a fedora and trench coat. You can't miss them." He turned to swipe his card and punch his code into the door again, opening it and calling down the hall. "Hey, Thad? Where'd you go?"

"Down here in the break room!"

Niles glanced through the doorway to the empty maze of cubicles he thought he'd heard someone working in before, but there was no sign of anyone. The back of his neck prickled as he continued down the hall, reaching the break room just as Thad was emerging with an airpot hanging from his hand.

"Hey," the receptionist said with a smile. "Those guys wanted coffee, so I decided to make some fresh. I started another pot for you and Rosie in there too, and I'll bring this one back after they leave."

"It looks like they already took off, Thad, but thanks. Why don't you head on home? I'll rinse out the airpots before I go. Thanks for the coffee."

"They took off?" Thad gave him a disgusted look. "Jeez, what kind of assholes ask you to make fresh coffee and then bug out before you're done?"

"Maybe something important came up. Do you think there's been news about Patrick?" He tried to damp down the flare of hope and fear in his chest, but he needed to get to his office and call Tim for an update, *now*.

Please, God, just let him be okay.

"Oh God. Right. Scratch that asshole comment." Thad looked sheepish.

Niles waved it off, the idea of finding out if there had been a development in the case becoming an obsession. "Have a good night, okay?"

"Yeah, sure, Niles. Thanks." Thad handed off the full airpot and returned to the lobby.

Niles looked at the airpot in his hands and turned briskly to take it back to the break room, digging for his phone once he'd set it down. Tim answered on the first ring, which said a lot about how antsy his convalescence was making him.

"Tim? Hey, it's me. Is there any news about Patrick?"

"What? No, not that I've heard of. Why?"

He sighed, his heart sinking. "Nothing. Never mind. I was being stupid. I just had the crazy idea that there might be. I'll come by the hospital later, okay?"

"Sure. You all right?"

He shrugged, though he knew Tim couldn't see it. "Define 'all right.' I'm still breathing. I guess that's a check in the pro column."

"Hang in there, baby. We'll get you through this. Want me to call Payne? Find out if there have been any developments I'm not aware of being laid up here?"

"Sure, that'd be great. I'll see you later."

He hung up before Tim could offer him any more well-meaning encouragement, then braced his hands on the edge of the sink, breathing in and out deeply several times before opening his eyes.

He could do this.

"At least there will be plenty of coffee. That'll make Rosie happy." He retrieved two mugs stamped with the Third Wave logo from a cupboard and filled them. He stared at the cream and sugar a moment, then reached for the seldom-used cupboard above the refrigerator, pulling down a bottle of Baileys and dropping a generous splash into each mug. He'd probably be better off settling in at his desk again and trying to recapture his flow, but he'd been interrupted anyway, so he might as well have a drink.

He ran into her rushing around the maze of cubicles, looking grim.

"Niles, get Thad if he's still here to come help. We need to make sure every computer in this place is shut down, and warn everyone with remote access to company email to not open any broadcast messages. IT has been alerted. There's something in the system, and judging from the way the virus software was struggling with it, it's big and bad."

"Fuck. Thad already left." He set the coffees down on a mail cart outside her office and started searching CubicleLand for computers that were left in standby mode by their users. While he was doing that, he heard Rosie on her phone.

"Angie, it's me. We just had a virus hit our system, and it's huge . . . Exactly, that's what I'm thinking too. It's not something the virus software recognizes, so it's not anything that's already known, which means it's new. Probably custom . . . Yeah, I've got our IT people coming in, but bring your computer guy with you. See you."

Adrenaline spiked when he realized Rosie thought this might have something to do with the murder investigation and the threats, making Niles feel like he'd been punched in the sternum. He *had* heard typing earlier on his way to the lobby. It hadn't been his imagination, and it hadn't been Rosie or Thad. Thad had shut his machine down; Niles had seen him do it. And he'd been on the complete other side of the office space from Rosie's office. It couldn't have been her computer he heard.

Had Charlie and Mike actually left? But they couldn't have gotten into the office, even if they hadn't, right? Thad wouldn't have allowed them back, not with the new security protocols in place.

Unless they'd slipped in somehow when they sent Thad on a phony errand to make coffee . . .

He looked around the maze of cubicles. Fuck, they could be anywhere, waiting for one of them to walk into their hiding space.

"Rosie?" he called, meeting her eyes as she popped up out of a cubicle. He gave her an intense stare, trying to say with his look what he didn't dare say aloud. "I think these are all shut down. Let's go out to the lobby to check Thad's computer and *wait for Angie* and the IT guys."

Those guys would have no idea who Angie was, right? They didn't know the cops were coming. They didn't know there was a security guard in the lobby now, did they?

Rosie opened her mouth as though she was going to ask a question, but then she caught on to Niles's laden stare. Her dark complexion paled a little, and she nodded.

"Just let me grab something out of my office first," she said, and Niles grabbed the cups of spiked coffee off the mail cart and followed her out of the cubicles, waiting in the door and trying to appear normal and unalarmed in case the guys were still skulking around. "Here, I got us coffee. No sense in it going to waste."

Whatever Rosie was about to say in response was forestalled as the tension and concern on her face transformed to full-on alarm. Something sizzled across his collar where his neck and shoulder met, followed by a throbbing burn along the path the initial sharp pain had taken.

As he yelled, Rosie dropped to the floor as if she'd been shot, though there was no sound. The coffee flew from both mugs in an almost graceful, slo-mo arc as he whirled to face whatever had struck him from behind. Which was when another shriek followed Niles's own.

"Fuck! *Fuck! My eyes!*" Patrick's stepbrother toppled over, clutching his coffee-scalded face. A forgotten knife fell from his hands, but before Niles could reach for it, he saw the cousin standing on a desk within one of the cubicles, holding . . .

Was that a *crossbow*?

The anti-cybertech terrorists who attacked Grace and Chino had used bows and knives, his brain supplied uselessly.

"Shut the fuck up, Charlie. It's just coffee. It'll cool down," Mike snarled, sneering at his cousin. He kept the bow trained on Niles. "You. Don't fucking move, queer."

Niles felt the back of his shirt growing cool and wet, and reached for where the junction of his shoulder and neck burned. His hand came away drenched in blood, and looking down, he could see crimson streaks rapidly soaking through the front of his shirt. Fuck, had a crossbow bolt skimmed his shoulder? Was that what hit Rosie?

No. The knife at his feet was bloody. Charlie had cut him. But why had Rosie fallen?

Or had she dived?

"Get up where I can see you, you spic bitch!" Mike called. "Or I'll slit this fag's throat."

Pressing his hand against his wound, Niles watched Rosie rise from behind her desk, her hands in the air. "I'm here. There's no reason to hurt him."

Mike sneered. "Fucking cunt. Diving for cover, hiding under the desk. You talk like you think you can fight, but when you have to stand up to a real man, you hide like the pussy you are."

Rosie blinked slowly. "Spic. Bitch. Cunt. Pussy. Do you have a single original insult in your vocabulary?" She brought her hands down, lifting her chin as she faced him.

Fuck. Niles could feel the blood slick between his fingers, growing tacky where it had been sitting for a while. How bad had they cut him?

He clenched his jaw and waited for the crossbow bolt to find him.

"There was something in that shit, man! It wasn't just coffee!" Charlie was moaning, huddled on the floor and rubbing his eyes frantically. "Fuck, it burns!"

"I said shut up, you fucktard!" Mike hefted the crossbow up, narrowing his eyes to take aim at Niles.

Rosie scoffed. "These are the guys who have killed four people, maybe five? Seriously? *This* is what you're bringing? You're a pair of fucking cliché buffoons."

"Fuck you, bitch. I gave you a chance to show me some respect. Now I'm gonna make you fuckin' respect me."

"Oh God. Are you honestly going to monologue at me? Just fucking shoot me already." Niles tried to shut her up with the power of his mind, but it wasn't working. Just like the warrior tank she played, she would taunt them and try to draw their fire away from him.

But he wasn't an acolyte with healing spells to close her wounds when she began to bleed. All he could do was slump here uselessly against the wall while he bled out. And he was. He could feel the numbness, the tingling, the darkening of his vision that said he was losing too much blood.

"Get your hands where I can fucking see them!" Mike snapped, and Niles realized he'd actually lost a moment of awareness.

"What? You think I have a Taser stashed in my handbag under my desk?" God. No one did derision like Rosie when she was pissed off. But her eyes cut to Niles quickly, and then back to Mike. "I remember you now. You were in the autograph line at the convention. You tried to make me look at your artwork while you pitched me a game idea. I knew I recognized the style of those drawings."

Jesus, fuck, Rosie, shut up! Niles let himself slip down the wall a little further, moaning.

He should have been frightened. Niles knew he should have been frightened, facing what would no doubt be his final seconds. But instead, he was just fucking pissed off. For the first time in his life, he wanted to commit violence, wanted to smash these fucking losers' heads in for all the ridiculous waste of lives, for the grieving families, for the pain and fear those young women must have felt before they died. For Rosie, facing off against them so bravely like she did every day of her life, and for Jordie who would lose the other half of himself, and for Tim who would never know Niles was already well on his way to falling in love with him again. And for what? It made no fucking sense, and he just wanted to scream his rage and bludgeon these two punks to death.

"You should have paid attention when you had the chance, bitch," Mike snarled, and Rosie rolled her eyes.

"There was nothing to pay attention to. Your art was okay, but your game idea was some of the most unimaginative, uninspired shit I've ever seen." She huffed a humorless laugh. "Is that really what this is all about? I hurt your poor widdle feelings so you had a fit of nerd rage? Wow. You must have been eating your guts out, knowing Patrick was working for me and you never would."

Niles could feel the blood dripping from the wound on his shoulder. It was bad, but stopping the bleeding was the least of his worries. It didn't matter if the gesture was futile or not; there was no fucking way he was going to die cowering before some sexist, homophobic bully.

He met Rosie's eyes, then flopped over, grunting as he hit the floor. A surge of blood rushed from his wound and down his chest as he crumpled, half on his stomach, half on his side, along the floor between Rosie's door and her desk.

"Oh fuck, Niles? *Niles*?"

Rosie scurried around the desk and dropped to her knees beside him, effectively shielding his upper body from their view as she bent over him. Her hands fluttered around his back and torso as if she didn't know what to do for him. "Jesus, I think he's bleeding to death. I need to call the ambulance. *Please*."

"Yeah, that's it. Not so badass now. Beg like the fucking bitch you are. He's gonna bleed to death, all right. You both are."

Niles reached under her desk and just barely snagged the strap of her handbag. Half the contents were already spilled across the floor. Clearly she'd been digging through it when Mike had ordered her to get up.

He fumbled blindly, trying to move only his fingers, not to give any hint that he wasn't unconscious on the floor, until he felt something hard and boxy. He pulled it out and shoved it toward Rosie's knee where it would still be hidden by her body as she hovered over him.

"Please—" Her voice cracked dramatically. "Look, I'll do anything. Just let me call for help."

Her fingers shook as they brushed his, and then she was in motion, swinging around before Niles had a chance to do anything else. He heard a startled cry and a crackle of electricity, and by the time he managed to grab the small cylinder rolling on the floor beside the handbag and then sat up, Fedora Mike was convulsing on the floor with two wires sticking out of him.

"Mike!" Charlie yelled, and somewhere in the process, he'd managed to pick up the knife again. He came charging through the door at Rosie. "Leave him alone!"

Niles rolled to his feet, putting himself between Rosie and Charlie, and he sent a mist of pepper spray into Charlie's already-scalded face. Charlie dropped to the floor, shrieking.

Details were starting to come back with the clarity of the adrenaline-induced fight-or-flight response. Underneath the cacophony, he could hear Rosie's cell phone on the floor where she'd dropped it behind the desk. An emergency operator's tinny voice was calling out. Rosie stooped and brought it to her ear. "I'm here. My coworker is bleeding badly. I need to put the phone down to try to stop the blood, but I'm here."

Niles felt his extremities begin to tingle again and sank back to the floor before he could pass out and fall over.

He didn't hear much after that with the sound of his own pulse roaring in his ears. He felt cold, shivering as Rosie grabbed a hoodie off the hook on her door to press against his shoulder. He vaguely heard Rosie talking to someone and realized the night guard had reached them, no doubt drawn by the screams. Had it really all happened so quickly that she hadn't even had a chance to come running before it was over? Or had it not gotten loud enough for her to be aware there was a problem until the end? Niles thought the guard might have been restraining Fedora Mike, who was still dazed, and the screaming Charlie, but Niles's vision was darkening around the edges again, so he closed his eyes and just focused on the ache where Rosie applied pressure to his wound.

"Jesus, I think he was going for your carotid. Good thing you moved—either that, or he's shit with a knife," she muttered.

He managed to blink his eyes open. "You're okay?"

"Me? I'm fine."

"When I saw you fall, I thought—"

"I dove down behind my desk when I saw someone come up behind you with a knife. I didn't think they saw me so I grabbed my phone and dialed 911. I was trying to get the Taser out of my bag, but I didn't have time."

Niles found himself laughing weakly, even though it hurt. "You're so badass."

"It's why I'm the boss," Rosie said warmly, and he felt her press a kiss to his forehead.

He heard more voices then. Police, he thought, and soon after, Detective Payne joined them. But it was Jordan's voice, sharp with panic and emotion, that he clung to. Jordie was here. He'd be all right. He wouldn't leave Jordie, and Jordie wouldn't leave him. He felt his brother clinging to his hand, refusing to let go even as the paramedics bandaged Niles up and loaded him onto a gurney. That grip allowed him to finally let go and let the shock take over, sending him into oblivion.

CHAPTER 22

T im laced his fingers tightly with Niles's where he sat on the edge of Tim's bed. Niles's left arm was in a sling, apparently to keep him from moving too much and pulling out the stitches at the base of his neck. Those bastards had gotten way too fucking close to killing him while Tim had lain here uselessly in the hospital.

"I don't see how they hoped to get away with it," Rosie was saying from one of the chairs in his hospital room two days after the attack at Third Wave Studios. Jordan stood leaning against the wall near the door, while Payne sat in another chair. Jordan looked as grim and furious as Tim felt.

Payne shrugged. "When he was blubbering and spilling his guts, Tweedle-Dum said they had this story all worked out about how Niles tried to molest them at the convention. He said a jury would be searching for a reason not to convict them for killing—and I quote—'some pervert fag and a feminazi bitch.' Sorry." She cast an apologetic glance at them each in turn.

Tim rubbed his aching head, then pulled his hand away when it encountered the bandage covering his meticulously reconstructed ear. "That doesn't make a lot of sense. They came pretty damn close to pulling off the perfect crime with Charity Anspach and Lakshmi Agrawal. Did they just get cocky?"

"I think they got addicted to the attention," Jordan replied. "The praise they were getting on the forums for that fan art of the murders was pretty intense."

Payne nodded. "Tweedle-Dum seems to think they were heroes. Rebels with a cause or some shit."

"And what does Tweedle-Dee say?" Tim asked.

"Tweedle-Dee was smart enough to keep his mouth shut and lawyer up. Not that it matters. Mike's actually a pretty amazing hacker, apparently, but he didn't wipe his computer before he went on his 'mission' to kill you. Bryan had a bitch of a time cracking into it, but it was all on there. His involvement on several men's rights forums, his posts about the Third Wave agenda, and even videos of Charity and Lakshmi, which he sent in emails and texts to Keilana. Seeing her friends murdered seems to be what finally drove her to suicide after she withstood a year of relentless harassment."

"What about Daniel?" Niles's voice was nearly inaudible, his head bowed. "What did they say about killing Daniel?"

"That's a little more complicated. There was nothing on Mike's computer about that, and Charlie's lawyer showed up before we could get anything out of him." Payne sighed. "But the one thing we were able to get from Mike was that he claims it wasn't them, but he knows who did it."

"Any idea who he's gonna finger for that?" Tim demanded incredulously.

"I'm not sure, but we're looking into the alibis for the other guild members who were here for the convention. The ones who were actually there when Charity and Lakshmi were attacked are already in custody. We're just waiting on extradition from their states of residence." Her mouth twisted. "He thinks he can bargain for immunity on the other charges."

"What?" Tim coughed when his voice approached a yelp,

clearing his throat. "I mean, what? Tell me the DA laughed his way out of the precinct."

"Yeah, there's no way he's going for that. He's pretty sure this is a ploy to try to dodge the one charge that would carry a hate crime penalty. But if Mike's information is good, he might be able to weasel his way into a reduced sentence."

"I don't like that," Niles said grimly. "Bad enough they tried to kill us, but they murdered three people and bullied a fourth into suicide—a crime for which they probably won't ever be charged even though they're guilty as sin."

Tim, surprised by the hard, unforgiving edge in Niles's voice, gave him a sharp look. Then he glanced over to see Jordan watching his brother with concern as well.

"How's Patrick doing?" Tim asked, and Niles flashed him a grateful look.

Angie shrugged. "Still doesn't want to see anyone or answer any questions. He'd been knocked around pretty badly, and he was dehydrated when they found him tied up in Mike's apartment. We're pretty sure they were planning to burn him alive, just like Marc in those drawings, but he'll be okay."

"Why don't we let these guys get some rest?" Jordan said, pushing himself away from the wall. "Niles, you need to get home. We can debrief on all this later, after everyone has healed up a bit."

"Sounds good," Rosie agreed, rising and gathering her coat. "I'm going to go work at home, since my office is a goddamn crime scene. I have a meeting tomorrow with the EEU brass I have to prepare for. They're all shitting themselves about the publicity this is generating, and we've got to convince them it's a good thing somehow." She didn't look much happier than Niles.

Payne followed suit. "I'll go with you. I still need to finish the last act." She narrowed her eyes at Tim when he snickered. "You got something you wanna say, Wyatt?"

"Yeah," Tim shot back with an amused challenge in his voice. "Admit it. You're hooked."

Payne opened and closed her mouth a couple times, then strode for the door. "Shut up," she threw over her shoulder, making them all laugh. Even Niles cracked a smile.

"Niles, you want a ride home?" Jordan asked pointedly as he shrugged into his coat.

Niles shook his head, and anger surged through Tim again as he saw the bandage sticking out from under the collar of the button-down Niles had changed into when they'd released him from the hospital that morning. "No, it's just a few blocks. I'll walk. Clear my mind."

"Okay, bro. I'm going to head over to Rosie's as well, then. We have some stuff to work on." Jordan stepped up and gave Niles a careful hug, ducking to meet Niles's lowered eyes, his expression tender and earnest. "Hey. Get some rest. We're all okay now."

"I'll try," Niles whispered, leaning into his brother a moment before letting go.

When the door closed behind Jordan, and he and Niles were alone, Tim lifted a hand, stroking down Niles's back. "You in there, baby?"

Niles took so long to respond, the answer might as well have been *no*. "I just— I can't shake it."

"Can't shake what?"

"The anger. Until the other night, I never realized I could actually, truly *hate* someone, you know? I don't want to hate *anyone*." He folded his hands in his lap, speaking down to them rather than facing Tim.

"What part are you angry about?"

"All of it. Those dead young women, all the grief and fear Rosie has had to deal with from men like those guys, how they were going to take me away from you before we got a chance to really figure things out." His voice grew tight, and he cleared his throat. "They were going to take me away from Jordie. I can't— I can't imagine trying to live without him, so how on earth was he going to live without me?"

"I don't know," Tim murmured. He pulled on Niles's arm until he finally turned. "C'mere."

Niles settled in carefully beside Tim. The shifting and shuffling hurt, but he refused to so much as grunt until Niles was tucked against his side.

"I don't have any answers, baby," Tim breathed into his soft hair, stroking the side of his face. "I don't know what makes people do things like that, except hate. But I know that no matter how much you hate them, no matter how angry you are, you could never be like them. So let yourself feel the anger for a little while if you need to. It doesn't make you a terrible person. It just makes you human." He kissed Niles's temple. "I'm glad they didn't take you from me."

Niles lifted his head, finally fixing his gaze on Tim. "So, are you in this for the duration?"

Tim blinked. "You mean us?"

"Yeah, us. Because I gotta tell you, I really don't want to fall any further if this is just—"

"Hey. Shh." He pulled Niles to him and kissed him firmly before he could finish the thought, though the abrupt movement hurt. "I'm in, all right? I'm all in."

Niles broke the next kiss to stare at him a moment longer, then nodded once and settled in beside Tim again. "Okay."

Niles fell silent for so long, Tim might have thought he had fallen asleep if not for the fact that his breathing was still quick and irregular. Tim was happy to let him lie there, though he knew soon he would have to ring the nurse's station for some more pain meds. For now, though, he was just grateful to have Niles beside him at all.

He didn't want to burden Niles with the panic he had felt when Payne had called him and informed him that Niles had been attacked. To think that he'd just barely begun to make use of the second chance he had been given with Niles, only to lose him, was more than Tim wanted to consider. Ten years ago, he'd been stupid enough not to hang on when he had Niles in his arms like this. He wasn't going to make that mistake again.

"I love you," he whispered, kissing the top of Niles's head again. Niles looked up at him, blinking in surprise. "I do. I did back then, and I still do. I never stopped. Never."

The kiss Niles gave him now was slower and gentler. It was pure Niles, all the tender sweetness and innocent sincerity Tim had fallen for so long ago. It lingered until Niles shifted to try to press closer, and Tim couldn't suppress a groan of discomfort.

"Shit, sorry!" Niles pulled back, reaching for the call button. "You need meds?"

Tim nodded, trying to catch his breath against the throbbing pain radiating through one side of his torso. He let Niles summon the nurse but grumbled when he rolled off the bed before she arrived. "Where do you think you're going?"

"I think I'm going to head home. I may call Patrick Rutledge along the way."

"Why?"

"Because I can't stop thinking about what it must have been like for him, living in the same house with those guys. Then to have them attack him like that—"

Tim frowned. "Maybe you should steer clear of him awhile, at least until we've got answers to the rest of the questions, particularly about Fortesen's death and how Patrick came to be kidnapped by his cousin."

Niles clenched his jaw, stepping aside when the nurse knocked and bustled into the room. "I'm not going to argue with you about this, and I'm not going to abandon him. He needs someone to support him; he needs to know he's not alone, that Mike and Charlie can't hurt him anymore, that we're there for him. He needs to feel safe."

Tim groaned, even as he felt the meds the nurse pushed into

his IV begin to work on his pain. Shit, that was the good stuff.

"Fine, just—be careful, okay, baby?"

Niles looked like he was ready to argue again, then nodded.

"Okay. I'll do that."

———

Despite the November drizzle, the Nob Hill shopping district along Northwest 23rd was bustling on this Sunday afternoon, offering Niles some distraction with its preholiday bustle. There was an energy in the renovated historical district that never failed to lift his spirits. It helped him draw a deep breath and pull out his cell phone to dial Patrick's number.

He turned at the next intersection and continued uphill toward his house while it rang, hanging up with a disheartened sigh when it went to voice mail. He didn't want to leave Patrick a message. He wanted to talk to him, make sure he was okay.

Perhaps he didn't want to talk to Niles, though. Maybe Patrick blamed him for what had happened. He'd been so grateful for Niles's little kindnesses, so bright-eyed and eager while he had worked. And look what it had gotten him.

Was his and Rosie's crusade really worth it?

The ringing of his phone jerked him out of his morose musings, and he scrambled for it when he saw Patrick's name on the caller ID.

"Mr. River?" There was a tremor in Patrick's voice, and Niles felt the knot in his chest loosen.

"It's Niles, Patrick," he said gently, opening his gate to his front walk, then latching it behind him. "How are you?"

"I'm all right, I guess." An uncomfortable silence followed, then Patrick sighed heavily. "I don't know what to say. I—I'm not supposed to say anything. I'm not supposed to even be talking to you. The lawyers—"

"Whose lawyers?" Niles mounted the steps and sank onto the porch swing.

"Charlie and Mike's."

"They can't intimidate a victim into not talking. That's illegal. If you're in trouble, Patrick, I want to help you. You don't have to be afraid anymore."

"I just—" Niles heard a deep male voice shouting something in the background. "Oh God, I have to go."

"Patrick? *Patrick*?" The phone beeped in his ear, telling him the call had been disconnected, and Niles let the phone fall onto the swing beside him, before bracing his elbows against his knees and burying his face in his hands.

If there were a way to reset the clock a few weeks back, to before this whole nightmare began, he'd do it. He'd warn Lakshmi and Charity to be careful who they were approached by at that convention. He'd find some other way to convince Anthony to back off and accept their breakup so that he wouldn't act so crazy and cause suspicion, which then drove him to push Tim into the street . . .

So much senseless, unjustifiable hurt in such a short time. Surely there could have been a way to circumvent it all? Something he could have done?

He felt something spark in his chest, a feeling he'd once described to Jordan as being exclusive to storytellers, the birth of a new tale. He couldn't call it inspiration, really, because the need to create the story didn't so much inspire as consume him. Pushing himself out of the swing, Niles grabbed his phone and let himself into the house. He dug into his messenger bag, which Jordan had salvaged from his office, and pulled out his MacBook Air, carrying it to his desk to begin making notes.

It wouldn't be like any other Third Wave game he had written. No high or low fantasy. No sci-fi or cyberpunk. It would be a modern-day role-playing game, a whodunit with a time-travel twist, a choose-your-own-adventure tale for the digital age. The player character would be an everyman/everywoman, completely ordinary, until tragedy unfolds around the PC. And then it would become a matter of traveling a few days into the past, racing against the clock to piece together the clues—as well as to make the correct decisions with regard to the NPCs they meet along the way—to rewrite the events leading up to the tragedy and change the narrative.

And at the heart of it, of course, would be Third Wave's theme of equality, intersectionality, acceptance, and antiprejudice. Jordan would give him some gentle shit for the blatant wish fulfillment, of course, but—

But what?

His hands stilled on the keys and then fell away. He didn't like the sneering tone of that inner voice, but the hopelessness he'd been trying to keep at bay since he'd learned the murders were linked to the games he wrote kept digging insidiously for a foothold in the back of his mind.

Even if he could tell the story, what would it accomplish? Would regressive troglodytes be provoked into further bloodshed if he dared to write another tale of bigots being the bad guys and underdog minorities being the heroes? What was the point of shouting his vision into a darkness that privileged people felt murderously compelled to preserve?

His phone rang with Jordan's ringtone, and he closed his laptop on his notes before answering. "What's up, Jordie?"

"I was about to ask you the same thing. You sulking?"

"Yeah, pretty much. It's bordering on self-indulgence. What's the use? Might as well give up. Nothing's ever gonna change. Blah, blah, hopeless, morbid, blah."

"Well, knock it the fuck off. If you're not gonna rest like I told you to, then open up your damn computer and keep writing."

"You know, I closed my computer to answer this call, in which you're now telling me to open my computer."

"Yeah, but you'd stopped writing, hadn't you?"

"Listen, smart-ass—" The phone beeped in his ear, and when Niles checked, Patrick's name was on the call-waiting screen. "I gotta go, Jordie. Patrick's calling me, and I really want to speak with him. I'll talk to you later."

"Okay. Tell him we're all thinking of him and hoping he's okay." He hung up as Jordan was shouting, "Keep writing!" in his ear and thumbed the touchscreen to answer Patrick's call. "Patrick? You okay?"

"Yeah. I'm okay." Patrick's voice sounded thick and clogged, and he cleared his throat. "I know I don't have a right to ask, but could we get together to talk?"

"Of course. Would you like to meet somewhere? I can come to get you—"

"No. No, please. I have bruises. I don't want people staring. If it's all right, I'd rather come see you. My mom and stepdad are having a hard time, you know, with Charlie and all. You can't be here. Can I come over to your place?"

"Absolutely. I'll text you my address."

Niles disconnected the call and sent the text with hope burgeoning in his chest once more, smiling as he reopened his laptop and took his brother's advice.

CHAPTER 23

"Son of a bitch!"

Rosie's head shot up from where she was hunched over her laptop, perusing the report Jordan had brought her on how public recognition and perception of Third Wave was shifting with all the—frequently unwanted—publicity they'd been getting. Across the room, Angie pushed her chair away from Rosie's desktop computer, letting it roll as she swiped a hand over her hair and shot the machine a disgusted look.

"Problem?" She couldn't help the smirk that curled one corner of her mouth at the sight of Angie's frustration. There was always a certain element of sadism involved in ushering some unsuspecting soul through a game whose twists and turns one already knew.

"Marc. That little shit!" Angie flung her hand toward the computer and scowled. "He sold me out!"

"Ah, that."

Angie gave her a narrow look. "You can quit gloating now. Where the hell did I go wrong?"

"You didn't."

"Come again?"

Rosie shrugged. "You didn't do anything wrong. No matter what choices you made along the way, Marc was going to betray you to the terrorists in the end."

"But *why*?"

"The game takes place over the course of about six months, through most of which he's been their hostage. Stockholm syndrome sets in, or he's just trying to survive, or he can't take any more and will do whatever it takes to appease them. He's meant to be tragic, a victim, not a villain."

"Who's not a villain?"

Rosie turned her attention from Angie to see Jordan poking his head out from her kitchen, where he'd been making a new pot of coffee so he and Rosie could keep working. "Marc. Angie just got to the point where he sets the PC up to be attacked by the terrorists."

"Hmm, poor guy." Jordan dropped onto the far end of the sofa from Rosie. "Not that I've gotten that far in the game, but Niles has told me all about it."

"Wait. *You* haven't played the game?" Angie gave him an incredulous stare.

"Only enough to be conversant about it when doing PR. Niles is the gamer, not me. I can't sit still long enough."

"Can you believe we allow him to work for us?" Rosie grinned. "An infidel in our very midst."

"Give it a few more years," he shrugged. There was something missing behind his banter, a fleeting frown as if he were shoving aside something he wanted to say. "I'm sure you and Niles will manage to convert me eventually. Now, about this EEU meeting . . ."

WHEN NILES ANSWERED THE DOORBELL, Patrick stood there rubbing his palms on the thighs of his jeans as though they were sweating. His brow was beaded with moisture, though whether it was perspiration or rain, Niles couldn't say.

Niles took a deep breath and tried to calm himself. "Come on in, Patrick. Can I get you a Coke? Some tea? Anything?" Okay, so his inclination to fuss and try to make Patrick comfortable was probably going to make him feel the exact opposite.

"No, thanks, Mr. River."

"It's Niles, remember?" He smiled gently and squeezed Patrick's shoulder comfortingly, urging him out of the open doorway, then closed the door behind him. He didn't miss the startled glance Patrick gave him at even that innocuous contact. Niles let his hand fall away. "I'm sorry. Come in. Have a seat."

"It's okay," Patrick murmured, shuffling down the hall toward the living room, then sinking down onto the sofa. "I just don't get why you're being so nice."

"Why wouldn't I be?" Niles followed, seating himself across from Patrick to give him some space. "I don't blame you for what happened. You're not your stepbrother or his cousin, and you're not responsible for them. I can't imagine what it must have been like for you, living in that situation, but I want to help make things better for you."

Patrick's hands writhed in his lap, twisting and twining. He stared down at them, not meeting Niles's eyes. "I leaked those spoilers. I gave them the details they used to— I'm sorry. I was trying to impress them."

Something clenched around Niles's heart. "You wanted them to approve of you?"

He heard Patrick swallow. "I wanted into their guild. You don't understand. Not really."

"What don't I understand?"

"What it's like to be the odd one out. The easy target. The one who gets fragged first in every PvP match." Patrick's eyes flitted up to meet his for a moment, glimmering with a sheen of tears. "You're gay, but that never happened to you, did it, Mr. River?"

Now it was Niles's turn to rub his hands on his thighs, feeling ridiculously guilty for something over which he'd had no control. "No, I suppose it never did. I had friends who supported me when I came out. I had my brother."

"I never came out." Patrick looked away again, his voice dropping to a whisper. "But they knew. They always knew. It didn't matter how good I was, how hard I tried to fit in. They knew."

"Who? Your stepfather? Your stepbrother and his cousin?"

Patrick nodded. "Them. Everyone. Mike lived with us, you know. His dad was in jail for beating his mom to death. He and Charlie were always together. It wasn't until I went to work for Third Wave that anyone thought I was worth talking to. Then they just wanted inside info about the games. But it was nice that they were paying attention to me for once, you know? At least as something other than a target."

Niles nodded. "I'm sure it was."

Patrick didn't answer. "They finally did invite me into the guild. I had friends, you know? They wanted me around. When they asked me to come with them to help punk those two cosplay girls, I went. Of course I went."

"You—" Oh shit. Oh no. Ice shot down Niles's spine, every strand of his body hair standing on end. "You were there," he whispered.

"They were my friends. I told them about the scene they could recreate when they asked. But then she started bleeding. I didn't know they were going to hit her for real!" Patrick's voice cracked, his words tumbling out faster, hysteria edging his tone, and Niles sprang to his feet.

AT THE DESKTOP COMPUTER, Detective Payne muttered another curse, and Jordan glanced over at her in amusement. She caught the gaze and glowered. "This is some jacked-up shit, let me tell you. *Damn!*"

"You're at the final fight?" Rosie asked from her side of the desk, looking up from the proofs Jordan had handed her as they moved on from the EEU meeting to the preliminary marketing for the Gairi DLC.

"Yeah. Just saved the game because hell if I know which way this is gonna go. They're gonna let me exchange myself for Grace and Chino, but I gotta let Marc go too. Fucking traitor. I oughta be able to space his punk ass."

"See, this is where you get to the 'role-play' part of 'role-playing game,' Angie." Rosie laid the proofs on her desk and rose, crossing the room to sit on the table next to the computer.

Jordan squashed a sense of impatience at the interruption of their discussion. It wasn't like he and Rosie were talking about anything that couldn't wait a few minutes while she flirted with the detective, but something was tightening the muscles at the back of his neck, and he wanted to wrap it the hell up.

"You're looking at Marc and his actions as Detective Angela 'Take-No-Shit' Payne. But in the game, you're Marc's foster sister," Rosie explained. "You grew up with him. Spent your whole life protecting and looking after him, mentoring him. And yeah, he betrayed you. But his actions don't erase all that history. Not unless you decide your character is someone who would overlook all that and only care about the betrayal."

Detective Payne harrumphed and muttered something too low for Jordan to hear, but Rosie laughed. The sound grated on Jordan's nerves, and he shoved himself up out of his chair. "I'll let you two lady-geeks take a gaming break while I call my brother," he announced, digging for his phone.

"How's Niles doing?" Rosie asked. "I haven't wanted to push

him about coming back to work yet. I thought I would give it a few more days."

"He's okay. Trying to see if he can still salvage something with Patrick. You know him and his causes."

"Patrick?" Rosie went still, and she and Detective Payne locked gazes for a moment. Jordan wasn't quite sure what was in that look, but the tension creeping up the back of his neck redoubled.

"He wouldn't try to meet with Rutledge, would he?" Detective Payne asked.

Rosie made a pained face. "Of course he would, if he thought he could help."

That was when it finally clicked for Jordan what they were getting at, with the parallels between Patrick and Marc and Marc's betrayal. His stomach twisted as he tried to convince himself that he'd feel a lot more alarmed if Niles was actually in danger, but the nagging tension refused to abate. He didn't believe in that "twinscience" shit, no matter how staunchly Niles defended it.

Meeting Rosie's anxious eyes, he thumbed the speed dial and pressed the phone to his ear, waiting.

———

"PATRICK, STOP." Niles barely registered the ringing of his phone where he'd left it over on the kitchen island. It was Jordan's ringtone, and right now his brother would just have to wait. "Listen to me. Don't say anything more. You need to call your lawyer—a lawyer of *your own*, not one defending Charlie or Mike—and then you need to talk to the police. I don't— Shit, I'm not a lawyer. I don't know what the law is with being an accessory or whatever, but if you witnessed the murders, you need to come clean about it or you'll be, I don't know, obstructing justice or something."

"No." Patrick's voice hardened, and he shook his head emphatically. "I'm not going to testify against them. Don't you *get it?*" He swept his hands through his hair, making it stand in disorderly tufts. "*They let me in.*"

"They were *using you,*" Niles said gently. "In fact, I'm pretty sure they're planning to pin Daniel Fortesen's death on you. They're claiming they didn't do it, but that they know who did. *You need a lawyer.* I'm sure Eliza Muldrake can refer someone. Let me call her for you."

His phone stopped ringing for a moment, then started up again as Jordan tried to call a second time. Niles continued to ignore it, all his attention on Patrick's agitated fidgeting.

"Fine. Let them blame it on me." He gave Niles a stubborn look. "Might as well go to jail with them. At least then I'll still have friends. I won't be home alone with my stepdad while he tells me how worthless I am."

"Don't let them do that. It's not your fault. You don't deserve—"

"How do *you* know?" Patrick shouted, leaping to his feet to pace between the back of the sofa that separated the living room from the kitchen and the island. "How do you know it's not my fault?"

"Because I know you. You're a good guy. You wouldn't—"

"You don't know *anything!*" A sweep of Patrick's arm sent a stack of mail and Niles's phone scattering through the room just as Jordan tried ringing through for the third time. Patrick kicked at the phone, and it fell silent with a crunch. The concern that had blossomed in Niles's chest when Patrick began making his unexpected admission ratcheted up to alarm, and Niles found himself backing away slowly.

"You want to know what I did when they beat up those girls? Huh? *I laughed.* I wanted to puke, but they were all laughing, so I laughed with them. For once it was a couple bitches they were giving shit to instead of me, so I *laughed!*"

"Patrick? Hey, can you calm down? I'm on your side, okay? I want to help you. Can you sit back down?"

"I let them do it." In an instant, the tension drained out of Patrick's body. His shoulders slumped, and his voice took on a plaintive, almost childlike tone. The skin under his bulging, red-rimmed eyes was wet. "I didn't want them to turn on me, so I let them do it. But then Charlie was in the parking lot, and he overheard you talking to the police about the murders, and they realized the cops had found the connection, and they told me . . . they told me you had to be taken care of. I didn't know what to do, so when I picked up your reporter friend and he saw how upset I was, I . . . I told him everything. And he told me we should go to the cops, but they were tracking my phone and . . . I watched them run him down. And I told myself it would be okay. What did I care about a couple fake geek girls and some fag reporter? At least it wasn't me."

Niles didn't want to hear any more. He wanted to get to a phone and call someone—anyone—who would come and make Patrick stop. But he couldn't stop the question from slipping out when he asked, "Did they attack Jordan? Did they hurt my brother?"

The look Patrick gave him was so raw and wounded, Niles felt his own eyes burning. Patrick's shoulders began to shake. "I did that. I didn't— I thought it was *you*."

Niles's mouth fell open. He shook his head, trying to deny what he was hearing. No. Not Patrick.

"After they ran that other guy down, they said I had one final chance. You knew I was supposed to pick him up, so you had to go. But I couldn't— I couldn't let them do that. So I said I would do it. I told them I'd prove myself. I wasn't trying to kill you —*him*—I wasn't. I just needed to make it look good. I didn't even know it was Jordan until after I—" A sob erupted from Patrick's chest, and he sank to the floor, weeping. "I wouldn't have hurt him. I wouldn't ever want to hurt him. I swear it!"

He wanted to hate Patrick, wanted to hate a man who had injured his brother, who had abetted so much senseless violence. But all Niles could see in front of him was a broken boy, bullied to the point where his own moral compass had been smashed beyond any hope of repair. He could only feel pity, and a terrible, terrible grief.

"Listen to me, Patrick. Are you listening?" Patrick's racking sobs eased up enough for him to nod as Niles scrubbed at his own face and cleared his throat. "I need to go grab the landline phone from upstairs. I'm going to call a lawyer for you, okay? I want to help you. Will you promise me you'll stay here? I'll only be gone a few seconds."

Patrick pulled his knees to his chest, curling into a ball. His eyes were vacant and lost as his gaze slowly tracked toward Niles. "I'll stay."

CHAPTER 24

J ordan swore when his attempt to call Niles went to voice
mail for the umpteenth time. Detective Payne's car had one
of the bubbly light things, so they were making reasonably
good time, considering it was nearly rush hour in downtown
Portland, but his gut feeling that Niles was all right had become
less certain since they'd left Rosie's condo to check on him.
Maybe he was projecting his own anxiety onto Niles, but he felt
certain Niles was frightened now. He knew it the way he'd
known Niles was disheartened earlier. It was easy to take that
surety for granted when nothing was on the line, but when it
mattered, Jordan didn't dare trust what amounted to little more
than intuition. He needed to see Niles safe with his own eyes.

"Still no luck?" Detective Payne radiated an aura of control
and competence. *Relax*, it said, *I've got the situation under control.
Let me do my job.* Did they teach that at detective school? Because
if it was supposed to be comforting, it was failing rather spectac-
ularly. He would have liked to have seen her a little more
agitated, to know getting to Niles and making sure he was okay
was a little more crucial to her than just another day on the job.

"He would never ignore one of my calls like this." Jordan

glared at his phone as if it had let him down by not yielding an answer.

"We're almost there," she murmured, slowing to give traffic time to clear an intersection before she ran through it against the light. "You can stop clutching that Oh-Jesus handle so hard. I aced all my driving tests."

"Not unless you have a crowbar," Jordan shot back with a tight smile he was pretty sure came off more like a grimace. "Tell me why there aren't other units rushing to meet us at Niles's house again?"

"I've called for the nearest beat car to make a security check, but they just radioed in that there's been a collision involving the streetcar, so all nearby units are going to be handling that." Her fingers flexed on the steering wheel. "It's fine."

"Can you at least turn on your siren?"

"No. We have no reason to consider this an emergency. We're just making sure everything is okay."

"He wouldn't ignore my call," Jordan repeated. "That's more substantial than just some tenuous link to a game."

"Phones get lost, dropped in the toilet, run out of charge, just plain stop working. So let's just consider ourselves cautiously optimistic until we're sure we have a problem, okay?"

He wanted to thank her for at least attempting to be reassuring, but he couldn't waste the mental capacity to find the words to explain that there was no possible way he could be reassured short of reaching Niles and seeing for himself. He wasn't sure he could make her understand that his world would quite literally end if anything irrevocable happened to his brother. Instead, he thumbed the speed dial again—knowing as he did so that it would be futile—and watched cars angle off to the side of the busy city streets to permit them to pass.

They turned onto Niles's street and made their way up the car-lined hill to the Victorian near the top. Detective Payne parked illegally at the entrance to Niles's driveway and turned off the car, killing the bubble light. That was when Jordan's unease spiked into full-blown alarm, a surge of terror he knew came from Niles.

"Oh *fuck*," he muttered, groping blindly for the handle and charging for the house, ignoring Detective Payne's calls to stop.

THE CORDLESS PHONE wasn't charged, of course. That was just his luck. He never used the damn landline and kept forgetting to put the phone back on the charger, so it figured it would be dead the one time he actually needed it. Groaning, he tossed the handset on the bed and strode into the upstairs guest room, opening the closet where he stored his miscellaneous crap. He was pretty sure he had an actual corded phone in there somewhere.

"You called the police." Patrick's voice, coming suddenly from behind him, made Niles jump and nearly topple a stack of holiday ornament boxes. There was something strained and ragged in his tone that put Niles on full alert. He spun to see one of his kitchen knives clutched in Patrick's hand, and his heart lurched with a jolt of fear. It wasn't some huge, dramatic butcher knife, thank God, but even a seven-inch chef's knife could do plenty of harm.

"The phone is dead, Patrick. I didn't call anyone." He tried to keep his voice calm, but he couldn't help the waver that crept in. All of Patrick's earlier grief and remorse was gone; his face was stony, and his eyes bleak. That was far more frightening than anything Niles had seen from him yet. "I'm looking for another phone so we can call a lawyer, just like I promised."

"Don't lie to me!" Fury reddened Patrick's face, and his body quivered with it, his knuckles whitening on the hilt of the knife. "I just saw them pull up!"

"I didn't call them." Niles felt the jamb of the closet door at his back and wondered if he could manage to get inside and slam the door to shield himself if Patrick snapped, which was looking increasingly likely from the trapped, panicked way his eyes were darting around. "I wouldn't do that to you. I want to help you, I swear. Please, just let me help you."

"What am I going to do?" The knife lowered a few inches, and Niles felt the tension in his shoulders sink with it. Patrick's voice cracked, and his red-rimmed eyes filled with tears again. "*What am I going to do?*"

"First thing you need to do is put the knife down. If the police are here, if they see you holding it, they're going to consider you armed. They might think you're a threat. Put it down, Patrick. Just put it down. No one wants to hurt you. Please, just put it down."

"Niles!"

His breath whooshed from his lungs in a relieved sigh when he recognized Jordan's voice accompanying the pounding of footsteps downstairs, but Patrick went the opposite direction, going ramrod stiff.

"Oh God! He's going to know. He's going to know what I did!"

Horror froze Niles for an instant, a split second in which Patrick moved, slashing at his own wrist with the blade in a single, violent stroke. There was no hesitation, no indecision, just a sudden streak of crimson coloring the edge of that razor-sharp Japanese steel. With a shout of alarm, Niles dove for Patrick when he tried to switch hands, and felt the rip of pulling stitches in his own wound as he moved.

———

THE FIRST THING Jordan saw was blood staining both Niles and Patrick as they fell to the floor together, each shouting incoherently. A knife spun away from their struggling bodies, and the sight of it felt like a wrecking ball to his solar plexus.

"Niles!" He charged into the fray, where it seemed Niles was trying to pin a writhing Patrick down.

"Patrick! God, Patrick, stop!" Niles clutched one of Patrick's arms, which was streaked copiously with blood. "Jordie! Give me something to stop the bleeding! Hurry!"

Jordan began tearing at the buttons on his shirt, but Detective Payne was already there, thrusting a towel at Niles. "Ambulance is on the way," she announced, her alto sharp enough to cut through Patrick's yelling and Niles's panicked muttering.

"Are you hurt, Niles?" Jordan demanded, running his hands over Niles's bloodstained shirt.

"I don't think so. Oh God, Patrick . . ."

"I can't tell whose blood is whose." He peeled back the collar of Niles's shirt over his wound, wincing when it stuck to Niles's skin. The bandage was saturated and blood had seeped around the edges. "I think you pulled some stitches."

"I'm fine." Niles shook him off. Patrick's thrashing slowed courtesy of their combined weight and finally halted. He lay still, panting and groaning, and Niles kept a death grip on Patrick's forearm with the towel. He glanced around to see Detective Payne had her weight on Patrick's lower legs, keeping them immobile.

"Hey." Jordan gripped the towel Niles was holding in place and pushed him away. "Let me keep pressure on that. You let Detective Payne check your shoulder."

Niles glanced up from Patrick then, looking absolutely shattered. The pain in his eyes made Jordan's throat tighten. "Jordie, he— I tried to— But he— Oh *God* . . ."

"Hey. Hey. It's okay." Swallowing against the lump in his throat, Jordan leaned forward, pressing his forehead to Niles's. He closed his eyes and let himself feel his relief that Niles was all right, that they were together and nothing was going to happen to him. Niles shuddered and then leaned into Jordan, slowly relinquishing his grip on Patrick's arm.

He felt Niles move away, heard Detective Payne murmuring to him, heard the siren of the ambulance drawing closer, but he kept his eyes closed, his head bowed in a silent prayer of thanksgiving. Niles was okay. The world wasn't going to end today.

When he finally did open his eyes, Patrick's were open as well, and he was staring up at Jordan with a hopeless, bewildered look.

"I'm sorry," he whispered, his voice cracking. His eyes pleaded for something Jordan had no idea how to give him. "I didn't mean to hurt you. I would never hurt you. *I'm so sorry.*"

When the paramedics crowded their way into the room, Patrick was sobbing, his face pressed against Jordan's thigh as he pleaded over and over for forgiveness.

CHAPTER 25

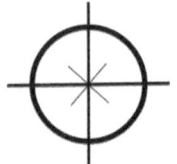

Six Months Later

"Well, that's it, then." Tim watched as Niles picked at his fingernails. Rosie stroked his shoulder. He'd been silent since they'd gotten back home from the courthouse, and neither Tim nor Jordan knew what to say to him.

"You did all you could for Patrick," Jordan murmured, laying a hand over Niles's to still his fidgeting. "He got probation and court-ordered psychiatric help instead of prison, thanks to you."

Tim nodded, watching them closely. "Without you, Charlie and Mike would have taken him down with them. They sure as hell tried." It had been an act of pure spite, it seemed, at least on Mike's part. Charlie was merely, as always, following his cousin's lead. But Mike had made every effort during his trial to shift blame over onto Patrick, as well as his other guild-mates.

As it was, the jury had come back finding him and Charlie and their other guild-mates guilty on all counts—*except* for the murder of Daniel Fortesen, which was the only one that would have carried a hate crime penalty, and the one they had tried hardest to pin on Patrick. Testimony had devolved into Mike and Charlie's story against Patrick's, and once the defense lawyers pointed out that Patrick was getting immunity from aiding and obstruction charges in exchange for his testimony, he lost credibility with the jury. So no one was facing justice for Daniel's death, a fact that Tim could see eating at Niles.

"Doesn't feel like it's enough." Niles looked up and tried to muster a game smile. "He didn't deserve what he got."

"He watched those girls get murdered, and he did nothing," Jordan said firmly. "He didn't try to stop it, he didn't report it to the cops. Niles, all things considered, he got off lightly."

Tim pressed his lips together and refrained from agreeing with Jordan. He and Niles had been over this again and again in the months since Patrick had tried to kill himself. In a way, Niles had been right. Patrick Rutledge *was* a victim, not a villain. But the fact remained that he could have tried to stop what his stepbrother and cousin had been doing, yet, whether from fear for his own safety or a need for inclusion or both, he hadn't.

"Bullying does things to kids beyond just the obvious harassment," Niles murmured. "It drives them to desperate extremes just to make it stop, just to win a few moments of peace and acceptance. They didn't just hurt Patrick. They warped him."

Tim laced his fingers with Niles's and squeezed, while Jordan wrapped his arm around his brother's shoulders and let Niles lean on him. Another morose silence fell before Rosie spoke up. "And with that, I have an announcement to make. EEU has asked me to resign as Third Wave's CEO. The negative publicity hasn't died down, the protests and attacks in the media on gaming in general—Third Wave in particular—haven't let up enough. And though they stuck with us until the trials were over, they've lost the stomach for the fight. So now I'm too controversial and polarizing a figure."

They gaped at her, though Niles didn't look particularly surprised.

"By 'asked for your resignation,' I assume you mean EEU has

given you a choice between resigning and being fired?" Jordan asked.

She nodded, and Niles mirrored it, grimacing. "I figured they'd do that to you sooner or later. I've had my own resignation letter signed and ready to submit for months now. There is no sense in me trying to work there without knowing you have my back."

Rosie gave him an understanding smile. "I wish I could say you were wrong, but we all know how it's going to go. *PF3* is released now, out in the world where no one can mess with the vision we had for it. The Gairi DLC is released and the Issis DLC is far enough into production that whoever they bring in to finish it can't do too much damage. But from here on, they're going to play it safe with their titles. You're not going to find any support from them if you try to push the boundaries."

"We'll start over again, Rosie," Niles said firmly. "From the ground up, just like we did before. Once we have a new game concept that's solid enough, a distributor will fall in line. They're not going to stop us."

"No, they're not." She rose and kissed both Niles's and Jordan's cheeks, then pulled on her coat. "I think I'm going to go out tonight and get drunk. You guys in?"

"Out to a club?" Jordan asked, and both he and Niles groaned. "Come on, Rosie!"

"Oh, suck it up. You can deal with guys giving the pair of you speculative looks for one night. This is probably going to be our last night as a team with Third Wave. Let's celebrate it."

Niles sighed. "Fine. I'm in. Call me at seven and let me know where to meet you."

Jordan echoed the agreement, and Tim found himself nodding because there wasn't much for him to add to the discussion. Rosie left, leaving him alone with Jordan and Niles.

"So what's this about the two of you not wanting to go out? You used to do it all the time when we were in college," Tim said, looking between them. Niles snorted softly and hung his head.

"That was before we realized that every horndog in the clubs was going to proposition us for a threesome," Jordan explained. Niles's face pinkened as he buried it against Tim's shoulder.

"Oh bullshit," Tim scoffed. "I don't buy it."

Niles lifted his head and arched an eyebrow. "Excuse me?"

"Not every guy has a twin fantasy. I sure don't. No offense, Jordan."

Jordan shrugged, barely suppressing a smirk. "Oh, none taken."

"Really?" Niles's eyes glittered with mischief as he glanced over at his brother, then shifted abruptly to straddle Tim's lap, pushing him back against the cushions of the sofa. He leaned in and his breath brushed Tim's left ear. "You sure about that?" he whispered before catching the lobe between his teeth.

"Mmm." Tim's moan trailed off in a soft sigh, and his hands settled on Niles's hips, pulling him closer. He turned his head to capture Niles's mouth. "Yeah, I am," he whispered before their lips sealed.

There was nothing sweeter than kissing Niles. He was sugar and smoke and yielding softness, and he positively melted into Tim every damn time. Tim's arms wrapped around his torso, dragging him in tight, and his tongue reached deep into Niles's mouth, determined to steal not just the kiss but his breath and even his very ability to think.

But just as he took charge of the kiss, he faltered, jerking when something warm and wet caressed the shell of his right ear.

"*Really* sure?" Jordan demanded before he bit it as Niles had just seconds ago. Tim gasped and froze, shuddering while Niles continued to kiss him lazily, working across his face and down his neck.

The way Jordan nibbled on his ear was different than what

Niles had done. There was no sweet teasing, just a wicked demand. His teeth grasped harder, bringing an edge of almost-pain, and the way he sucked a line down Tim's throat said he wasn't going to relent.

Niles's tongue lapped the hollow between his throat and clavicle. Jordan's teeth scraped the stubbled skin of his neck. And all Tim could do was arch and moan at the dual sensations. He was hard where Niles's groin ground against his, so incredibly hard he thought he might pop at any second just from a little necking. Hands closed over each of his nipples, and he could tell by the firmness of the grasp that they didn't belong to the same man.

"Oh *Jesus*," he breathed as they continued to make love to his throat. His hand wedged itself between his body and Niles's, though Tim wasn't quite sure what he was going to do with it, except try to get some of their damn clothes out of the way because it was getting to the point where necking wasn't enough and now he needed *skin* and *flesh* and *touch*.

He didn't even realize as he fumbled with that first button that he was ready to strip down with both of them there until the attentions to his neck and nipples eased off slowly. Gradually, they eased away, their breath cooling the moisture their lips and tongues had left on his throat. In perfect unison, they drew back and turned toward each other, their identical faces just a whisper apart. Tim held his breath, something in the very pit of him needing to see them close that distance, needing to see how sublime it would be to witness Niles's beauty mirrored in a moment of passion.

But instead, swiftly, Jordan moved up and placed a hearty, smacking buss on Niles's forehead and was off the sofa before Tim even realized what was happening.

"See you at the club tonight, bro," he said with a wide grin and a saucy wink to Tim. Then he adjusted his erection with a complete lack of self-consciousness and strode away, leaving Tim blinking at a very smug Niles in utter disbelief.

"You . . . are in *so* much trouble," Tim panted. Niles's dick was hard against his own, his face flushed and his eyes sparkling, but his mischievous smile was far, far too self-satisfied. With a growl, Tim shifted, rolling Niles underneath him on the sofa in a single lunge.

Niles laughed, smiling brilliantly as he embraced Tim with his arms and legs, and tugged him down.

THE END

AUTHOR'S NOTE

**Trigger warning for disturbing content, including examples
of real harassment**

When I wrote this book in 2013, it was inspired by the experiences of Anita Sarkeesian of FeministFrequency.com and Jennifer Hepler, formerly of Bioware.

I was also heavily influenced by the backlash I've seen against feminists and LGBTQIA+ activists on social media, including Tumblr, Twitter, and YouTube.

Little did I know what was to come next, or just how bad it could get. Just as this book was completing the editing stage in late summer of 2014 when a new word entered the vernacular: GamerGate.

This "movement" was started when the ex-boyfriend of Zoe Quinn, the developer of a popular small game about mental illness called *Depression Quest*, released a manifesto accusing her of trading sexual favors for favorable reviews of her games. Trolls from 4chan quickly seized upon the excuse to harass women in gaming and called it a crusade about integrity in video games journalism, using the hashtag #GamerGate.

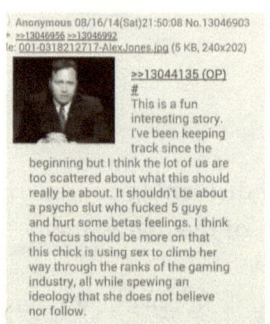

Example 1: *"Well you see anon, it's like this: she is a cunt so naturally she does not have anything to offer except access to her holes. Can a cunt create a masterpiece? Write a play? Make a Game of the Year? No. Therefore, it is fair to conclude that she received favorable reviews from Kataku in exchange for use of her cum receptacle."*

Example 2: *"This is a fun interesting story. I've been keeping track since the beginning but I think a lot of us are too scattered about what this should be about. It shouldn't be about a psycho slut who fucked 5 guys and hurt some betas feelings. I think the focus should be more on that this chick is using sex to climb her way through the ranks of the gaming industry, all while spewing an ideology she does not believe nor follow."*

They were very organized about it, plotting the best way to try to inoculate themselves against backlash and prevent their threads from being deleted, and to manipulate so-called "social justice warriors" into turning against Quinn.

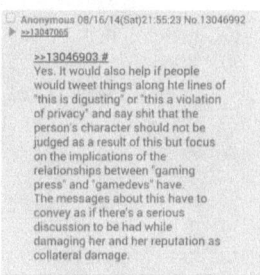

Example 3: *"it would also help if people would tweet things along the lines of "this is disgusting" or "this is a violation of privacy" and say shit that the person's character should not be judged as a result of this but focus on the implications of the relationships between gaming press and gamdevs have. The messages about this have to convey as if there's a serious discussion to be had while damaging her and her reputation as collateral damage."*

The GamerGate trolls quickly widened their scope. They used the crusade as an excuse to renew their harassment of Sarkeesian, and took aim at other targets. Game developer and current Massachusetts congressional candidate Brianna Wu was driven out of her home by threats. Trolls—led by former Breitbart contributor, racist, and pedophilia advocate Milo Yiannopoulos—even celebrated her dog dying and tried to dox her veterinarian while she was dealing with that.

Twitter Harassment of Brianna Wu

In October of 2014, as I arrived in Chicago to attend GayRomLit 2014, Anita Sarkeesian was forced to cancel an appearance at Utah State University after a terror threat was made, promising a "Montreal Massacre-style attack" (the reference is to the 1989 massacre of female engineering students at École Polytechnique in Montreal.)

This is what has happened, and is still happening, to people trying to make a difference in gaming culture.

For more information on feminist and LGBTQIA+ issues in gaming and popular media, check out Zoe Quinn's book, *Crash Override: How Gamergate (Nearly) Destroyed My Life, and How We Can Win the Fight Against Online Hate*

See Also:

- fandomsandfeminism.tumblr.com
- fatuglyorslutty.com
- destructoid.com/halo-3-homophobia-evolved-nsfw-audio--56000.phtml
- gaygamer.net/category/lgbt/
- Rational Wiki: A Timeline of GamerGate
- The Crash Override Network, a crisis helpline for victims of online harassment

Thank you to Jennifer, Zoe, Anita, Brianna and the many, many other brave women in gaming who have been targeted by harassment simply for Gaming While Female. Hopefully someday our beloved hobby will be safer for us all.

Please also consider supporting INeedDiverseGames.org, because the only reason the stories of the women I've mentioned got the amount of attention they did is because this harassment happened to white women. People of color and LGBT people in gaming, like Rosie and Niles in my book, receive all this sort of harassment amplified. INDG is fighting to change that.

ACKNOWLEDGMENTS

Thank you to author David Sullivan, who was my police procedure consultant, for his input, and to author P.D. Singer, for her beta read midway through, which helped me get moving when I was stuck. And thank you to Sarah Frantz for her help in brainstorming early on.

Sea Change

SAUGATUCK BOOK 1

AMELIA C. GORMLEY

SEA CHANGE, SAUGATUCK BOOK 1

One Summer Can Change Everything...

Topher Carlisle's always been the black sheep—literally—in his middle-class family. Biracial, gay, and genderfluid, his family doesn't think he'll amount to much, and he just might believe them.

After a bout of severe depression has put both his academic and financial prospects in danger, he accepts his best friend's offer to stay in her family's summer home while he works to make up the shortfall of his athletic scholarship. But his tendency for self-sabotage is strong and soon a terrible mistake in judgment leaves him homeless.

From the moment he sees Topher, artist Jace Sieger knows that this is someone he needs to capture on canvas. He's no stranger to poor life choices, and he sees something in Topher worth nurturing.

The challenge, though, is chipping through Topher's prickly defenses to reach the sensitive, traumatized soul beneath. With the help of his friends Geoff and Robin, maybe, just maybe, they can convince Topher he's worth something after all, and that a few mistakes don't make him irredeemable.

What starts as a casual vacation fling grows into something that will change both of them forever.

(This novel is a newly-released and retitled second edition. It was previously available under the title Saugatuck Summer.*)*

STRAIN

In a world with little hope and no rules,
the only thing they have to lose
is themselves.

AMELIA C. GORMLEY

STRAIN, THE EROTIC, POST-APOCALYPTIC THRILLER!

In a world with little hope and no rules, the only thing they have left to lose . . . is themselves.

Rhys Cooper is a dead man. He's spent years hiding from the virus that wiped out most of the human race, but an act of futile heroism has him counting down his remaining days. The timely arrival of superhuman soldiers offers some feeble hope—but only if Rhys can reconcile himself to doing what is necessary to take advantage of it.

Sergeant Darius Murrell has seen too much death and too little tenderness, seeking out survivors only to put the infected out of their misery, or send the uninfected to a safe haven he and his fellow Juggernaut troops can never enjoy. Rhys's situation is different, though. Not only is there an improbable chance that Darius won't have to put a bullet in Rhys's head, but he has somehow managed to get under Darius's skin.

The virus Rhys must infect himself with is sexually transmitted, and optimizing his chance of exposure requires him to submit as often as possible to Darius—and the other soldiers. Though the boundaries of morality have shifted in this harsh new world, what they must do has them asking if their humanity is too high a price to pay for Rhys's survival.

THANK YOU FOR READING!

If you enjoyed this book, please be sure to support authors so we can continue to write the books you love. One great way to do this is to recommend the book to your friends on social media. Another is to review it at Goodreads and/or whichever site you purchased it from. Thank you!

OTHER BOOKS BY AMELIA C. GORMLEY

THE IMPULSE TRILOGY

Inertia

Acceleration

Velocity

SEASONS IN SAUGATUCK

The Field of Someone Else's Dreams

Sea Change

Risk Aware

THE STRAIN TRILOGY

Juggernaut

Strain

Bane

PLAYER VS. PLAYER

ABOUT THE AUTHOR

Amelia C. Gormley published her first short story in the school newspaper in the 4th grade, and since then has suffered the persistent delusion that enabling other people to hear the voices in her head might be a worthwhile endeavor. She's even convinced her hapless spouse that it could be a lucrative one as well, especially when coupled with her real-life interest in angst, kink, feminism, and pretty men.

When her husband and son aren't interacting with the back of her head as she stares at the computer, they rely on her to feed them, maintain their domicile, and keep some semblance of order in their lives (all very, very bad ideas—they really should know better by now.) She can also be found playing video games and ranting on Tumblr, seeing as how she's one of those horrid social justice warriors out to destroy free speech, gaming, geek culture, and everything else that's fun everywhere.

http://ameliacgormley.com
http://ameliacgormley.tumblr.com

[f] facebook.com/ameliacgormley

[t] twitter.com/ACGormley

[g] goodreads.com/ameliacgormley